STRIKE ME DOWN

STRIKE ME DOWN

MINDY MEJIA

WHEELER PUBLISHING
A part of Gale, a Cengage Company

Copyright © 2020 by Mindy Mejia.
Wheeler Publishing, a part of Gale, a Cengage Company.

Wheeler Publishing Large Print Hardcover.
The text of this Large Print edition is unabridged.
Other aspects of the book may vary from the original edition.
Set in 16 pt. Plantin.

LIBRARY OF CONGRESS CIP DATA ON FILE.
CATALOGUING IN PUBLICATION FOR THIS BOOK
IS AVAILABLE FROM THE LIBRARY OF CONGRESS

ISBN-13: 978-1-4328-8140-5 (hardcover alk. paper)

Published in 2020 by arrangement with Emily Bestler Books/Atria Books, an imprint of Simon & Schuster, Inc.

Printed in Mexico
Print Number: 01   Print Year: 2020

For all my sisters, blood and beyond,
who know their own strength

NORA

Numbers, like people, have no inherent quality. Their value lies only in their relation to others and what they represent. Good. Bad. Strong. Weak. These are descriptions given by the counter. The counter weaves a story into the numbers, a narrative combining quantity and quality, fact and fiction. Numbers by themselves are invisible, much like the counters.

Take fifty thousand. In and of itself, the number had no significance, but add a resource (people) and a quality (frenzied) and now the number mattered. Fifty thousand confused and frantic people all looking for one person.

The counter.

Her.

Nora rushed through the promenade.

"Her name is Nora Trier. She's in the stadium and we need your help to locate her as a person of interest regarding Logan Russo's disappearance." The voice boomed over the sound system, reverberating off the glass dome.

Tides of shock swept through the stadium as the news sank in. Logan Russo, legendary athlete and feminist icon, the hero they'd all flocked to see and cheer with during tonight's championship fight, was missing. Her Twitter account was silent and her Instagram, dark. The police had searched her penthouse apartment, finding nothing except broken glass and blood.

And Nora was the reason she was gone.

Nora pulled a clip out of her hair and shook the dark blond length into her face. People stood up in their sections, craning their necks and pointing in every direction. Keeping as far to the side of the walkway as possible, Nora donned reading glasses, clipped her Strike badge to her jacket, and lifted her phone to her ear. Everyone she passed peered at her. She returned each look with equal and unabashed suspicion while speaking rapidly to no one.

At the skyway exit, two security guards checked the few people who were already leaving, holding their phones up against the faces filtering out into the downtown Minneapolis night. When one of the guards tilted his phone, she saw her own picture on the screen.

"No, I've already worked sixty hours this week and I'm not putting in any more overtime." She flashed her badge irritably at one of them, who hesitated before Nora leaned in and whispered, "Screw this bitch, right?"

Grunting, he waved her past.

She'd gotten twenty paces into the skyway that stretched long and almost empty, a shadowy tunnel suspended in midair, when her phone buzzed and a series of messages started popping up.

They live-streamed it.

Get out of there.

Now.

Where are you?

The bridge crossed over the top of an intersection where squad car lights flashed. She was texting back when a voice shouted behind her.

"Nora!"

For forty years she'd been invisible, a quality she'd not only taken for granted, but turned into her greatest asset. She was the unseen eye, the counter nobody counted, who wove numbers into dark and avaricious stories.

Her breath hitched in her chest as she

looked back and saw it — the figure standing with the security guards and pointing at her from the other end of the bridge. The other people walking back to their condos and high-rises started yelling and lifting their phones. A few of them hurried toward her, but they were incidental. It was the one who'd alerted them she cared about, the one who might have been following her the whole time. He broke into a sprint the moment their eyes met. Turning, Nora pushed through a set of double doors and barreled into the maze of abandoned passageways, the second-story city her only hope.

She wasn't invisible anymore.

■ ■ ■ ■

OPPORTUNITY

■ ■ ■ ■

NORA

"Fraud kills."

Nora allowed the words time to land on the crowd, a full audience of mostly twenty-somethings with brand-new CPA licenses still crisp inside their wallets.

"You've all heard, at some point in your lives, the lie that fraud is a white-collar crime, a victimless crime." She paced the length of the stage, heels marking the distance between the darkened aisles.

"Sam White was the founder and president of Computech, a microchip manufacturer that weathered the tech crash with little more than a shrug and a few treasury stock purchases. They employed ten thousand people and maintained manufacturing facilities in China, Mexico, and Ohio, with headquarters in Minneapolis."

The screen behind Nora flashed to a wall-sized scene of a rocky beach where a group of people squinted into the sun. Two teen-age boys corralled a pair of dogs while a middle-aged couple, both fit and wearing their gray with ease, corralled the boys. The entire family was frozen mid-laugh.

"Sam White built Computech from his parents' garage into a Fortune 500 company in less than two decades. For five years they boasted the highest gross profit percentage in the tech sector worldwide, until a whistle-blower inside the company exposed a major misstatement scheme. The SEC opened an investigation into securities fraud, share prices plummeted, and three weeks after the scandal broke in the *Wall Street Journal,* Sam White shot himself in the head."

The room, massive as it was, had fallen completely silent. No one sipped their complimentary coffee. No one checked their phones. Two hundred faces stared at the one smiling down at them, the larger-than-life father hugging his son to his dead chest.

Nora glanced at the picture, a familiar swill of emotion clotting her throat, but her voice carried clearly as she swiveled back to the young accountants eager to kick-start their careers. "Sam White was forty-seven years old when he died. Computech de-clared bankruptcy less than two months into

14

the SEC investigation and thousands of people lost their jobs, including me.

"I was the whistle-blower."

Fraud, whether it was a petty cash scheme or a multibillion-dollar revenue inflation, required three essential elements. The first was opportunity; the thief needed access to the assets or financial statements. The second ingredient was pressure. Maybe that meant a gambling problem and a silent, ballooning debt or a sick family member accumulating hundreds of thousands of dollars in hospital bills. The pressure could be professional — the imperative to outperform competitors or meet investor expectations — but whatever the form, the person was under stress. They spent nights awake, withdrawn from family life, suffering from headaches, upset stomach, constipation, muscle tremors, and chest pains. They had trouble performing sexually.

Both of those elements — opportunity and pressure — existed ubiquitously. Millions of employees around the world were entrusted with financial authority simply because someone had to write the checks; someone had to approve the journal entries. And stress was the postrecession way of life, the corporate imperative to do more with less. Despite having the opportunity and feeling the pressure, employees didn't commit fraud until the final, game-changing factor came into play: rationalization. The thief had to find a way to reconcile the crime within their individual moral framework. They created a narrative in which their actions were justified, even righteous. They *deserved* what they stole. They deserved so much more.

"Sam White took a skydiving trip with his family the summer before I discovered the fraud." After two hours of lecturing on the basics of fraud detection, Nora always wrapped up the presentation by circling back to the beginning.

"I hadn't noticed the behavioral pattern, but it was there in plain sight. Sam loved parasailing, skiing in the Rockies, and jumping out of airplanes. He had a risk-taking personality."

Nora felt the eyes in the room, full of silent questions pressing in on all sides, but every time she locked on a face in the audience, their gaze skittered away, as if embarrassed to be caught paying attention. They wouldn't make it as forensic accountants if they were afraid to look without flinching, to unearth what lay beneath through the power of a protracted and deliberate stare.

16

"We operate in an economy that glamorizes risk. It's embedded in the very heart of the American dream — the entrepreneurial spirit. Business owners constantly risk failure with every decision they make, and the bigger the risk, the potentially bigger the reward. When a high-stakes risk pays off, when a company hits on the product of the year, the money and recognition instantly follow. The risk-taking personality is compelled to chase bigger and bigger rewards. It feeds them and can override many of their ingrained ethical checkpoints. Does every skydiving CEO commit financial statement fraud? Of course not. But your job, your ethical duty as CPAs, is to monitor the risk environment of your company and understand the elements of the fraud triangle.

"Opportunity. Pressure. Rationalization. This is the birthing ground of crime."

A dozen people approached Nora afterward, asking follow-up questions or sharing their own war stories about corporate theft. Nora made the appropriate noises, handed out her firm's business cards, and offered general, conservative guidance while the seminar handlers herded them into the hallway so they could set up the next presentation.

As the attendees dispersed, Nora glanced toward the opposite ballroom where a crowd still gathered around their presenter, a tall, lanky man who'd gravitated to the food table and was making short work of the remaining croissants. He chatted, laughed, and gestured with a coffee cup while the staff tried in vain to clear the buffet. When he spotted Nora watching him, arms crossed and one eyebrow raised, he winked.

"Excuse me."

A tender pantsuit, who must have been hovering in the background, complimented the lecture before nervously clearing her throat and asking the question Nora had learned to expect since she'd started giving this talk five years ago.

"Did you feel responsible?" the girl asked. "For Sam White's death?"

"I didn't commit the fraud or put the gun in his mouth." Nora thanked her and watched her leave.

"You didn't answer her question."

Corbett MacDermott stepped up beside her, brushing bits of croissant off his shirt. Nora ignored her partner's pointed look. She didn't have to answer the question, not for Corbett, because he already knew what she wouldn't say.

"Let's go."

It was hard to watch a company collapse, run into sixty-year-olds working as cashiers because their pensions were worthless, and testify in trials that put your colleagues in prison, without feeling at least partially responsible. It was even harder when your boss had been your father's best friend. For as long as Nora could remember, the Whites and the Triers had vacationed together. She'd spent summers babysitting Sam's kids, beating one at tag and the other at chess. Later, Sam hired her right out of college as a junior accountant at Computech, constantly bragging that she was his big gun in the finance department.

When Nora uncovered the company's scheme to inflate profits, she'd gone straight to Sam, assuming he would be as outraged as she had been to find the fraud. Instead, Sam gaslit her, telling her she didn't understand complex accounting. Then he tried to bribe her with a higher salary, and finally he resorted to guilt: Nora wouldn't ruin him, would she? Not after everything Sam had done for her.

"We're family, Nora," he said, reaching over the evidence she'd compiled and covering her hand with his perspiring one. "I need you to help protect our family now."

Nora nodded, gathered her notes, and went to look up the number for the SEC. Less than a month later, Sam was dead.

After Computech collapsed, Sam's wife had a breakdown. The kids Nora had once babysat started sending her hate mail. Even her own parents stopped talking to her. Nora got used to lying awake nights in bed, staring at the rotating blades of the ceiling fan. She inventoried the peas on her dinner plate, lined them up in neat rows of ten before scraping the food into the trash. She thought about moving away, but before she could decide where to go a different path presented itself.

An older man greeted Nora in the court-house lobby as she left one of the trials. "I believe you're out of a job, Ms. Trier."

The card he handed her was thick and embossed. *Jim Parrish,* it read. *Parrish Forensics.*

"I've got a few irons in the fire." She had three unreturned calls in to temp agencies and a head hunter who'd actually laughed in her face. Whistle-blowers might have legal protections under the Sarbanes-Oxley Act, but no one wanted to hire someone who rocked the boat.

"Have you considered forensic accounting?"

Nora had never actually heard the term before, which in retrospect should have been embarrassing. She said something about *CSI* and swirling tubes of DNA at crime scenes, which made Jim chuckle.

"We stay away from bodily fluids, but the principle is the same. Fraud costs this great country of ours forty to fifty billion in direct, measurable dollars every year. Corporate boards, CFOs, and CEOs like yours who don't care about the lives of their employees or customers, so long as they can squeeze a few million more. It's bloodless, calculated crime and forensic accountants are the ones who are smart enough to not only catch them, but explain to a judge and jury exactly how they did it."

He nodded at the business card. "We make the bloodless bleed."

Nora still didn't understand exactly what forensic accounting entailed, but she was also sleep-deprived, exiled from her family, and living off the last thousand dollars in her savings account. She pocketed the card and offered Jim Parrish her hand.

That was fifteen years, a hundred audits, countless investigations, and sixty-five convictions ago. The summer after Nora came on board, Jim hired Corbett MacDermott, an Irish transplant who specialized in artificial intelligence, and he and his wife began having one baby per year like they were doing a companion experiment in organic intelligence. Corbett liked to stroll into Nora's office at the end of the day and talk about cases while she worked over three monitors and her analysts bustled in and out. Both of them bought into the partnership at the same time and they celebrated with a round of beer at Ike's, which had turned into a round twice a week ever since.

"You've got to let Sam White go." Corbett said as they walked into the skyway, leaving the conference hotel behind.

"He's been dead for fifteen years." Nora replied. "I think he's sufficiently gone."

"You know what I mean."

"How was your seminar?" While she'd taught the principles of fraud detection, Corbett had lectured on developments in artificial intelligence, a topic that consistently drew audiences from across the country.

Corbett chuckled. "Steering me back into my box, are we?"

Nora smiled and pointed to the sandwich board of one of Corbett's favorite lunch spots. "Your pork belly ramen's on special today."

"And now she's speaking my love language." Laughing again, he elbowed her in the shoulder as they joined the pedestrian traffic flowing above the streets of downtown Minneapolis.

Nora had always appreciated the planning and design of the Minneapolis skyway. She'd taken an underground tour of Seattle on a business trip once and marveled at how the entire elevation of the city had risen one story, leaving a ghost town of empty storefronts and subterranean alleys beneath it. The Minneapolis skyway was similar, except the actual ground hadn't shifted at all. The streets, sidewalks, and plazas remained where they'd always been, crowded with food trucks in the summer and coated with a gristle of snow and ice in the winter. The skyway simply layered another city on top of all that. Glass-encased walkways connected every skyscraper in downtown, a ten-mile labyrinth of convenience stores, salons, bakeries, sushi counters, farm-to-table hot spots, burger joints, and pop-ups for every conceivable Kickstarter product and signature-starved petition. It was the largest system of enclosed, second-story bridges in the world and, for Nora and Corbett, it was home.

"Where are we going for lunch?"

"You're on your own." Nora swerved to avoid a group of businessmen as her partner stopped abruptly in front of a pizza place. Corbett never watched where he was going in the skyway. He didn't have to. The crowd parted around him like pedestrian male privilege, or maybe tall person privilege, while he obliviously perused the lunch counter menu.

"They've got Hawaiian barbecue pizza."

She checked her watch and shook her head. "Strike's in twenty minutes. I don't have time."

At this point, she'd barely be able to grab the gym bag from her office and get to Strike's building before class started.

"Ah, come on, Ellie."

Nora sighed. No one else called her that. Most people didn't even know her full name was Elnora. *Ellie* was too light, too easy on the tongue. Ellie was someone who changed her schedule around at the drop of a hat, who acquiesced to her friend's cajoling.

"They aren't holding any lunchtime classes next week. I don't want to miss this one." She'd reached the top of the waitlist for the exclusive gym six months ago, and since joining, Strike's kickboxing sessions had become an integral part of her week. It was the exact opposite of the mental challenges that filled her work days; Strike was visceral, a world distilled into sheer physical effort and power. It was also her only chance to see Logan.

"Fine, fine." Corbett gave up. "I'll fend for myself."

They moved back into the crowd and turned a corner past a six-story waterfall cascading into a pool at the bottom of an atrium. Just before crossing the final bridge to Parrish's building, Nora reached into her blazer pocket to grab a few folded bills.

"You're not still giving her money."

Nora didn't bother replying; they'd had this fight too many times. She checked for security guards as they crossed over the intersection, then grinned at the woman lumbering slowly next to the glass.

"Hi, Rose."

"Briefcase lady!" Rose, an elderly homeless woman, straightened up when she saw who'd stopped in front of her.

Nora shook the older woman's hand, pressing the bills into her palm.

"You busted that heart out of your briefcase yet?" Rose asked the same urgent question of every passerby on the skyway, until

25

she got locked out of Parrish's building and headed to the shelter at night. The same went for purses, laptops, and backpacks; Rose was on a mission to liberate all the hearts in downtown Minneapolis. The building's security left her to it as long as she didn't panhandle, which was why Nora made sure to be discreet.

"Any day now, Rose." Nora touched her arm, winked, and kept walking, while Corbett scrolled through his email at her side.

"She's a lush."

"Said the Irishman."

"Doesn't take Irish eyes to see that one keeps her heart in a bottle." Then Corbett stopped in his tracks, almost causing a collision with the person behind him, and cursed at his phone.

"What is it?" Nora checked her watch again. She had less than fifteen minutes now. "I have to go."

"We both do." He stalked to the elevator banks and shook his head. "Change of plans."

Nora followed him into the elevator and checked her email to find a meeting request for a new client. There was no company name, but it was flagged as a white-glove prospect, which meant all available partners were required to attend. "In ten minutes?

26

Are they joking?"

"Apparently it's an emergency."

"Whose emergency?"

Before they could discuss it further the elevator doors opened to reveal a near frantic Rajesh, their newest partner in the firm.

"Ah, thank God you're both back. Jim is already in the executive conference room and the client will be here any moment. Please." Rajesh waved them out of the elevator and bustled behind them down the hallway. "We'll have an hour. I'll do the introduction and then we'll hear what they need. Can you imagine if we took it? What an opportunity. They're famously private, closed door, not a single equity offering as far as my sources can tell."

"Who is it?" Nora asked, but Rajesh had already doubled back toward reception to welcome the mystery company who'd just hijacked Corbett's lunch and prevented Nora from going to Strike today. She gritted her teeth as they stepped into the conference room where an admin was laying out settings of spotless china.

"How did the seminars go?" Jim asked, leaning back in his chair at the head of the table.

"Fine. The usual crop of new accountants."

"Our bright future." Jim smiled. "I'm sure you both showed them the way."

"We always do." Corbett sat down and pulled the tray of biscotti closer to him.

The admin set a cup of steaming green tea in front of Nora along with a meeting agenda that made her spine straighten with a shock of excitement.

Strike, Inc.

She stared at the client name at the top of the paper and ran a quick hand over her hair, smoothing any loose strands back into the chignon. Despite all these months of attending classes, she'd never worked up the nerve to actually speak to Logan. Now an entire host of nerves flip-flopped under her skin. When Rajesh ushered their guest into the room, Nora closed her eyes and took a steadying breath, but the voice behind her wasn't the one she'd expected. The deep, crisp notes filling the air didn't belong to Logan Russo.

Nora turned and saw a trim, handsome man in a full-vested suit. He shook Jim's hand with a measured intensity, and the silver sprinkled through his dark hair matched his watchband and tie, all combining to form one gleaming, deliberate package. It was a man she hadn't laid eyes on in months, who — in fact — she'd counted on never seeing again.

When he pivoted to Nora, his smile didn't alter the slightest fraction, but the light in his eyes changed. He remembered her, too. As she struggled to understand what was happening, he offered her a perfectly groomed hand.

"Gregg Abbott, Strike."

GREGG

She didn't say *Nice to meet you* or even *You look familiar.* None of those lying Midwestern pleasantries from Nora Trier. She met my eyes steadily, shook my hand with a dry palm, and when the overeager partner gestured for everyone to sit down, she folded her dove gray suit back into her executive chair, ready for whatever came next. Even if what came next was me.

I'm not what people expect when they hear *Strike.*

Strike, for most of the country, means Logan Russo. They see her signature swirl braid, the bald determination glazing the eye that stares them down over the top of a boxing glove. They see her when they're browsing a gas station aisle for protein bars and they see her while they're watching commercials during Sunday's NFL game, but most of all they see her every time they throw a secret late-night punch at the bathroom mirror, when they think no one's up besides them and their demons. They see Logan, only Logan, because that's what we told them to see.

Gregg Abbott — cofounder of Strike, husband of Logan Russo — is just a guy who sits in meetings. I sat down now, and took stock of my surroundings.

Parrish Forensics wasn't what I expected, either. Elegance exuded from the sleek fortieth-floor conference room and the paint-splashed canvasses along the wall: indigo on butter, orange against navy. There was no mistaking the crimson on chalk white. It was blood splatter, a crime scene exploded and examined at microscopic range, and I couldn't tell if it was meant to assure or discomfort the viewer. The same could be said about Nora Trier and the rest of her partners around the table. Most accountants gave you that long-suffering, "no one understands the importance of my tedium" sort of vibe, but this group had a different energy completely.

Jim Parrish was the same hale, jovial boomer who smiled from the white screen of his bio photo on their website, emanating all the energy of his résumé. I could picture him downing wheatgrass shots as he exposed the World Com scandal and running marathons while he linked a five-billion-dollar money laundering ring to several South American governments. He probably had enough enemies to fill a stadium, the type of hatred that keeps you young.

I'd taken the chair on Jim's left and Rajesh, the partner who'd met me out front, sat facing me.

"We are gratified you reached out to us, Mr. Abbott."

Rajesh Joshi was no challenge to read. He'd referenced his past professional life within the first minute of greeting me in the lobby (establishing credentials) and drew his shoulders up to hold himself a half inch taller than his spine wanted to stretch (seeking dominance). He wasn't a short man, average in most dimensions, although his head was disproportionally big, exacerbated by a hairstyle that reminded me of a rippling motorcycle helmet. I wondered if it intentionally emphasized his skull, whether head size to accountants was the equivalent of comparing dicks.

"Parrish Forensics provides expertise in a number of areas." Rajesh nodded to the assistant who controlled a PowerPoint from one corner of the room and took me through the standard company presentation, their mission statement, which read like a code of conduct for the United Nations, and the various services they offered. Forensic investigation, including asset misappropriation, money laundering, and financial statement fraud. Litigation support. Expert witness testimony. Divorce and estate property valuation. International expertise and resources, on-the-ground investigations around the globe.

While he talked, I took stock of the other two partners. Corbett MacDermott, a ruddy guy with a strong chin, was the only one in the room who wasn't trying to look pleasant. Unlike Jim and Rajesh, he was tie-free and jacketless, wearing an off-the-rack button-down rolled up to his elbows. Not a brawler, not a wimp. A man who could give or take a punch, but wouldn't be sorry to hear the bell at the end of the round. He looked, in fact, like he'd love to hear a bell right now. And finally, there was Nora Trier, watching the presentation as though she hadn't seen it a thousand times before. Occasionally she and the ruddy guy exchanged glances and there was something more there — a partnership beyond the business.

"The only continent we haven't found money in — yet — is Antarctica," Rajesh laughed at his own joke as he wrapped up the pitch. The last slide included the Strike logo and a shot from our website, which he left on-screen as they all turned subtly toward me, my cue.

I looked at each of them in turn.

"Strike is the fastest growing premium athletic brand in the country. We formed in 1999. Logan had already done some endorsement work, but together we developed a line of nutritional supplements and hit the market at the exact moment protein powders were exploding. From there we expanded into sponsorships, apparel, and urban gym experiences. We have over five million email subscribers to Logan's blog and we've trained dozens of youth state boxing and professional UFC champions. Our last year-end showed a net worth of $920 million. Based on our revenue growth, I assume we've passed the billion mark now."

You showed me yours, I'll show you mine.

"I've read numerous articles about Strike's trajectory, and I can personally confirm your sea salt cashew protein bar is excellent." Rajesh laughed, enjoying the reflected success of having a billion-dollar company at his table. "We understand Strike is a privately held corporation with two equal shareholders." He paused and glanced at me.

"That's correct. Logan and I each own

fifty percent. We're the founders, owners, and board of directors."

"Has the company ever undergone a formal audit?" This from Jim.

"It's never been necessary. We're self-made. We've financed every step we've ever taken, including the move this year to add thirty new gyms to our portfolio, doubling our physical footprint in the United States and moving into select markets in Canada."

"An aggressive expansion." Jim took a sip of his coffee.

I couldn't help it; I leaned in. "We all have a fight inside us, waiting to be unleashed. Skinny, short, fat, weak, old, happy, it doesn't matter. There's an animal within, a highly evolved aggressor that isn't conference room compatible, and Strike provides a channel for that ferocity right in the heart of the city, amid all the boardroom handshakes and neckties and professional courtesies. I've seen sixty-year-old women throwing side kicks that would decimate you, and twelve-year-old at-risk boys with their eyes on fire, like they're falling in love for the first time. Strike is primal; it feeds the animal and hones the human."

Each partner reacted separately to the pitch. Most onlookers would see an interchangeable assortment of executives, but there were tiny differences opening like fissures all around me. It was completely unlike the single-minded drive we had at Strike, the common goal we held supreme among us. These people were four islands who happened to be sharing a sea. Rajesh seemed like he was going to burst into applause, bobbing his head and smiling, although I'm not sure if he absorbed anything past the one billion in net worth. Corbett swirled his coffee and nodded, while Jim leaned farther back in his chair, acting the benevolent audience to the sales pitch. Nora was the only one who seemed unaffected. Her back was straight, a perfect stack of vertebrae. They didn't arch with false confidence or bow in intimacy, but sat easy and natural one on top of the other, a tower built of balance and grace. She set her pen down, a careful diagonal across the meeting agenda, then met my eyes squarely and spoke for the first time since the meeting began.

"The business model seems successful, Mr. Abbott." (A pat and a shoulder together.) "So, what is it that brings you to Parrish today?"

This was it — the point of no return. I could simply get up, excuse myself, walk out of this office suite and try to find another solution, another way to save Strike. The urge was so strong my legs tensed, ready to stand. But that wasn't the plan. Our mission statement was for the company to win at all costs. It's what we'd all worked toward for so long. The company was the most important thing.

I swallowed and returned Nora's look. "Strike is in trouble."

"How?" she asked, the first real curl of emotion flicking behind her eyes.

"We're hosting an event next week, a kick-boxing tournament called Strike Down. Fighters from all over the world will be competing for twenty million dollars in prize money."

Jim cut in. "We know. We've got a box, don't we, Nora?"

She looked down and played with a corner of the paper. It was her first self-soothing gesture of the meeting and I didn't entirely understand it. She was embarrassed to be a fan? Or was it something else?

"We organize partner outings," Nora explained. "Plays, Broadway shows, cooking classes. I suggested the tournament as our entertainment for this quarter."

"You won't be disappointed." I smiled. "Strike Down is going to be unlike anything the martial arts world has seen. In addition to the professional and amateur fights for both men and women, we'll have live technique demonstrations, meet and greets, a full range of exclusive products for sale, social media voting for fan-favorite contenders, and a surprise experience we haven't even unveiled yet."

"So, where's the trouble?"

I took a breath. "The prize money . . . it's gone."

"Withdrawn?"

"Apparently it was never funded. We had enough in the bank at the beginning of the year, but it's all been spent. The accountant is worthless — sorry — and said we've run over cost on our new clubs, which is bullshit. Ten thousand here or there, maybe, but this much overage is impossible."

"You're missing twenty million dollars." Nora said. "And you need to find it by . . . ?"

"Next Friday." A surprised noise came from Rajesh's side of the table, and I became aware of the rest of the people in the room again. Nora flashed Corbett a look, flaring so quick I almost didn't catch it, and the Irishman's eyes fell back to his coffee. Jim Parrish's jaw tightened one screw click, the tiniest adjustment. There were things swimming under this conference table, dark forms I couldn't see the shape of, but I felt the ripple of their current.

"We can stall the winners on their payout for a few days beyond the end of the tournament, but not more. Our reputation is too important to jeopardize."

"Mr. Abbott, our next opening for new engagements doesn't even begin until August. We pride ourselves on timely investigation, but —" Rajesh spluttered.

"We'll pay the premium for immediate service and provide any access you need: on-site, remote, software, hardware, twenty-four-hour support for your people. Please, we have no other options. The event is sold out, but we've sunk that revenue —"

"Cash, not revenue," Nora corrected.

"— back into the tournament. The stadium rental, the setup, tech, and staffing. We'll barely break even. We have to find that money."

"How much is your line of credit?" Corbett asked.

"I told you, Strike is self-determined. We don't rely on anyone but ourselves." Which was why asking for Parrish's help was this hard.

"So, no insurance, then."

"Property and casualty, of course, alternative risk — but nothing that would cover this."

Corbett twirled his pen, obviously checking some box in his head between *idiot* and *bankrupt.* Maybe *bankrupt idiot.* None of them understood that financing and insurance, public stock offerings, all of that corporate dealing was the opposite of what Strike symbolized. We had fought our way from the ground up. We didn't take handouts. And we'd always solved our own problems, until now. Rajesh opened his mouth, but I held up a hand.

"I have a . . . suspicion . . . about where the money went." The partners waited, postures straightened in rapt attention now, the lure of twenty million dollars brightening their hunter eyes. "As I mentioned, my wife and I both have a fifty percent stake in the company, equal authority to open accounts, initiate transactions, approve transfers."

I paused, my eyes straying to the PowerPoint slide still glowing on the wall. The Strike logo. Everything we'd worked toward for twenty years.

"Are you saying you suspect your wife — Logan Russo — of embezzling the money? From her own company?"

I blinked away from the screen. "It

wouldn't be about damaging Strike, not to Logan. She doesn't think the way you or I do. It's hard to explain, but she's a celebrity, a fighter. Everyone in the world knows her, but no one is allowed close enough to get under her guard."

"Aren't you?" Corbett asked.

"Our marriage has always been . . . complicated." My gaze didn't stray anywhere near Nora's side of the table. "It's impossible to know, sometimes, where our personal lives end and the company begins. But things have deteriorated in the last year. Something happened recently that she's blaming me for. And this is her primal response, to hit me where it will hurt the most."

"Mr. Abbott," Nora said, interrupting the Irish partner, who looked like he wanted to question me further. "If we accept the engagement, we'll be conducting the investigation with absolute impartiality. The evidence alone will inform our conclusions, and not anything said here. Your personal opinions are merely that. We'll be the ones to determine the truth regarding what Ms. Russo — or anyone else at the company — did or didn't do."

There was a fire in her eyes now, illuminating her immaculate professionalism and reminding me, for no tangible reason, of my wife.

"You'll find out for yourselves." I swallowed, appealing to the room at large. "She's been sabotaging Strike from the moment she announced this tournament to the world."

The Big One

January 25, 2019

I'm going to get personal today, guys. It doesn't happen often, but today's a milestone and you've shared so many of them with me so here's one back at you.

Strength.

Everyone wants it, reveres it, boasts about it, without the first fucking clue what it is.

As a kid I thought strength was earning a black belt. I kicked through boards and felt them splinter under my feet. I thought strength was a guttural yell, an opponent stumbling backward in the ring. In my twenties that turned into a title, a trophy, and the endless climb toward championships. By my thirties I thought strength meant expanding my reach, turning my passion into a career, a company. In my forties I decided strength was found in giving back, doing more to help my community and passing on the maybe four-and-a-half things I know.

I woke up a few days ago as a fifty-year-old woman in a villa in paradise. That's not a metaphor. I thought fifty deserved a holiday — a beach surrounded by lush palm groves and filled with enough lounge chairs and Bahama Mamas to properly salute the last half century. I didn't meditate or reflect. I didn't come up with some bullshit advice no one wants to hear. What is fifty, anyway? Enough trips around the sun to feel the rain in your bones or to send ungrateful little versions of your DNA into the world, if that's your thing. And enough time, at least for me, to figure out what strength really means.

When I woke up that morning, fifty years old, I didn't want to lounge or drink. I didn't want to tour pastel tributes to colonialism. I was Midwestern-sweaty, my winter skin blistering and winter lungs stinging with one pure need.

I wanted to fight.

I cut the trip short, flew back to the frigid heartland, and went straight home. *Our* home. I surprised everyone at the club after the regular evening beatdown and invited the trainers to strap on their gloves, all the faces our Minneapolis members know and love to hate. Jessica, senior trainer and legendary glute buster. Rae, our happy hour warrior. And of course Aaden, who graduated from the Strike Next after-school program to become one of the fiercest fighters I've ever trained.

I went into the ring with every single one of them and I fought them all into the ropes, all of them who, let's be honest, were giving the old lady a pass — except Aaden. Guys, he knocked me on my ass. This kid can jab you from three paces away. He can kick you from the fucking locker rooms. When I first met Aaden, I asked if they had kickboxing in Somalia and he said no; they liked football but they never had a ball. You don't need a ball to be a kickboxer, I told him. You were born with all the equipment you need. And damn do I hate being right. Aaden gave me a beating I'm going to feel until fifty-one. He was a blur of tendons, a tornado of roundhouses, and when he threw a cross-hook-uppercut combo this boss-gone-bottoms-up took a cartoon flop straight to the mat. While I was lying there, doubled over laughing in pain and spitting blood at the hands offering to help me up, I knew exactly how I wanted to celebrate my birthday.

Strength is knowing when to get the fuck

out of the way.

This is a milestone, guys, and not because I hit the half century mark. This week, the *New York Times* rated Strike the #1 premier urban gym in the United States. We have locations in twenty-nine major cities and teach self-defense, martial arts, and body conditioning to thousands of members who understand what strength is, because some of you have been fighting all of your lives. This isn't my milestone; it's yours. You've risen up. You've beaten back the odds. You've found the strength inside yourselves and tapped it every day, called it into the ring again and again.

YOU are the employees who file awkwardly into Strike for a team-building exercise and an hour later knock your manager sideways with a left hook you never knew you had.

YOU are the city kids who catch two buses to spend the afternoon pummeling a body bag and learning one-arm defenses against common grab assaults.

YOU are the women who barely notice the glass shards as you punch through that ceiling. Your resistance has given my life purpose, has galvanized me, and together we've made something that's stronger than all of us. YOU are Strike.

Today I'm making it official. I'm handing this company to you.

Get ready for Strike Down.

Fighters, whether you're from all over the metro or all over the world, men, women, amateurs, and pros, I'm calling you to downtown Minneapolis this July to compete for twenty million dollars in prize money.

You read that right. Twenty million dollars from Strike to you.

And I'm not done yet. In addition to eight figures of cash, I'm going to be choosing one of the champions to become the next face of Strike. Your face on the posters. Your gloves framing the walls.

Strike isn't me, not anymore.

Strike is you.

There is strength in knowing when to let something go so it can become greater than you. Fifty fucking years and I've finally found that strength. Now the future is up to you.

Today's Workout (Did you think I'd forget? I'm not that old yet.)

- Basic warm-up shuffle with upper body combos for five minutes.
- Round kicks to the knee, waist, and shoulder. One minute cycles per side.

Ten rounds with thirty seconds' rest in between.

- Fifty push-ups. You're celebrating my birthday, too.
- Repeat round with front kicks, then hold chair pose for ninety seconds.
- Half mile cooldown jog and stretch.

NORA

As Rajesh explained their vetting process for new clients, Nora pulled up the blog where Logan had announced the Strike Down tournament. It had originally posted five months ago, just after she'd joined the gym. She hadn't read any sabotage in the content at the time, and — apart from knowing the money was gone — she couldn't find anything alarming now. What did Gregg Abbott think his wife had done?

Gregg Abbott. Cofounder of Strike. Logan Russo's husband. When Nora had met him, months ago and half a country away, she'd had no idea he was any of these things.

Nora sat through the rest of the meeting quietly. Like most new clients, Gregg didn't understand why Parrish couldn't accept the job immediately.

"We must complete the evaluation first," Rajesh sounded apologetic, "to ensure our firm has no conflicts of interest before we begin an investigation. In the event our findings lead to any criminal or civil charges —"

"I'm not going to drag Strike's reputation through a public trial. I just need the money back. Now."

"Nevertheless." Rajesh inclined his head, politely ending the debate and the meeting.

"How long will this evaluation take?" Gregg asked, rising from his chair.

"As long as we need to assure our independence," Nora replied, drawing his attention as she moved to the door. "We'll advise you as soon as possible. May I walk you out?"

His eyes widened almost imperceptibly, but he quickly nodded and shook hands with everyone before falling into step alongside her. As they walked back to reception, Nora caught the scent of maple and musk. He smelled as good as she remembered and he looked even better: summer gold skin, precisely shaved jaw, and amber eyes that missed nothing. He wasn't wearing his Atticus Finch glasses and that was probably for the best.

She nodded as they passed several analysts in the corridor. "You never mentioned how you became aware of our firm, Mr. Abbott. We always ask new clients."

He paused when they reached the foyer, glancing at the receptionist before replying. "It was on a recommendation."

"From someone in Atlanta?"

He cleared his throat. "Yes, it might have been in Atlanta."

At least he was honest about it. The least she could do was return the favor. The elevator dinged, but instead of shaking hands and saying goodbye like she would with any other business associate, she stepped inside. As soon as the doors closed, she turned to face him.

"Let's be clear."

"Let's." He didn't completely drop the pretense of formality, but took a step closer, narrowing the gap between them. Nora resisted the urge to back up.

"Atlanta was a one-night stand." She didn't blink, didn't allow her volume or tone to change from what it had been moments ago. "It didn't mean anything. We didn't even exchange full names, so I have no idea how you found me here."

"You had some business cards on the dresser in your hotel room. I took one when you were in the bathroom."

"Why?"

He didn't reply for a moment. His eyes softened and he swallowed. "I wanted to

51

see you again." Then, shaking his head. "Not like this, obviously. I didn't know the prize money was gone until our quarterly financial review this morning, but when the accountant told me, you were the first person I thought of."

His hand lifted, bridging the distance between them, but at that moment the elevator stopped to let in a group of people. They both pivoted to the front and stood silently for the rest of the ride.

Nora focused on breathing. This was exactly why she didn't sleep with people in the Twin Cities. Her cardinal rule, since the day Jim Parrish hired her and gave her a new path, was to never mix the personal and professional. It hadn't mattered that she'd done the right thing with Sam White; she'd still lost everything — her job, her family, even her childhood had somehow been taken away, the memories fractured and shadowed by the knowledge of how it had all ended. How *she* had ended it. But Nora wasn't stupid. She didn't make the same mistake twice.

When the elevator reached the skyway level, she and Gregg exited. The lunchtime crowd had thinned. Groups of chattering coworkers had given way to suits on their phones, either going to meetings or starting their weekend early. Nora headed west toward Strike's building with Gregg at her shoulder. He was shorter than Corbett. Whenever she walked through the skyway with her partner, they always looked like the odd couple, but she and Gregg moved smoothly together. Their pace was quick, in sync, and noticing that fact made Nora distinctly uncomfortable.

"Would you have any qualms if I headed this engagement?"

"None at all." His answer was immediate. "Why do you think I came to you?"

"Do you believe me to be impartial?"

She looked over to see his eyes scanning her face, her hair, as if searching for the right answer, but there was no hesitation in his reply. "Yes."

A heat rose between them and Nora looked away to find Rose, her homeless romantic, nodding and grinning as they approached. Nora glared at her and shook her head. Rose cackled as they passed.

"If Parrish accepts this assignment, we'll be investigating you. We'll be investigating your wife. We'll turn your company and your lives inside out. Is there anything you want to tell me now? What are we going to find?"

They stopped outside the entrance to

Strike. The lunch class she'd missed was just getting out and Nora spotted familiar faces — red, sweaty, and triumphant — leaving the gym. She should have been among them.

"You're going to find twenty million dollars."

"In one week? I might catch the thief, but if the money was stolen it could be anywhere in the world by now. Finding the money is impossible."

"Not for you."

"You don't know anything about me."

He moved a few feet down the hall, out of sight of the gym members and staff. "I checked on your company this morning. Your partner Rajesh wasn't bragging back there. For a small firm, you carry a big stick." His voice lowered. "And I personally know you are thorough, creative, and attentive to every detail."

She swallowed and found her mouth had gone dry.

"I need you, Nora." He reached out and shook her hand — his grip warm yet professional — before leaving to go inside.

Nora walked back into the skyway between their buildings, leaned against the glass as traffic rushed underneath, and put her face in her hands.

What the hell had she done?

Most people didn't realize accounting wasn't about numbers. Anyone could learn the basics of a balance sheet, but an investor wouldn't buy stock in a company just because some *numbers guy* said it looked all right. Maybe the numbers guy was a major stockholder who wanted his share price to go up. Maybe he was married to the CFO. Maybe he was an anarchist who liked setting things on fire. Numbers were meaningless without integrity. Stockholders relied on the ethics of accountants, on the work of men and women who counted inventory and visited property holdings to make sure they actually existed, who checked that sales were genuine and invoices weren't stuffed in a drawer, and to do all that an accountant had to be absolutely neutral, without bias or even the appearance of bias.

Forensic accounting had even more rigorous standards because every testimony became an invitation for attack. Defense attorneys checked Nora's background on a daily basis. Her identity theft protection software pinged like a heart monitor during big cases, when entire teams of legal interns

55

tried to find even a hint of shade in order to convince the jury that Nora's testimony was unreliable. They found nothing. Her cardinal rule to dissociate all personal and professional interests had made her into a model investigator. For fifteen years, Nora had thrived on the basis of her integrity, her independence.

But when it came to Strike, she was anything but neutral. And it had nothing to do with Gregg Abbott.

Pushing away from the skyway glass, Nora turned around. Through the second-story floor-to-ceiling windows she could see the Strike studio hung with rows of punching bags. This was the exact spot where she'd first seen Logan Russo. Nora had been crossing the skyway on her way to some appointment, and stopped dead in her tracks. Had it been almost a year ago now? One year since she'd stood here, transfixed by the blazing fighter in the window, an olive-skinned woman who strode between the bags, correcting fighters' postures and demonstrating kicks. She wasn't beautiful. Spare and dense, she was a miracle of flesh on whom too many clothes would be tragic. She'd worn a ripped tank top and shorts that day. Her dark eyes had glowed with humor, her black hair slicked into a low bun. Nora had traced the shadows in her arms as she moved, the line of her jaw as she threw her head back and laughed. The woman worked her way through the bags until Nora couldn't see her anymore, but it was impossible for someone like that to ever disappear. She would burn through the back of your eyelids first. Nora had stood frozen at the glass for another minute, waiting for the woman to come back into view. When she didn't, Nora walked into Strike and added her name to the waitlist to join the gym. Six months later she'd taken her first class.

That first session, Nora had hovered nervously in the back. She'd bought several books about martial arts form and technique — one had even mentioned Logan as a condescending aside "testament" to the growing presence of women in the sport — and Nora had memorized the basic punches. Jab, hook, cross, uppercut. She strapped and re-strapped the black boxing gloves she'd received with her locker key, oddly comforted by the padded restriction of movement in her wrists. When Logan appeared and cued up a song she'd never heard, a song probably meant for millennials or whoever came after millennials, she felt old and out of place. She followed along to the warm-up, though, drawn out of herself by the woman at the front of the studio.

Logan Russo was a cyclone, a brilliant burst of energy orbiting the room. She made them forget they were lawyers and hassled fathers and accountants, and turned them one by one into warriors. Halfway through the first class, as they worked through a combination drill of punches and kicks, Nora felt a hand circling her arm.

"Don't collapse your elbow or you'll lose all the power in your back."

Nora nodded at her punching bag, not daring to turn around, to trace the grip back to the woman attached to it.

"Here." Logan shifted behind her and held Nora's elbow down by her side. "Hit the bag."

Nora obeyed, feeling her knuckles burn while the bag barely stirred. Logan didn't comment, but lifted Nora's elbow straight out to the side and placed her other hand on Nora's sweat-soaked running shirt, pressing the point between her neck and her shoulder where masseuses found hidden tendons that released shards of white light through her body. "Now hit it again."

Nora did, and the muscles underneath Logan's hand engaged and flexed, shooting energy into her arm.

"Well, hello, gorgeous trapezius." Logan's gravelly voice curled with humor as she patted Nora's back. "Now keep hitting it. Don't give that fucking elbow any opportunities. It wants to defend. Make it attack."

Then she moved to the next student, while Nora became aware of her entire body in a way she hadn't been since she was a teenager. She felt the connection between muscles, tendon, organ, and bone, all firing with a new, unnamed excitement. The awkwardness faded and she felt, for the first time, like she was strong.

After that first class her hands were meat, raw and bruised even through the protective gloves. Her knuckles mesmerized her. It was like she'd never seen them before, and maybe she hadn't. She tried to remember what Logan's knuckles looked like when her ungloved hand encased Nora's elbow, but she'd been too nervous to look. She'd focused only on the bag, Logan's instructions breathing hot against her back, and the pounding of her own heart.

Nora concentrated on her technique after that, reserving a spot in every available lunch class and trying to lose herself in the forest of bags. When Logan paced the rows,

Nora crouched further into her stance, guard up, always pivoting away from the sleek black hair and piercing eyes.

They did push-up breaks. They did Heisman drills. One day an entire obstacle course of tractor tires was laid out when they arrived and they had to leap over them with their legs bound, pull themselves into the ring, and try to land a punch on Logan, who shouted them all on with throaty curses. Another day giant bolts of fabric had been stretched across the room, effectively dropping the ceiling to five feet off the ground, and they had to do the entire session in a squat. Nora couldn't walk down a flight of stairs for two days afterward, taking elevators everywhere and tracing the outline of wasted muscle in bed at night.

Nora knew she wasn't the only devotee in the Logan Russo cult. A sea of eyes followed Logan's every move, and peals of sweat-flushed laughter echoed when she told stories about the absurdity of having a door-man ("The building says he can curate our mail upon request. Isn't that the fanciest fucking term for a felony you've ever heard?") or being invited to a gala for the mayor's urban outreach initiative ("My shoulders have hulked through more sleeves than Marvel could CGI-imagine. I'm having nightmares of reaching for a meatball and spraying sequins into some senator's drink."). She drew them in with the illusion that they were all friends chatting on some rooftop bar, before annihilating them with a drill that brought them gasping to their knees.

Nora thought of dozens of responses, witty things she could say to Logan as she walked by, but none of them made it past her lips. Instead she threw silent punches and kicks and hurried to the locker room afterward to change. Because what could an accountant ever say that would interest someone like Logan Russo?

Now Nora stood in the skyway, staring at Strike. Her muscles should be aching and sore, humming from the noon class she'd missed. Instead they felt empty, restless, inadequate. She brushed the spot on her elbow where Logan had once corrected her form and tried to feel the skin as Logan would have, wondering whether the fighter had sensed an opponent, a creep, or a friend. Whether she'd sensed anything at all.

She was nothing to Logan Russo. And yet.

In the meeting, Gregg said something had happened in their marriage recently, something Logan blamed him for. A flush of guilt rose up as Nora realized he might have been talking about Atlanta. She might be the thing that had disrupted their marriage. Backing away from the glass, Nora retreated across the skyway and into the Parrish building. It wasn't rational, this feeling. She'd done nothing wrong, but right and wrong never mattered when things became personal. It was messy, dangerous ground.

I need you, Nora.

It was the same thing Sam White said when he'd pleaded with her to save his company, to put her friendships and her heart first. And Sam White had ended up dead.

GREGG

Three hours later I walked out of downtown in the company of the smartest, most driven women in the world. The senior managers of Strike all marched ahead of me, eager to get their steps in and reach the towering glass of U.S. Bank Stadium, site of the Strike Down tournament.

Our last order of business for the day was a preliminary walk-through of the stadium, but that didn't stop Brennan, Director of Events, from doing a mobile rundown of where everything stood.

"All the staffing is confirmed for security, ushers, and concessions. Merch is arriving today and tomorrow. The vStrike prototypes are en route. The last box for the preliminaries has been taken, so we are officially sold out on all nights. I've notified —"

"Brennan."

She paused, fingers hovering over her tablet.

"We're four days away."

"Right. Four days." She flipped the tablet to show us a countdown clock in the bottom corner of the screen. Laserlike concentration. No detail too small to be noticed and handled. But underneath that, buried in the lift of her eyebrows and rush of her vowels — excitement.

"You're going to have to breathe at some point between now and the start of the tournament."

Laughter erupted through the group and even Brennan smiled as we crossed an intersection. "It's one of the bullet points."

"Good." I held up my hands. "Sold. Out. Congratulations, everyone!" I shouted over the clapping and cheering that erupted around me. I tried to feel it with them, to take in this moment that we — that Strike — had created, but the weight of the missing prize money still churned in my gut. When I turned toward C.J., the Director of Marketing, she waved me off, grinning into her phone.

"I'm already tweeting it."

I should have told them. Every single one of these women was just as devoted to Strike, had given as much of their time and talent to this tournament as either Logan or I. They deserved to know that everything might come crashing down on our heads, but I couldn't bring myself to do it. Not yet. This was a moment they deserved to savor.

When we got to the stadium the staff were waiting for us. They escorted our group inside and we filed onto the concourse overlooking the field. No one spoke for a minute. Except for a few workers milling in the aisles, the sections and the floor were completely empty. It was a sixty-five-thousand-seat, thirty-story blank canvas, and in four days it would become the epicenter of the martial arts world.

C.J. walked over to me. She'd been with Strike longer than any of the other directors, since we took the leap from merchandise and supplements and started construction on our first gym. Holding up her phone, which meant she was either live-streaming this or planning to slice it into a more polished piece for later, she grinned and asked me a question.

"Gregg Abbott, did you ever think you'd be here?"

"Not me, C.J." I paparazzi-palmed the camera. "Interview someone else."

"I'd ask Logan if she were here."

We both let that lie, then she pocketed the phone and turned to face the belly of the stadium with me. The amount of space was mind-boggling. You had to be insane to pull off an event of this magnitude. Insane, or in love.

"No, really, Gregg. When you went to Palicka vs. Russo, could you ever have imagined this?"

I smiled at the massive stadium, remembering.

"I didn't have to imagine."

It was twenty years ago. I'd been in Las Vegas for a conference and someone handed me fourth-row tickets to what turned out to be Logan's greatest, highest-rated match of her career. I'd heard of Logan Russo before, the undefeated Italian fighter they called the Mill City Miracle, but the odds that night favored Palicka, an up-and-coming Czech who was supposed to rob Logan of her title. I put a hundred dollars on the Czech and walked into the lights of the MGM Grand Garden Arena, unaware that my entire life was about to change.

Logan decimated Palicka. On the KO, she landed a side kick to the challenger's face that broke her nose and sprayed blood all over the mats, and I barely saw it. I was mesmerized by the flex of Logan's calf, the ripple of perfectly arced quads at the moment of impact, glistening with moisture and salt and indomitable victory. She watched her opponent fall without a flicker of change in expression, then she paced the far end of the ring, shaking her head at the count of the ref, and I swear she wanted the Czech to get up, like the KO had robbed her of something more vital than a retained title could give back.

I was nothing and everything in that moment. A loser who'd placed the wrong bet. Not even a story. Just a spectator to the blood-splattered day my life began.

I spent the rest of that night looking up everything the internet knew about Logan Russo, which in the late nineties wasn't much. I talked to various staff until I found out she was staying in a penthouse suite at the MGM and bribed one of the concierges to tell me she was scheduled for a massage in the spa the next morning. I booked a facial and hot shave.

I'd been in the relaxation room a little over two hours when she came in, dressed in the spa robe and slippers. She looked startled at first, as though she'd expected to have the room to herself. If we'd met in 2019 everything would have played differently. She would have been jaded, suspicious of random men acting like they didn't see her. She probably would have called hotel security to run interference. But this was pre-Y2K, before the towers fell, before W had been elected, before smartphones, and long before strong was the new skinny, and so Logan just gave me a once-over before lying on a chaise lounge, facing away.

I waited three minutes, time for her to get comfortable but not long enough to forget I was there.

"Congratulations."

She glanced over and the hand she'd braced against her ribs instantly dropped to her side.

"Thanks." Her voice was a surprise. Hoarse and low, the kind of voice that works its way into your subconscious.

"You were unbelievable. No tricks. No tells. The sheer ingenuity and power . . ." I trailed off, letting her fill in the spaces, before holding up the paper I'd been reading. "The sports section doesn't do it justice."

Then I turned away, hiding behind the pages, and waited.

She could have walked away then, or closed her eyes and pretended she was alone. She could have gone ahead and called security to toss me out, spa slippers and all. She held the power to decide what happened next, if anything.

A minute passed where all the words on the newspaper blurred into a haze of black and white. I turned a page, pretending to read, until she cleared her throat and asked my name.

We traded the usual tidbits — work, life, origin stories — the stuff that fills Tinder profiles now. At one point an attendant brought water with sliced lemon. Logan sipped it, made a face, and pushed the glass aside.

On an impulse, I stood up and held out a hand. "Let's get some real food."

We went to Venice, the faux Venice down the street, for a victory breakfast. Logan ordered an egg white omelet and a drink that almost made her cry. It was called the green goddess smoothie and she finished it in three orgasmic gulps. I laughed and ordered two more, another for her and one for me because I had to try it now, too.

We talked about Vegas, the unnatural nature of the city itself, a mirage in the desert, while we sat by a Venetian canal and drank liquefied gardens. It was a perfect date, the kind of date that wasn't. I told her crazy stories about growing up in Chicago, making her bust out in infectious gut-laughs, while stealing bites of her omelet and offering her some of my steak and eggs in return. We watched the people who'd been out all night stumble down the canal in their miniskirts and booze-stained Cherry Poppin' Daddies blazers.

After we finished eating I threw a few bills on the table and stood, tipping a smile toward the boulevard. "Let's keep those tendons loose."

We walked the surreal canal, then headed down the Strip where a guy — who was trying to give us flyers for prostitutes — recognized Logan and followed us for half a block, miming punches at our backs.

"Do you know what's strange?" I asked as the guy leapt and jumped behind us, shouting to all his flyer pals. "Yo, this is the Mill City Miracle! Logan fucking Russo!"

She didn't answer. She seemed like she was struggling not to cram the flyers down the guy's throat.

"I couldn't taste the parsley or cilantro at all. They combined forces to create some bright new super herb. It's still here." I touched my neck and sighed. "I was going to try to kiss you, but now I just want to ride out the smoothie aftertaste for as long as I can."

Her laugh lit up the whole street and the flyer guy melted into irrelevance. We talked protein shakes then, and how Logan had spent years tweaking her homemade formula for maximum performance.

"Most protein powders are geared toward men, toward male hormones and physiology. You should see my kitchen — it's like a mad scientist lab of bottles and machines. I buy dried peas in bulk and grind them down. There's pea dust everywhere."

"And I didn't think I could find you more attractive."

We wandered back into MGM almost four hours after we'd left, only to find Logan's manager and coach panicking at the front desk. They hadn't called the police — yet — but had spent most of the morning searching for their lost champion. She'd forgotten about a press conference that was supposed to have already begun. They whirled her away and I followed, snuck into the back of the room, and ignored the repeated glares of her manager.

During the Q&A, a reporter asked what it was like to be breaking the glass ceiling of combat sports. Logan shrugged and said, "I get that question every time I win a fight, so I have to wonder — how fucking thick is this glass? Because I've been breaking it my entire life." Every woman in the room cheered, literally cheered, and the hair on the back of my neck stood up. My body

71

absorbed the significance of the moment in a way my head couldn't yet fully grasp.

When another reporter asked Logan what she planned to do next, her eyes met mine. A smile lifted one corner of her mouth, but all she said was, "You'll find out."

I didn't see her after that. Her manager hustled her out of the press conference and when I asked the friendly concierge, he said they'd gone straight from the reporters into luggage-loaded limousines.

A week passed. A week during which I kicked myself continuously for not giving her my card, not kissing her when I had the chance. I'd played a cool hand and all I could do now was return to Chicago and wait, imagining all her possible futures without me. A marriage to her bald coach, a couple bullheaded kids, a no-frills gym where she trained the next generation of athletes, and features in sports magazines titled, "Where Are They Now?"

One week after I'd lost the hundred-dollar bet, my assistant put through a call.

"Hi, it's Logan."

I sighed, a tide of relief pushing me back into my office chair.

"Thank Christ. I can't get that goddamn breakfast out of my head. Be honest. Do you think there was weed in the smoothie?"

She'd laughed, low and happy. "Might be why I can't duplicate it."

"What have you tried?"

We talked for an hour about smoothies and shakes, then moved on to roundly abuse the protein bars on the market. At the end of the call, I looked up at the cracked and water-stained ceiling tiles of my Gold Coast office. The brand management business, so far, had not afforded better amenities.

"You know that glass ceiling the reporter mentioned? The one you have to keep breaking over and over?"

"Yeah?"

"When you obliterated Palicka, you didn't hit her repeatedly in the same place like some fighters do, weakening the whole by focusing on a single point. You beat every square inch of her body. When she tried to defend her core, you went for her head. When she leaned her upper body back, you attacked her base."

"You pay attention."

"Let me be completely honest. I was half-erect the entire time. I'm getting hard now just thinking about it."

She laughed. "I'm trying not to think what that says about you."

"Obviously it says I'm booking a flight to Minneapolis right now. And the next time I see you I'm not letting you get whisked away to some press conference without a fight."

"Oh, you're a fighter now?"

"The intent here is that I be the lover and you be the fighter."

"I can live with that." Her voice was breathier now. "So, the glass ceiling . . . ?"

"The glass ceiling." I dropped my voice to mirror hers. "It's not a thing you can punch in one place and expect to break through. You have to attack it like you attacked Palicka. You have to hit it in places it doesn't even know it has."

"Like where?"

"I'll tell you Friday. I'll be there in time for breakfast."

By Friday, I'd gotten hold of a contact who lent me the keys to an old Pillsbury test kitchen on an abandoned floor in one of the downtown skyscrapers. Logan and I spent the entire morning blending, sampling, arguing, and flirting. We made a giant mess of spinach, celery leaves, orange rinds, and sugar snap peas, then had sex on top of all of it. Sometime that day, we decided to form a company and name it Strike.

Now, two decades later, I was stepping back into an arena, but this time with a billion-dollar company on the line.

"Keep up," C.J. called as the Strike directors trooped down to the U.S. Bank Stadium field. I followed at a distance, watching them block the setup for the main events, working their magic to bring this tournament to life.

I checked my phone, but there was no news yet from Parrish Forensics.

I hadn't been completely honest with Nora earlier. Yes, I'd checked out her company, but not this morning. I'd looked her up months ago, immediately after I'd gotten home from Atlanta, and what I'd found was formidable. Nora Trier, forensic accountant, was as relentless in a courtroom as Logan Russo was in the ring. And now I was pitting one against the other.

The tournament lights were about to ignite. Logan would be in center stage, and once again I'd be watching from the shadows. I just hoped I hadn't already lost everything on this bet.

NORA

"I can't stay long." Corbett seemed preoccupied as he and Nora slid onto their usual stools at the end of Ike's massive two-sided bar. "Katie's cooking a tenderloin tonight."

"New baby?" Corbett's wife tended to make extravagant meals whenever she announced the next addition to their herd.

"Not mine if that's the case."

"Vasectomies can spontaneously reverse."

The bartender set their drafts down and gave the mahogany a knock for his regulars before working his way down the bar.

"I had 'em take my balls, too, for good measure."

"That explains why Rajesh keeps circling and sniffing. He's so confused."

Corbett laughed and shook his head. Despite the quaking in her gut over this new client, Nora felt an answering smile tugging at her mouth as she clinked her glass against his.

The Friday happy hour crowd was the usual mix of loosened post-work ties and tight preshow dresses. Ike's was an institution in downtown Minneapolis, a street-level bar built of gleaming wood and dark, nestling corners. Heavy curtains blocked out the urban glare and everything that buzzed impatiently beyond the windows.

Normally Corbett filled their happy hours with anecdotes and family stories, but today he seemed more interested in staring at his beer, and in the absence of his usual energy, the two of them lapsed into silence. Nora had never been great at casual conversation. She could have a two-hour debate about the appropriate amount of internal controls for small businesses, but commenting on the weather seemed as brainless as an emoji text string. She didn't admit it to anyone, but she actually prepped for small talk with clients; she read BuzzFeed articles, kept track of popular TV shows and local news so she could chat with seeming ease about *Game of Thrones* (that ending!) or whichever road construction project was creating the most headaches. It was an investment, just not the tax-deductible kind.

When Nora could get employees engaged

in small talk, they started to forget why she was there. She became a faceless friend, an anonymous confidante. They opened up about more things — weaknesses in the business or witnessing improper behavior — pointing out possible avenues of investigation that saved Nora's team valuable time. Chatting for hours with strangers, though, was exhausting. After a long day of client interviews, her jaw would ache from smiling and her sentences bloomed bright and brittle, "like a robot impersonating a human" Corbett once joked.

"Thanks," she'd deadpanned and then drained her beer in a way that would put a robot to shame.

"But a really good robot. An Inga-quality robot." Corbett had designed the computer program named Inga, so in a way it was a compliment, like Frankenstein comparing a villager to his monster.

Once, last winter — and perhaps to prove she wasn't a robot — she'd convinced him to try a class at Strike. It was bring-a-friend-for-free day. He'd grudgingly filled out the forms and sweated through half the session until Logan came by and tried to correct his form. When she jabbed his ribs under his "chicken wing" elbow, he fell into the bag and groaned, "Good god, woman. I'm an accountant. My opponents cheat their investors, they don't take potshots at my ribs."

"Are you kidding me? I saw that movie." She'd laughed into the mic. "Who saw that Ben Affleck movie, *The Accountant*?"

Shouts went up among the thumping of bags. "We've got Affleck right here, guys. Let's see how much ass he can kick."

He didn't walk normally for days and refused to ever go back. For weeks afterward, he called her Affleck and she called him Chicken Wing. But regardless of whether he teased or challenged her, asked for advice or offered it, he brought out a casualness in Nora that she'd thought only lived in other people. She'd never had to prep for conversations with Corbett.

When their beers crept past the halfway mark and they passed on another round, Nora sighed. She was running out of time. Katie's tenderloin was cooking, the fat bubbling to an inevitable crisp.

"Can we talk about this client?"

In the hours since she'd escorted Gregg Abbott out of Parrish Forensics, Nora had tried to focus on her other cases, but even as she reviewed field status reports and prepped testimony for a court appearance, she could feel herself rearranging things, considering what she could reschedule or hand off to subordinates to clear a space in her head big enough to examine that spine-tingling voice with its impossible deadline. One week. A twenty-million-dollar chase. It wouldn't be the largest fraud of her career, but it would be the most challenging, an all-out sprint requiring every trick and tool and ounce of energy she had. The lure was almost irresistible, but — she had to keep reminding herself — taking it was out of the question.

She was trying to choose her next words, dreading Corbett's reaction, when he pushed his chair back and said, "You're taking it."

Nora blinked. "What?"

"They passed the vetting process this afternoon, and Jim told me to make it happen. He and Rajesh are preparing for that conference in Singapore and I'm taking the family to the North Shore for the weekend, so that leaves you." He drained the rest of his beer and set a bill next to the empty glass.

"You're assuming there are no threats to my independence." She sat up straighter, trying to slow this whole conversation down.

"Don't make a fuss about your membership," Corbett said. "It's not an issue. How much do you pay to go there?"

"Five hundred dollars a month."

"Jesus Christ."

"I don't have a gaggle of children to feed and clothe."

"Or a wife who considers Amazon her own personal warehouse." He muttered, reaching across the bar for her beer, and took a healthy swig. "How much of your monthly disposable income does that represent? Ten percent? Fifteen?"

"Closer to ten."

He shook his head and scooped his cash back off the bar. "You're buying this round. You should've bought every round this month."

She tossed out a twenty without comment, grinning despite the rumbling of unease in her gut.

"The membership's negligible," he continued. "It's not an investment, anyway. Month to month?"

She nodded.

"It's a discretionary consumption, just like eating at a restaurant. You put all this through the framework already." It wasn't a question. The conceptual framework for independence worked like a living machine at the edges of their minds. "And if it really bothers you, you can always suspend your membership for the duration of the case. Or, Christ, join another gym. For a hell of a lot cheaper."

He was right; it was just a gym and there were a host of others downtown, but even the idea of them repelled. They wouldn't smell like the sweat that emanated off the bags; their walls wouldn't echo with Logan's voice, pushing them to be stronger, jab faster. *Guards up! You never know what's coming at you next.*

"I'm not worried about that. The membership doesn't compromise my independence."

"See, there's no problem. You can take it." He stood up to leave and before she'd figured out the best way to phrase it or map all the possible responses, she grabbed his arm and swung him back around.

"I had sex with Gregg Abbott."

It wasn't what she'd meant to say. It wasn't the reason she felt conflicted, but before she could tell him more or try to explain the feeling twisting her stomach, Corbett's expression froze. He looked directly at her for the first time since they'd sat down, his mouth open, and all the good things he'd thought her to be seemed to drain slowly from his eyes.

"Ellie, you're married."

■ ■ ■ ■

"Jesus Christ." Corbett had left the dark crush of Ike's happy hour and pushed his way out to the sun-broiled downtown streets. He walked fast and hard, but Nora kept up. "You *slept* with him. You slept with *him*." He kept repeating it, changing the emphasis to a different word each time, as if trying to find the one that would finally make sense. She felt shock reverberating through him and didn't know how many knots of their friendship were loosening, becoming unsecured.

"I didn't know who he was at the time. But now . . ."

They stopped near a crowd waiting for the light to change and Nora stared at the trucks and cars honking their way through the intersection. "Gregg said something happened to him and Logan recently, an event she blamed him for. Maybe she found out about the affair."

"You're speculating." Corbett's voice dropped into short, clipped tones.

"I know, but it would make sense. Most people resist polyamory."

"I can hardly believe I'm having this conversation right now. Mike's a good man.

And you're a mother, for Christ's sake."

"I told you, we have an—"

"An open marriage." He shook his head like gnats were buzzing in front of his face. "What does that even mean?"

The light changed and the crowd hurried into the crosswalk, Corbett and Nora among them.

"It means we don't rely on each other for every physical and emotional need. You know Mike." She gestured helplessly. "He's affectionate, demonstrative. He was born to cuddle with someone while watching TV, and I . . ." She shrugged.

"You were born to expose liars and cheats and you think that means you have to keep everyone in your life at a fifty-meter distance." Corbett shook his head. "This makes perfect sense coming from you, Ellie. I shouldn't even be surprised."

She hadn't expected him to understand, but even so, the bite in his words struck deep. Woodenly, she moved to the talking points she'd developed in her head, the ones she'd saved in case they ever had this conversation.

"I know this resides completely outside most people's comfort levels, but it's rational. Monogamy doesn't make sense. Love isn't a finite resource; it's not depreciable."

He barked out a humorless laugh. "What, is it like goodwill, then? Do you perform yearly impairment tests on your marriage?"

"I'm saying use doesn't deplete it."

Corbett didn't reply, but he looked more and more agitated. They arrived at their building and headed down to the parking garage. Nora floundered for the right thing to say, some way to convey the necessity of all the choices she'd made for the last fifteen years. Was there any way to translate the architecture of a life to someone standing outside it? To show them that if one single pillar was moved, everything could come crashing down? But Corbett was done trying to deconstruct her; he'd already shifted back to the more pressing topic.

"Gregg Abbott came to Parrish for you," he murmured, so low she almost didn't hear it. "He wants it to be you."

"I made it clear to him today that I'm impartial," she shook her head, then — thinking of Logan — amended, "at least as far as he's concerned."

Corbett didn't seem to notice her qualification. They walked into the garage and stopped next to their adjoining parking spots. An emotion crossed his face, twitching at the corners of his eyes before it disappeared and his expression hardened. "If

85

that's true then you can take this case."

"But . . ." she trailed off.

"Listen to me. He thinks you're biased. He thinks he can influence you." Corbett stepped closer, grasping Nora by the shoulder, and for a moment they stood frozen, rooted to the dark cement floor in the bowels of the city. When Corbett spoke again, his voice sounded like a stranger's. "He has no idea who he's dealing with."

Nora lived in Steeplechase, a housing development tucked in the wooded hills south of St. Paul and built on the site of an old horse ranch. Some of her newer neighbors didn't know the history of the land. They thought they had a knack for growing heirloom tomatoes and Nora merely smiled at their enthusiastic endorsements of organic gardening; mentioning the decades of horse shit fertilizing their lawns wasn't on her list of neighborhood conversation points. Veering away from the sprawling mansions, she drove into a cul-de-sac of townhomes that backed up to the abandoned horse trails snaking for miles through the woods. Before she'd joined Strike, she'd disappeared into those trails every night.

Inside, the kitchen and great room were empty. She found Henry in his room, playing some fighting game on his computer. He was locked in hand-to-hand combat when she knocked on the open door.

"Geez, Mom, you scared me." He didn't flinch or even blink an eye.

"Don't say 'geez,' it's slang."

"Jesus, Mom, you scared me." He smirked without taking his eyes off the screen. The other fighter spun a 360-degree somersault in midair, ending with a kick that shot blue flames into Henry, who immediately lost half his energy. Her son didn't hesitate before attacking again, though, running headlong into another blinding shot from his opponent. She didn't allow him to play shooting games, so he consistently found ones like this that skirted the edge of acceptable violence.

"Can I watch?"

He shrugged, which meant yes in ten-year-old. She pulled up a stool that was too small for either of them, a relic of his younger years she'd yet to donate to Goodwill, and sat down. During the school year she helped Henry with his homework, an hour they spent together after dinner where she coached him through long division and the scientific method, but in the summertime she had no place in his daily routine. He and Mike were an exuberant party of two, always off on some biking adventure, attending ball games or cat video festivals. They sent Nora pictures which she scrolled through in airports or while sitting in court waiting to testify.

"Why didn't you duck that?" she asked, as another jolt of blue flames caught Henry's fighter square in the chest. She resisted the urge to comb her fingers through his shaggy blond hair. He never liked being groomed.

Henry shrugged.

"You keep running into those fire things. Can't you back up or dodge him?"

"For a minute, maybe, but Nathan's like eighteen levels higher than me. He's gonna kill me anyway. If I'm gonna die, I wanna die big."

"Geez, you don't get it, Mom," someone mimicked from behind her and Nora turned to see Mike leaning in the doorway. "Did you just get home?"

Nodding, she stood as Henry's fighter jumped, flipping around in a physics-defying attack. He flew through the air, mouth open, a halo of energy radiating from his feet and fists, and for one brief second Nora thought he might win, but before Henry could land the move, the other fighter blasted a jet of blue energy at him and Henry's avatar fell to the ground, dead.

"See, I told you," he said. "At least I went out big."

Nora surveyed her son's room, looking for an excuse to stay longer, but he kept an improbably neat space. His Lego creations were displayed on the window ledge, dirty clothes all piled in the hamper. He'd even pulled his bedspread up over the mattress. The room, like the boy, was almost completely autonomous.

"Can I have dinner at Nathan's house?" Nathan lived in the mansion side of Steeplechase with his heirloom tomato-growing parents.

"Your mom just got home. You've barely seen her all week." Mike pushed away from the doorframe, but Nora waved him off. What ten-year-old wanted to sit through adult conversation when he could spend the evening playing with a friend?

"No, that's fine. You can go."

A few minutes later Nora watched Henry walk up the cul-de-sac, a hint of young man already lurking in his meandering stride. He was getting so tall.

Nora's mother always said a parent's job was to become obsolete, and they'd enacted their philosophy thoroughly with Nora, removing themselves from her life so quickly she felt breathless from it. Her father refused to speak to her in the wake of his best friend's death and her mother gave up after a few stilted phone calls. They'd invested more than Nora had realized in Sam White's company, and had been forced to sell their house when the Computech stock turned to junk. They lost their life-style, their friends, yet it had still been a shock when they chose to lose their daughter, too. But she had to give them credit. They'd warned her they would make themselves obsolete, and they did.

That was why — when Henry took these small steps away from them, when he exerted his budding independence in something as simple as a video game or his dinner company — Nora smothered the instinct to hold him closer. It was better this way, she repeated to herself as he disappeared around the end of the street, better for him to be the one to turn away first. She encouraged every gradual step so, when she became obsolete too, he wouldn't even notice.

"How was Logan boot camp today?" Mike joked when she came back into the kitchen.

He hadn't shaved in a few days, and the scruff suited his round, peach-colored face and twinkling eyes. He padded barefoot over to the table and set a salad down next to two bowls of pasta. The candles on the dining room table were lit, but she didn't join him.

"I didn't go to Strike today." She couldn't tell him that Strike had come to her. All of their clients and investigations were strictly confidential.

"Afternoon delight?" Mike cocked an eyebrow hopefully. Nothing in a marriage was ever equal and, in that way, their agreement to see other people was just like washing the dishes or taking out the trash. Mike, it seemed, always had more. More chores. More dates. Which was maybe why he was more excited on the few occasions Nora had a conquest to share.

"That would have been preferable." Nora picked up the briefcase she'd left by the garage door and fiddled with the handle. "We had an emergency client meeting. Corbett wants me to lead the investigation."

"You were gone practically all of June. Now it's going to be July, too?" Mike took a drink and set the wineglass down hard enough to make it ping against the table.

"This would be in Minneapolis."

"Oh, well, I guess that's better."

Nora shifted from foot to foot, still hovering on the far side of the kitchen. When she'd first joined Strike, Mike had already known it was Logan Russo's gym. They'd even watched some of Logan's old fights together on YouTube, Nora silently mesmerized while Mike provided a shouting and whistling soundtrack to the announcer's commentary. What would Mike say if she told him she'd accidentally slept with Logan Russo's husband? And that she was more worried about what Logan would think of her, than whether the fighter had stolen twenty million dollars? It was insane, absurd.

"Look, sit down. Eat. You can tell me all about it."

"No, I can't. You know that."

Mike stopped chewing and put his silverware down. He squeezed the bridge of his nose between his index fingers, leaning back in his chair.

"You come home, but you don't want to see Henry. You don't want to talk to me. You don't want to eat. What's the problem?"

She swallowed and told him the only thing she could. "I'm worried about my independence."

His laugh was immediate and devoid of all humor. Shaking his head, Mike picked up his glass and took another drink. "Trust me. You're the most independent woman in the world." Then he snuffed out the candles and continued eating, alone.

Nora went to her office and opened her computer. After staring blankly at the screen, she took a deep breath and emailed the other partners.

She told them she had no conflicts. She said she was ready to lead the Strike investigation. And she had no idea if either of those things was true.

GREGG

Sunday was supposed to be a day of rest, but the Sunday before Strike Down was hands down the least restful day of my life. The entire headquarters, everyone from the Director of Human Resources to the locker room attendants, showed up at U.S. Bank Stadium at five in the morning, ready to transform the venue into a kickboxing mecca. I'd been there since four, and greeted everyone with coffee, smoothies, protein bars, fruit, even doughnuts — yes, doughnuts, because I was not above sugar and empty carbs today. We conducted mini meetings, directed the setup of everything from the main ring in center field to the giant gray boxes — marked simply vStrike — lining the concourses, hung banners and signs, supervised the construction of the exhibition vendor booths, and stuffed more swag bags than the Academy Awards.

We held contests: who could do the most

push-ups wearing kickboxing gloves, who could run the fastest carrying boxes of programs, who could finish a protein shake first (me, in the only competitive event where I stood a chance). The races kept everyone engaged and excited, until someone asked the inevitable question, "Where's Logan?" Then I had to deflect, distract, and move them on to their next jobs.

I met with the entire security staff around lunchtime and took them through the non-negotiables.

"Everyone goes through the metal detectors. No exceptions to the no-bag policy. Watch for drunks, brawlers, and loners."

"Loners?" One of the guards laughed.

I leveled him with a look until he wiped the grin off his face and the murmurs around him faded into silence.

"Logan will have two personal bodyguards at all times. The bodyguards will pull you in for additional coverage during events with the biggest crowd exposure — primarily the meet and greets and opening ceremonies. No fan touches Logan unless she touches them first. Is everyone clear on that?"

I stared at the joker until he nodded, followed by the rest of them. As I handed the briefing back over to the head of security a notification buzzed on my phone. I moved to an empty corridor, my pulse picking up the same way it had every time I'd gotten an email in the last forty-eight hours. But unlike the last three hundred emails, this was the one I'd been waiting for.

The message was simple, direct, exactly what I expected.

Dear Mr. Abbott,

Your request for investigatory services at Strike has been approved and will commence Monday, July 1st. The senior partner in charge of this engagement is Nora Trier. Our team will arrive at your office 9:00 a.m. tomorrow. Please sign and return the attached contract prior to the scoping meeting, and insure the relevant employees are in attendance.

Regards,
Parrish Forensics

For the first time in two days I felt like I could breathe.

Twenty million dollars. It should have been pocket change. Most corporations could call the bank and get a loan, but Strike wasn't that kind of company. A bank would ask for audited financial statements, a business prospectus, the kind of bullshit Logan and I had always refused to deal with. We'd avoided it by sinking everything we had back into the company, and Strike had always rewarded our fidelity, until now. Now our fate rested with one woman.

I sent most of the management team — the *relevant employees* — home after dinner with instructions to be in the executive conference room the next morning. I didn't tell them why. I hadn't even talked to Logan yet, and I told myself it wasn't because I was scared.

Marketing tweeted until midnight (#are youready for #StrikeDown) and by one in the morning most people had left, exhausted and wired. Monday would be for finishing touches, Tuesday morning was reserved for media behind-the-scenes and advance hype, then the opening ceremonies and preliminaries would kick off on Tuesday night.

I walked home around two, retracing my steps from almost twenty-four hours earlier. Most of the Mill District buildings were shuttered, resting before the dawn of the new week. A few aimless drunks asked for change, one woman sat at a bus stop, her hard eyes scanning the shadows, and a siren echoed in the direction of Little Mogadishu, but otherwise the city could have been mine. I'd never felt that way growing up in Chicago, where I was just one more bee in the constantly buzzing hive. Here, though, the parks breathed with you, the river flooded your veins. Minneapolis made you believe the world was within your grasp.

It was the first thing that struck me when I flew in to see Logan after we met in Las Vegas, twenty years ago. The downtown skyline seemed quaint, small enough to reach your arms around and take for your own. I'd already done my research, though. I'd learned the history of this town. Empires had begun here and I knew — from the first morning Logan and I splattered the walls of a test kitchen with juice and leaves, sweat and heat — that Strike would rise to join their ranks.

I relocated to Minneapolis within months of that trip. Logan took me to the court-house to "make an honest man of me" and I moved into her shitty north-side apart-ment where she trained and slept and seem-ingly hadn't vacuumed in ten years.

"The rent is dirt cheap," she'd shrugged. "And I'm hardly ever here."

I made sure of that over the next few years. I opened an office slash personal gym for Logan downtown where we spent twelve hours a day, developing product lines and advertising campaigns. We traveled to every fitness expo across the country, converting fans into customers, and the fan base Logan had was astounding. They waited outside studios when she did television interviews. They mobbed her at title fights. The volume of email and physical letters she received on a weekly basis put Santa to shame.

I'd never been around a true celebrity before, but Logan just laughed and said, "Honey, you ain't seen nothing yet."

We started with energy drinks and recovery shakes. In 1999, no one wanted to hear that we used organic ingredients sourced in the heartland. No one cared about probiotics or sustainability. They wanted to see Logan — to be her — so we put her eye on the package, staring over the top of her boxing glove and hungering for the fight, and told the country they could have a piece of the legend.

For some people, though, a piece wasn't enough. Two years after I moved to Minneapolis we got home to find a man had broken into the apartment.

Rat faced and rail-thin, I thought at first he was an addict looking for money, but the second he saw Logan, he started pleading, whining that he was her soul mate and crying about how she'd used and betrayed him.

When he lunged at Logan, she delivered a cross punch to his jaw that cracked his teeth together and sent him reeling to the floor. His expression froze in a strangled mix of pain and ecstasy. Blood began trickling out of his mouth onto the carpet.

Then he pulled out a knife and stabbed himself with it.

He didn't die. Logan stomped on his hand and I jumped on top of him before he could hit any major arteries. The police found several pairs of Logan's underwear, a sports bra, a set of her hand wraps, and a half-filled vial of Rohypnol — the date rape drug — on the guy after he was taken to the hospital. We didn't have the language then that we do now. Now he would be diagnosed with Celebrity Worship syndrome on a borderline-pathological scale. Back then the cop just said I was lucky that lover-boy hadn't gone over jealous and attacked me first, then he frowned and advised us not to eat anything in the apartment.

Logan and I had been of one mind on everything up until that point: Strike, marriage, life. I'd even agreed to living in that shitty place because it let us invest more back into the company, but I refused to let her stay there after that night. All I could see was the guy's bloodstain in the carpet; all I could hear were his panting moans while we'd waited for the ambulance. Logan, however, dug her heels in.

"These are my roots. I'm not letting some crackpot scare me away from my own bed."

She scoffed when I hired a real estate agent and started touring the new condo buildings in the revitalized Mill District. "They're completely overpriced."

Eight hundred thousand seemed like a lot of money then, even to me.

"They have doormen. And security systems."

She wouldn't admit it, but I wasn't the only one who fell a little in love when we walked into the penthouse for the first time. Two stories, an open-concept space with exposed brick and hardwood floors, a soaking tub with one-way glass views of the Mississippi, all high above the prying eyes of obsessed fans.

Logan kept the apartment on the north side, just to prove she didn't have to give it up, and she went there from time to time over the years, maybe to train, maybe to remember. I didn't ask. I just moved our lives across the river, only a few blocks from where — less than two decades later — Strike Down would be held.

The night was muggy and airless as I walked the few blocks from U.S. Bank Stadium and fobbed into our building.

Nodding to the night security guard, I took the elevator to the top floor.

Logan, who never slept anymore, was still up. The rowing machine whirred rhythmically from the gym, probably waking the downstairs neighbors, who had learned long ago not to complain. I should have gone straight to her and showed her the email from Parrish, watched her reaction when I told her the prize money was missing, but I couldn't bring myself to do it. Not yet. I went to the bar and poured myself a scotch, then took it to the terrace and stood at the railing overlooking the water.

Pillsbury's Best and Gold Mill Flour glowed from opposite banks of the river. Of all the condos we'd seen after a man stabbed himself on our carpet, I knew I wanted this one. This was where the Mississippi had powered the flour mills for a hundred years, where empires were ground from wheat and water. Minneapolis had once been the biggest flour producer on the planet, feeding a world that hungered for bread. It sounded as wholesome as it must have looked — a wintry prairie town where flour dust whirled like snow in the air. Every empire, though, is combustible. Maybe it's twenty million dollars. Maybe it's enough flour to turn a mill into a powder keg. But one day in

102

1878, on this very spot, someone lit a match.

"What are you doing?"

I hadn't heard the rower fall silent. Logan stood in the doorway to the terrace, arms crossed and barefoot. Years of relentless training, even after she'd retired from the sport, had sculpted her beauty into more exquisite detail. The lines of her body were unforgiving. A perfect column of sweat darkened her wife beater from chest to groin.

"Having a drink," I said. "I just got home."

"It's two in the morning."

"I'm aware of that." I swirled the liquid, setting its sharp smoke loose. "Everyone asked about you today. They all wanted to know where you were."

"I'm sure you told them something. Spun it just right, the way you always do."

There was a fight waiting underneath the words. She wanted me to confront her, to attack, but I couldn't afford the battle. Not in the face of a war.

I took a breath. There was no more delaying what had to be done. "There's a meeting at nine a.m. with some accounting consultants. After your early class."

"Sounds thrilling."

"Will you please attend? It's important. The prize money for the tournament, it's . . ." She tilted her head, waiting, until I finally admitted. "It's gone."

I expected her to act shocked or confused, to drill me with questions about what happened, but she didn't. Instead, a ghost of a smile crossed her face and I felt my gut clench.

"For you, darling? Of course."

"Okay. Good." I downed another mouthful of liquor, watching her turn to go inside. "I know this year hasn't been easy —"

It was the wrong thing to say. She froze and every muscle on her body seemed to tense, or maybe she didn't even know how to relax anymore. "Don't say another word."

"— but it's been months."

She turned and there was murder in her eyes. "You don't know anything."

The scotch seeped into my stomach, peaty and bright. I pushed myself off the railing and felt the truth rise like a reek I could no longer ignore.

"I know you can't sleep without him."

For a second, it was like it didn't happen. Her face was smooth, blank, reflecting the empty dark of the night around us. Then she exploded across the balcony, so quick all I could do was jerk into the barrier and lift my arm. The snifter kept lifting. She forced the drink out of my hand and threw it across the terrace, where it crashed into the door, shattering the glass and the crystal into a thousand pieces.

"Charming." My voice was steady, betraying nothing. "Even Aaden had more maturity."

She took another step closer, pressing me to the edge of the balcony and I could almost smell the flour dust shimmering like gunpowder in the air, ready to ignite.

"If you ever fucking say his name to me again, I will throw you off this building. You'll be as dead as Aaden."

A spasm of pain crossed her face and she shoved me once, hard, before turning and pacing back across the terrace. She walked over the broken glass with bare, unflinching feet, leaving a trail of blood in her wake.

■ ■ ■ ■

PRESSURE

■ ■ ■ ■

NORA

As a child Nora had been nondescript, a girl who qualified for no adjectives other than an indication of their void, but in her thirties she actually began to disappear, fading from places she'd inhabited for years. Waiters in restaurants started forgetting her drink orders. Runners she passed on the trails behind her house looked straight through her. Even jurors seemed to hear more than see her, as though she were a disembodied voice emanating from the witness stand.

Some women probably bristled as their consequence became inversely proportional to their age, but it felt like familiar ground to Nora. She already understood the fickleness of worth. Instead of trying to dress younger, or starting to color her hair, Nora embraced her obscurity. No one looked at her twice when she requested access to restricted files. She walked unnoticed through client server and records rooms. And no one held their tongues when, after prepping them with mundane chitchat, she asked the kinds of questions that carried ten- to fifteen-year prison terms. She'd had more than one gasbag accountant explain to her, in bored, clock-watching detail, exactly how they journaled their improper revenue schemes.

"You're like a damn priest, Ellie," Corbett marveled once. "Why do they always confess everything to you?"

"They don't know I'm in the room."

On Monday morning, just a few hours before the Strike investigation was set to begin, she sat in a room where she had virtually disappeared. Steam billowed in the air, condensing in droplets that fattened and connected to slide down her skin. Nora stared at the vague impressions of tile through the cloud and then closed her eyes, leaning back against the slippery wall. Maybe it was odd to sit in a room blasting steam in the dead heat of July, but it might be her last chance.

For months she'd passed through Strike's changing area with only a quick shower as she hurried back to work, never joining the other women who soaked up the luxurious amenities. In contrast to the sparse mono-

110

chrome gym, the Strike locker rooms were pure oasis: fluffy towels and locally made toiletries stacked among tropical plants; meditation rooms and massage services on demand; and a dry sauna or steam room for however you liked your heat. Nora always told herself she'd indulge next time, but she'd run out of next times.

Today the other members hurried off, rushing to start their days, leaving Nora alone in the lavish space. She inhaled the nearly liquid air, absorbing its bright eucalyptus tang, and relaxed further into the steam, trying to enjoy it and not calculate the cost of everything around her. She wasn't on the clock yet.

A noise startled her and she opened her eyes to see steam sucking out of the room and Logan Russo striding into the void. Like Nora, she wore only a towel and paused mid-step, arching an eyebrow. "I didn't know anyone was in here."

Nora sat up with a jerk. "Sorry, I was just finishing."

"You're apologizing to me for barging in on you?"

Nora's eyes skittered across the nebulous clouds reforming between them. "I suppose I did."

"Take it back. Then say you don't mind if

I join you."

She laughed nervously and flicked her fingers at the open bench. "It's your gym."

"No, it's our gym. That's why I asked."

"You didn't ask."

Winking, the fighter crossed the tile to sit in the middle of the bench, leaving several feet of space between them. Logan lounged against the wall, legs rolling open as her eyes closed. She didn't seem interested in further conversation and the white noise of the generator padded the space where awkwardness might have lived between two strangers in a small room.

Nora tried to relax. She leaned back woodenly and rested her hands in what she hoped was a natural position on her lap. After a few minutes spent attempting to calm her heart rate, she noticed something that took her mind off Logan's proximity and it was the last thing she expected: Logan's feet.

Logan wore the same sandals put out for everyone's use next to the steam room entrance, but her arches and even some of her toes had been bound with bandages. White gauze covered most of the skin on her feet and only half her toenails were exposed. She'd worn shoes during class this morning so this damage, whatever it was, had been hidden. Nora scanned Logan's sprawled legs, arms, and her chest above the towel. The rest of her seemed uninjured.

Not wanting to be caught staring, she made herself look away while considering possible explanations. Callouses, training injuries, some bizarre foot condition. The bandages, blizzard white in the hazy room, kept drawing her attention back despite her effort to appear nonchalant.

The steam stopped hissing, and the sudden quiet seemed amplified by the travertine tile, as if silence could echo. Just as Nora was about to get up and leave, Logan stirred.

"You're not one of the dawns," she muttered, waving a hand toward the gym. "The sunrise crowd."

"No, I usually attend the noon classes, but I wanted to come one last time before . . . Strike Down."

Another pause, and Nora hesitated, glancing at the door. Her pulse wouldn't settle.

"Second to last row, third bag from the left." Logan's eyes opened and fixed on Nora. "That's where you like to stand, right?"

Nora nodded, taken off guard. She didn't think Logan had ever noticed her. She never thought anyone noticed her.

Something else was different, though, something beyond the strangeness of sitting nearly naked in a cramped space with a celebrity. It wasn't the bandages or even the improbable fact that Logan Russo had recognized her. Logan's voice had shed some of its sharpness, her body rounded in places where usually only angles lived — a slope in her shoulder, a curve in her belly. Her face had been scrubbed clean, too. Logan always wore full makeup during Strike sessions, dark eye shadow and mascara for her signature smoky-eyed look, a palette of gloss and contours made into a seamless, camera-ready appearance. The face studying Nora now wasn't flawless. Lines crisscrossed her temples and the shadows lived underneath her eyes instead of on the made-up lids.

"It's okay," she said, seemingly amused by Nora's concentration. "You don't have to hold back like you do with your side kicks."

"I don't hold back on my side kicks."

Logan's mouth twitched, and she shrugged deeper into the wall. "You're too technical, but that's a good problem. Some people come in here all fire and no form. It's harder to get them to slow down and learn the right way to attack before they hurt themselves. But you — you're all technique and no fire. You've never had to fight for your life."

"Most people haven't."

"Most people you know."

They paused, measuring each other, then Nora surprised herself by leaning forward. "Why kickboxing?"

Logan smiled through the steam, a reaction so bright and big it lit up her entire face even as her eyes unfocused. "Kids and kicks."

"What?"

"That's what my dad used to say. Girls' hips were meant to deliver two things — kids and kicks. He taught me hips were power, the engine behind every punch and roundhouse. It's all there in the pelvic floor, deep in the glutes, hips and hams, where biology gave us the goods." Logan glanced over, still grinning in a way that offered a piece of the happiness, inviting Nora to share in it.

"He was your coach?"

"He trained me in our garage every night after work. Made me promise not to deliver a grandbaby before I'd delivered a title belt." The smile faded as she smoothed the edge of the towel over her leg. "He didn't have to worry about that."

Logan cleared her throat, falling silent,

115

but Nora wanted her to keep talking. She could listen to this unpackaged, unguarded Logan all day.

"What happened to your feet?"

"A snake bit them."

Nora lifted an eyebrow at the bandages. "Big snake."

"You have no idea." Logan lifted her legs, flexing her feet and rolling her ankles. "The pavement wasn't fun this morning. I'm going to have to find some softer routes to jog until they heal."

Nora sat up so quickly her towel almost fell off "There are miles of trails behind my house. Have you heard of Lebanon Hills? It's beautiful and secluded and not that far from downtown. I run there after work and on weekends. If you want . . ." Her voice trailed off as she realized she'd been about to invite a client on a personal date, had — in fact — been bursting with the idea. The investigation hadn't even begun and she was already on the verge of breaking her one cardinal rule.

Holding her towel, she stood and moved quickly to the door, making the steam churn. "I have to go. I'm actually quitting the gym for a while."

"Why?"

Logan sat up, and it was amazing how fast

116

the curves transformed into angles again. Her shoulders gleamed like they'd been sculpted from marble and heat. Nora didn't know where to look. Her muscles tensed. She wanted to escape, but it would be disingenuous if she left without explaining.

"I'm Nora Trier. Have you heard of Parrish Forensics?"

Logan's eyes narrowed, and Nora heard an intake of breath. Did Logan already know who she was? Had Gregg told her about Atlanta?

"You should have a nine o'clock meeting on your calendar."

Logan stood up and crossed over to her. The camaraderie of a moment ago condensed into something much more dangerous. Logan's hand closed over Nora's on the door handle.

"Tell me about the meeting."

Nora swallowed. "What do you know about the prize money?"

Logan took a step closer, but there was nowhere for Nora to back up.

"I know it's not enough."

There were no filing cabinets. That's what Nora noticed two hours later as an executive assistant escorted the half dozen members of her team through the mostly vacant

Strike offices. A low-slung living room set, framed with glossy-leafed plants where there should have been locked records. A sleek mahogany server room door with an embossed note that read, "Keep open for ventilation." Screensavers that made her itch to bump the mice and see how much data sprawled behind the curtains.

Logan wasn't anywhere to be seen. She'd left Nora standing in the steam room with dozens of questions swirling in her throat. Nora had tried finding Corbett to get his opinion on the bizarre exchange, but he wasn't in his office yet or answering his phone. Her texts went unanswered. She felt off-balance, uneasy, until Mike's voice echoed in her head from the other evening, saying she was the most independent woman in the world. Today she needed to prove him right.

Gregg greeted them in the conference room, dressed in an impeccable linen suit and vest, which stood in sharp contrast to the jeans and yoga pants scattered around the table. He'd briefed his team on the missing prize only moments ago, judging by the blind panic in the room.

"I don't want to waste anyone's time this morning. Your tournament starts tomorrow and the purse is gone." She looked to each face in turn after the obligatory introductions. "Parrish Forensics has been hired to determine how the cash shortfall arose and, if possible, recover the funds."

No one seemed to know how to respond. They stared at Nora with varying degrees of confusion and worry.

"Strike is a private company, fully self-determined. You answer to no one. This is both a strength and an incredible weakness."

The Marketing Director made a poorly disguised noise of outrage and a paunchy man at the end of the table — the controller who'd apparently discovered the shortfall — shifted in his chair to the beat of a vein throbbing in his forehead. Nora slowed her rate of speech to that of a patient elementary school teacher.

"When you have no accountability to anyone — an independent board, or a bank, or shareholders — you lack the built-in checks of your system. Your controls may suffer, if indeed you had any controls in the first place, to prevent mismanagement or fraud."

Anger built steadily around her, the pungent vibe of a room dying to prove her wrong. Sometimes opening meetings were too easy.

"Parrish isn't here to dwell on those weaknesses or pursue any wrongdoers. Our assignment for the moment is simple: figure out which gap is large enough to swallow twenty million dollars."

Gregg cleared his throat and addressed his people. "Before we go any further, I want to remind everyone that the content of this meeting and subject of the missing prize money is strictly confidential. No one outside this room is involved. Delegate any tournament work and if you can't find someone, I'll do it. I expect full cooperation with Parrish and a hundred percent effort from every department. If anyone asks, tell them the truth: these people are consultants performing an audit. Nothing more." He glanced at Nora. "From this point on, we're one team with one objective. And the clock is ticking."

"What about Logan?" one manager asked.

"She's here." Logan walked into the room. She wore a tank top and shiny white leggings that glowed against her skin, as though her darkness had ignited them. Her black hair was slicked back and her makeup was once again flawless, the facade in place.

Dropping into a chair on the opposite side of the table from Gregg, Logan faced Nora with an attitude of detached interest. Their conversation in the steam room might never have happened.

Conscious of Logan's attention, Nora proceeded to explain the tasks each Parrish team member would focus on, pairing them with wary Strike department heads as she went down the line. One analyst would dive into the statement of cash flows, looking for patterns and one-offs. Another would liaison with the IT department, searching for system weaknesses and possible hacking attempts. The third would focus on the transactions within the accounting group, which earned another scoff, this time from the controller.

"And I'll be working primarily with the executive team and Inga," Nora finished.

"Inga?"

Nora nodded to one of her analysts, who swiveled her monitor around. An icon hovered in the corner of the dark screen, a bodiless head with downcast eyes and a benevolent, almost godlike smile cast toward the darkness beneath her.

"Meet the Amazing Inga, Parrish Forensics' most exclusive partner."

The controller forced a laugh. "Is that some kind of circus act?"

"We thought about naming her Hal, but Amazing Inga was voted more personable."

"Artificial intelligence?" The IT manager leaned forward, eyes as bright as a kid on Christmas morning. Nora nodded.

"Make no mistake; this isn't Siri. Inga is cutting-edge forensic technology developed by my fellow partner, Corbett MacDermott.

"Inga learns. She observes the communication patterns between people and then identifies where and when anomalies happen. She can detect changes in emotion or intimacy, when people are nervous, stressed, or become disgruntled. Off the record, Inga has found twenty-three office affairs and at least fifty, shall we say, budding romances. Between us, the boss-secretary cliché is not strictly unfounded."

Most of the Strike team laughed, breaking the tension in the room, with the IT manager laughing louder than anyone and looking like she'd be happy to toss another twenty million out the window for a chance to rendezvous with the Amazing Inga. The executive assistant didn't seem to find it amusing. Logan wasn't smiling, either. She stared at Inga's floating head on the computer monitor, as if making rapid calculations.

"On the record," Nora continued, "she's the most sophisticated robot in the world for locating pressure. People under stress, people who are being pushed to make choices they otherwise might not make. Pressure is one of the key elements of fraud and when we find the people who are under pressure, we know where to look to uncover the crime."

"Crime?" The controller, Darryl Nolan, half rose out of his chair, clearly not distracted by robot jokes. "Is this a criminal investigation?"

"We're not the police, Mr. Nolan. The information we find is confidential unless we are served a direct and properly executed subpoena, but twenty million has been drained from this company in six months. Either it was mismanaged or it was stolen. Whichever the case, our job is to find it.

"When we obtain access to your email server," Nora turned her attention back to the IT manager, who bobbed her head with the adoration of a puppy, "Inga will analyze the hundreds of thousands of pieces of communication that occur between your employees every year. She'll look through every email and chat message to determine where the pressure at Strike lives."

Gregg tipped forward. "With all due respect to Inga, I'm more concerned with where the money lives."

Nora glanced at Logan, who wasn't paying any attention to her husband. She stared at Nora with an intensity that made her feel cornered and exposed, like she was still in the steam room with her back against the wall.

"So are we," Nora nodded to Gregg, "which is why we use artificial intelligence. In the thousand cases where we've deployed Inga, she's never once failed us."

The meeting adjourned soon afterward, with each analyst accompanying their corresponding manager back to their departments. Everyone on her team was eager to get started, scenting — as she had — the irresistible lure of the chase. Five days. Twenty million dollars. The pressure was indisputably on.

GREGG

After the meeting I offered Nora a tour of headquarters. To my infinite surprise, Logan joined us. I hadn't thought she'd even show up for the meeting this morning. She'd promised to come when we spoke on the terrace last night, but she'd also threatened to kill me. Under the circumstances, lying seemed like the best-case scenario. Now that she'd made good on her promise, though, my stomach churned at the idea that the threat might also be true.

"I understand it's an extremely busy week for both of you. I'm happy to shadow you during your normal routines to conduct the interviews," Nora said as we left the conference room.

And get us talking while we were distracted. Smart.

"In or out of the steam room, right?" Logan joked and Nora flushed, looking momentarily flustered.

"You're a member?" I turned to Nora. When I Googled her after Atlanta I'd imagined seeing her again, not for sex — she'd made it clear she wasn't interested in continuing a relationship — but for a fleeting moment of connection, a nod across a restaurant, a glance in the skyway. I'd looked for her in every crowd in Minneapolis and she'd been at Strike the whole time.

"I was," Nora corrected, shifting uncomfortably. "I suspended my membership this morning, for the duration of the investigation."

We proceeded with the tour, me leading the way while Logan's spandex leggings and "Avocados for President" tank top flanked the other side of Nora's immaculate suit. It was a surreal thing to walk through the halls of my company with my wife and my . . . could I call Nora Trier a lover? I didn't know. If I'd had more practice cheating on my spouse, maybe I'd have learned the language. I wasn't even feeling the right things. I should have been terrified that Nora would mention Atlanta, but the thought barely occurred. All I wanted to do was shove Logan's face at Nora and shake her until she recognized what a decent woman looked like, the kind of person who didn't threaten to throw their husband off a balcony. If Logan had understood decency, Atlanta never would have happened. A lot of things wouldn't have happened.

We passed reception, where two towering body bags acted as columns on either side of the double doors, and moved into the administrative areas.

"Did we scare everyone away already?" Nora paused at an empty cubicle and tapped the mouse, prompting the monitor to boot up and flash a desktop photo of two fighters in a ring. One of the desk drawers was open an inch and she glanced at it before looking over the memos and a last-season Fitspo poster featuring Logan's blackened silhouette against the exploding flash of a camera, with a single line at the bottom. YOUR FIGHT WILL BECOME LEGEND.

"Most of the staff will be at the stadium all week, but we can call any of them back at any time. Obviously you'll have access to everyone you need. We simply ask for delicacy about the" — I felt Logan's stare and didn't trust myself to return it — "financial situation."

We moved on, past high-performance computers, treadmill desks, the self-service smoothie bar and balcony garden overlooking Nicollet Mall. Talking about Strike and the people who built Strike calmed me. "From the very beginning, we vowed not to be one of those companies who give their investors everything and bleed their employees dry. That's exactly the 'do more with less' corporate imperative that leads to disillusionment and burnout."

"Your motto is 'do more with more'?" Nora asked.

"It's one of the things Gregg and I always agreed on." Logan shifted from foot to foot, one or two degrees away from a boxer's shuffle. She acted as though I wasn't in the room and I wondered if Nora noticed how we both spoke exclusively to her. "Treating our employees like family. We don't just recognize and reap their accomplishments. We see the whole person, for exactly what they are."

There was a moment of silence before I forced a smile and led the way to the executive offices. Sara, my assistant, greeted us with a handful of brand-new, full-access security badges for the Parrish team. Nora accepted hers and followed Logan and me into my office.

I'd covered one entire wall with framed pictures, milestones from Strike's twenty years in business. There was the ribbon cutting at our production factory, promo images of our first bestselling supplements, and a *People* magazine cover of Logan. They'd written a profile when we opened our first gym, a fawning piece that was part essay, part Q&A with a sidebar recipe of Logan's favorite recovery meal, spinning her as an American champion turned maverick businesswoman, a singular force who was ready to bestow her strength onto a grateful public.

Nora surveyed those wordlessly before stopping in front of a picture of Logan with Elon Musk. "Wow."

"CEO TKO." I smiled.

CEO TKO was my brainchild, the corporate team building program we'd started a few years after the gyms gained traction. It was designed as a day for executives to literally get in the ring with their employees. The event came with a softball training session interlaced with business psychology and martial arts philosophy, and ended in the ring where senior leadership had to face off with anyone who wanted a round. On the day SpaceX came to Strike, Musk went 4–0.

Nora moved along the wall, tracking the photos of Strike's rise. There were endless images of Logan posing with celebrities and athletes, fierce, unsmiling Logan, her trademark look daring the camera, while the real Logan flopped onto my chair and put her feet on my desk. Another kind of dare entirely, and one I chose to ignore.

"This is a young company." Nora pointed to a shot of a group of kids surrounding Logan and a few other trainers.

"That's Strike Next," Logan piped up. "Our first graduating class."

We began Strike Next around the same time as CEO TKO. An after-school program for at-risk youth, kids came from all over the city to learn self-defense and fight technique. Part of Strike's membership fees went toward scholarships the kids could use for college. I moved to Nora's shoulder and looked closer at the picture. Standing in the back of the shot, like a shadow hovering behind Logan, was Aaden Warsame.

The Washburn Mill, the world's greatest flour mill at the time, had exploded from a single spark. I stared at the skinny Somali kid in the picture, with his jaw set and eyes bright. He'd seemed no different than the rest of them, trying to act tough in the presence of Logan Russo, following her every move, hanging on to her every word. Fans, yes. Disciples, even, but I hadn't been worried that any of these kids would open a vein on our living room carpet. I didn't realize Aaden Warsame was the spark that would blow us apart.

Nora turned from the wall with a bland smile, done with her photographic tour of the history of Strike. "The accountant didn't come off very well in the meeting."

"He's incompetent." I moved to the windows, eager for any distraction from that picture.

"Did you think so before last Friday?"

My mouth twisted into a grudging smile. "Sometimes."

"We'll do background checks on everyone, of course, while concentrating on the most likely candidates, namely finance employees and executives." Her eyes scanned both of us as she moved to the desk and dropped her briefcase on it, an unsubtle gesture that she was now in charge. "If the funds were merely mismanaged and overspent, we'll also be looking at your cash options. Bridge loans, divestitures, accelerated collections, and other ways to free the required capital by the deadline."

"Gregg doesn't mismanage," Logan interjected. "He spends lavishly, of course, as you've already seen. Nothing but the best for his baby."

"Logan —"

"But every move is deliberate. Obsessively planned and executed to perfection." She leaned back farther and crossed her arms.

"And look what we have to show for it. A billion-dollar company." A slight bow.

Nora had fallen still, tracking the volleys back and forth.

Logan flashed her a glance. "I'm sure Gregg will find a way to save Strike. He'd die for this company." Then, turning to me. "Wouldn't you?"

Ridicule, dare, and threat. Logan never threw a punch for just one reason.

"I wouldn't exactly peg my value to Strike."

"No one would."

A tense silence filled the room while all three of us shifted, recognizing the alpha, the predator, prowling within the others. Every movement became heightened, amplified. Before I could pivot the conversation, Nora stepped in.

"While I have both of you together, the only two shareholders of the company, I'd like to ask a few general questions."

She gestured to the conference table, but neither of us moved. Unperturbed, Nora folded her arms behind her back, the yin to Logan's yang, and paced smoothly between us. She asked about fixed overhead costs, the new club expansion, payroll and bonuses, and she seemed to file every answer — all from me because Logan couldn't have defined fixed overhead if it came with a title belt — into careful compartments in her head. Then she moved on to cover the management team, which employees had access to the cash and bank accounts, if there were any discipline or behavioral issues, and whose personal life might be in crisis. The last question, with the innocence of a saint or master criminal.

She didn't hide in the veneer of smiles or widened shoulders. Her voice didn't dip into the masculine range to grab for power. After decades of dealing with the athletic world where posturing was psychological warfare, a brutal, exhausting art, talking to Nora Trier was like breathing clean air after a lifetime spent in smog.

A half hour later, Nora turned away from the window and asked one final question.

"Have you experienced any theft in the past?"

"No." Logan's reply came like a gunshot. She was on her feet, staring me down, daring me to expose her lie.

"For God's sake, she's not the media. This isn't the time to —"

"No one has ever stolen from Strike." She

advanced around the desk, the terrible beauty of those trapezii and rhomboids looking unworldly in the mundane office lighting. I had created this. I had built an empire for her to stand on, had made a deal with the devil, and now it was time for my reckoning.

"Logan," I swallowed, standing my ground. Less than twelve hours ago she said she'd kill me for saying his name, and part of me wondered if she'd do it right now, with Nora watching. "We have to tell her about Aaden."

Nora

Name: Aaden Maxamed Warsame
Age: 24
Date of Death: March 18, 2019

Nora read the contents of the redacted police report while Gregg leaned against his desk, arms folded, head bowed, and Logan paced the room like a caged animal. She hadn't said a word since Gregg handed Nora the folder and murmured quietly, "He worked here."

Logan shot him a murderous look and clenched her fists as if refraining from ripping the paper out of Nora's hands.

The details were spare and painfully precise. A 911 call had been received just before five on a Monday morning, reporting the discovery of a dead body at the Strike gym. Responding officers confirmed the man had been killed by a single gunshot wound to the head. The trainer who found him had been unlocking the gym for the morning's classes. Logan Russo had arrived on scene shortly afterward, followed by Gregg Abbott, and the mother of the deceased.

Surveillance cameras showed Aaden Warsame entering the gym shortly after midnight. He badged in through the main doors, went to the front desk and wrote something on a piece of paper. Then, pulling a gun out of his coat pocket, he walked through the gym into the men's locker room, where no cameras were installed. The 911 caller found him dead five hours later.

Nora turned the page and caught her breath. The report included photographs: a close-up of the gun lying on the floor, a wide shot of the entire locker room, which had the same lavish aesthetic as the women's side, and, in appalling contrast to the spa-like atmosphere, images of blood splatter on the mahogany lockers, granite bench, and across the heated tile floor. Several shots of the body showed a young, unlined face, eyes that were open and blank, and a pool of dark, congealed blood flecked with bits of tissue and pale shards of what must have been skull.

She hadn't visualized Sam White's death, not the physical details of it anyway. She'd been too stunned by the fact of his suicide, too grieved for the family and friends, like her father, that he'd left behind. She'd never even known — until the coverage surrounding the Computech trial — that he'd been in his garage, sitting in his Lamborghini when he put the gun to his head. But now, seeing the body of Aaden Warsame, she felt wrenched back fifteen years. The details were too similar. The same weapon, the same wound, the horror of their deaths amplified by the luxury surrounding them.

Nora didn't know how long she'd been staring at the photo of Aaden Warsame's dead face. Blinking, she turned the page to a copy of a note the police had found on him at the time of death. It read, simply, "Logan, I'm sorry."

Security logs showed no one else badging in or out of the gym during the night. Aaden's fingerprints were the only ones on the gun and no other injuries, other than several strains and microtears in various stages of healing — all attributed to martial arts training — were noted during the autopsy. The death was ruled self-inflicted and the case closed.

Stomach twisting, Nora took a breath and closed the file.

"This happened here? I never heard about it."

"The incident was handled quietly, out of respect for Aaden and his family."

Nora had just sat with Logan in the steam room, had showered and dressed mere feet from where this man had died. How was it possible that only hours ago she'd been sorry she hadn't spent more time in the locker rooms? Now she didn't know if she could ever walk inside them again.

She moved to the conference table where both Strike owners had refused to sit, and held the back of one of the chairs to steady herself. She'd taken classes from Aaden once or twice. He'd been tall and almost too lean, as though still growing into his adult body. His smile was infectious, bright white against his dark skin, and his energy seemed boundless. A kid on the cusp of everything.

"And you feel this is relevant to the current investigation?"

"No." Logan's tone was flat and final.

Gregg sighed. "Some of the information blacked out in that report is . . . financial."

Logan made a move toward Gregg — What, was she going to hit him? — and without thinking Nora stepped between them.

All morning, she'd buried herself in professionalism, focusing one hundred percent of her energy on distancing herself from the two people in this room. She'd conducted the kickoff taken the tour, and interviewed them with as much detachment as she possessed. No one looking in during the last hour would ever think she'd slept with Gregg Abbott or enjoyed a cozy steam room chat with Logan Russo.

But those police photos had undone everything. They'd blown a giant, messy hole through her objectivity and now, somehow, she'd rushed straight into the middle of this land mine of a marriage.

Nora turned to Logan and spoke in a low voice, the same tones she used to coax witness statements out of scared or belligerent employees.

"It's just the three of us in the room right now. The door's closed and you can see I'm not writing anything down. We're only talking." Nora laid a hand on Logan's arm, and was startled to realize it was trembling. Anger, yes, but there was another emotion vibrating in the fighter's expression. Nora kept her grip light and her voice calm.

"I'm going to learn this information at some point this week. Either he's going to tell me or I'll find out on my own. That's what I do. And I can see that, whatever it is, upsets you. So wouldn't you rather be in the room when it happens? To make sure I understand the full and accurate situation?"

The office was silent for a moment before Logan swallowed and the tremors running underneath her skin seemed to shimmer in the very whites of her eyes.

"You're good."

A tiny smile lifted Nora's mouth before she released Logan's arm. "I'm the best."

Then she nodded at Gregg, who cleared his throat and began to fill in the redacted portions of the police report. The note to Logan wasn't the only thing the police found on Aaden at the time of his death. He'd also been carrying a slip of paper in his wallet.

"The paper had Strike's name on it and a bank account number. When the police looked through Aaden's checking account, they found three unexplained deposits."

"We checked all the company accounts. I had Darryl go through everything personally." Logan interrupted, flashing a look at Gregg. "There were no withdrawals for those amounts from Strike."

"How much were they?" Nora asked.

"Five thousand in January. Then two more deposits for ninety-five hundred each in

February and March, the last one just a few days before his death." Gregg nodded to the report still in Nora's hand. "The police checked, but there was no further information tied to any of them. They were in-person, cash deposits."

Logan moved to the pictures Nora had been looking at earlier, stopping in front of the one with all the kids. When she spoke, her voice was hollow.

"I knew Aaden Warsame for almost ten years. He was one of the first kids in the Strike Next program and he wasn't the strongest or the fastest — not then — but he worked harder than anyone I've ever met. He didn't cut corners or ask for a single goddamn thing from anyone." Her voice broke and she paused before turning to look at Nora. "Aaden wasn't stealing from us and I will destroy anyone who claims otherwise. Do you and your accountants understand?"

Nora held Logan's gaze. Dozens of unanswered questions fired through her brain, but she nodded. "I understand we've been hired to look for an amount much larger than twenty-four thousand dollars."

The two women faced off silently until someone knocked on the door and an assistant popped her head in, reminding

Logan of an interview with ESPN. She swallowed and walked out of the office, leaving Nora staring at the place where she'd stood.

Gregg leaned back on his desk and let out a breath.

"I'm sorry about that. Aaden was . . . special . . . to Logan."

"Special?"

"Certainly more than me." Frustration crossed his face, leaving as quickly as it had come. A buzz on his wrist signaled incoming messages, but he ignored them. The energy in the room had changed completely without Logan in it. Intimacy wound its way through his words: casual, direct admissions she wondered if he would say to other accountants. Or other previous lovers. "He practically worshipped her. I was worried at first. He certainly wouldn't have been her first stalker. People tend to become fixated on Logan."

She felt herself flushing, but Gregg spoke to the carpet, unaware of Nora's reaction. "Instead of distancing herself from him, she encouraged his ambition to become a fighter. She started training him personally."

"Gregg." The assistant was back. "Are you heading to the stadium? I'm getting calls like every two minutes."

"You've already been generous with your

time this morning." Nora picked up her briefcase. "Don't let me keep you."

He took a few steps toward the door, then stopped and shook his head at the floor. "Would you forgive me if I said I wished you would?" Then, giving her a regretful smile, held up an arm to usher her out.

After the charged scene in Gregg's office, Nora did the only thing she could. She worked. Her team set up operations and dove into Strike's books with a fervent determination, the challenge of the looming deadline propelling each of them faster and harder into their assignments. The IT manager patched them in, giving them full access to every drive and operating system, and hooked Inga into the email server where the AI computer began scanning eight hundred gigabytes of data.

They ran preliminary cash statements, performed comparative ratio analysis on Strike's account balances, and pored through the highest value bank transactions and vendors. Unlike most of their investigations, where the oversights or fraud schemes took years to develop, this was six months. Twenty million gone in six months. It wasn't some small, discreet wound slowly bleeding the company over time; they were looking for a gunshot.

A figurative gunshot, Nora had to remind herself when the image of Aaden's dead body flashed into her mind. Beyond the tragedy and horror of it, she didn't see how a young trainer's suicide could relate to the case at hand. She had to put Aaden Warsame aside, to file his death the same way she filed any other fact in an investigation, and not let it haunt her. Aaden wasn't Sam White. Twenty-four thousand wasn't twenty million. She had to be objective, and not see those open, empty eyes whenever she closed her own.

Dead man distracting me.

She texted Corbett at one point.

I'm still breathing, woman.

He sent it with a gif of a toothless, wrinkled senior citizen.

Now gifs distracting me.

You're welcome.

By the end of the first day, they'd identified the three largest outflows in the last six months — payroll, new club construction, and the tournament. Nora broke the team into groups and sent them down their respective rabbit holes while she concentrated on the major players. Only a few people at the company had the ability to divert that much cash that quickly.

144

As owners, both Gregg and Logan had full access to all bank accounts and unlimited authority to enter into contracts and make purchases or investments. According to their articles of incorporation, they had to have express permission from the other owner for any large investments, but if either of them wanted twenty million dollars, there would be little to stop them from taking it.

The other possibility was the highest-ranking finance employee, Darryl Nolan. Darryl, the sweaty white guy in the kickoff meeting who had been worried about criminal investigations. Darryl, who apparently hadn't noticed twenty million dollars was missing until last Friday.

Darryl Nolan required investigation.

There was an old joke accountants told each other. A business owner was looking to hire a manager and he interviewed each candidate with a simple question: "How much is $2+2$?"

The engineer pulled out his slide rule and shuffled it back and forth, finally announcing, "It lies between 3.98 and 4.02." The mathematician said, "I can demonstrate it equals 4 with the following short proof." The psychologist said, "It's not for me to answer, but we should spend some time exploring the question." The attorney stated, "In the case of *Swenson v. the State,* 2+2 was declared to be 4."

The accountant looked at the business owner, got out of his chair, and closed the office door. Then he leaned across the desk and said in a low voice, "How much would you like it to be?"

The accountant got the job.

Darryl Nolan, the controller at Strike, had either been told two plus two equaled twenty million, or he honestly had no idea it was four.

"The agreement was insane, I told everyone that from the beginning."

On Tuesday morning, Nora sat in Darryl's office, a dull space littered with Post-its, letters, and the general detritus of a man whose bottom had been wiped for far too long into his childhood.

"The agreement to rent the stadium? Can you elaborate on that?" Nora's senior analyst peered over her open laptop at the company's senior finance manager.

"You saw the contract. $250,000 a day? Is one and a half million a reasonable amount to pay for less than a week of rental space? And don't get me started on 'vStrike.' " He used air quotes. "It makes the stadium look like a garage sale."

The man seemed incapable of sitting comfortably in his chair. He'd been twitching and readjusting his girth for the last ten minutes while detailing examples of overspending at Strike. His salary, Nora thought, could be included as one of those examples.

"So, given your financial duty to the company, at what point did you caution the owners about their excessive spending? Did you prepare any reports? A cost benefit analysis? Request they review more competitive bids from other vendors?"

"You don't understand Gregg Abbott." The man took a swig of a liquid that resembled dark cough syrup.

"We'd like to." Nora folded her hands, smiling benignly.

"He doesn't do anything Kmart. Only the best quality suppliers, sustainable, green, LEED-certified, woman-owned, fair trade, award-winning for whatever the hell they're giving out awards in next."

Darryl went on about the exorbitant costs of Strike Down, shoving poorly executed Microsoft Excel tables across his desk for them to peruse. Nora's analyst raised her eyebrow a millimeter and Nora suppressed a smile; among accountants, there was no judgment like spreadsheet judgment.

They went through the tournament costs,

line by line, while Nora considered the man. She'd already learned a lot about Darryl Nolan. He'd been with the company for a decade, had no CPA or credentials beyond a bachelor's degree, and was married with two kids. His wife worked out of their moderately priced suburban home, making Disney-themed items to sell on Etsy. Neither of them overcharged their credit cards. They'd almost paid off a late model Chevy, attended a Lutheran church, and took annual trips to the Florida Gulf Coast for the Twins' spring training. In short, they lived within their means.

"We've examined the payment process," Nora broke into the discussion, lacing her fingers together. "It appears to be completely automated."

"Yep. An off-site company handles all the data entry. We can't change amounts or vendors or destination banks here; all we do is select yes or no. It's completely secure. I approve and Gregg releases the money."

"Not Logan?"

"She authorizes transfers when Gregg's traveling, sure, but she leaves the back office to the people who should be running it."

Which meant if Darryl wanted to approve phony payments, he knew which partner was disinterested enough to allow them out the door. The automation looked good, she had to agree, but no system was ever completely secure and an unsupervised accountant who knew a few tricks could easily find loopholes. Darryl Nolan had plenty of opportunity. Nora could smell some rationalization on him, too, talking about Gregg's big spending habits. A guy like this could watch money being spent on everything else and feel he deserved an equally inflated piece of the pie. Two plus two equals ten million? Sure, plus another ten for me.

The problem she had with Darryl, the ingredient missing from the fraud triangle, was pressure. His background check hadn't turned up any recent arrests or major health issues in his family. She'd had Inga read his social media posts last night while Mike snored in bed next to her, and found a parade of regurgitated memes and jokes with no measurable change in tone or frequency. She couldn't find a source of stress — either professionally or personally — that would make him steal eight figures in a matter of months.

"How did you come to work for Strike, Mr. Nolan?"

"My brother-in-law was one of Logan's coaches, so I knew her even before she was famous. She was always great. No bullshit, no pretense. With Logan, what you see is what you get, unless you're in the ring with her. Then you get a lot more." He laughed for the first time in the entire interview. "Anyway, when she started Strike she said something about needing a finance guy and the rest is history."

Mild nepotism, not uncommon in private, family-owned businesses.

"Did you even interview or did they just offer you the job?" her analyst asked.

"The three of us went out to lunch. Logan was on board, of course, but Gregg was kind of an ass at first. I heard he personally checked my references. What kind of a control freak doesn't leave that stuff to HR?"

So Darryl was Logan's hire, and apparently another member of the Logan Russo fan club. Would an admirer steal money from the object of his admiration? Perhaps, but he was starting to look more like an accomplice — someone who would be happy to do a highly regarded boss's bidding.

The analyst made a note as Nora stood, signaling the end of the interview. "Your current salary is a hundred and fifty thousand dollars a year, is that correct?"

He bristled, like most men did when she

undressed their wallets. "What about it?"

"Significantly higher than the average controller in this market. And you received a six percent raise last year, above virtually any comparable company in our database."

"I told you," he took another gulp of the sludge in his mug before herding them out of his office. "The best vendors, the best tech, the biggest, splashiest tournament on the planet. And now the biggest fucking emergency we could have in a week like this, all because he spent us into the ground. Gregg Abbott doesn't do average."

With that, Nora had to agree. Unlike average business owners, who wanted to conceal as much of their dirty laundry as possible, Gregg had given her team unprecedented access to Strike's books and people. He'd been open, candid, and unflinchingly honest, which made Nora wonder what exactly he was hiding.

If Gregg Abbott wasn't average, his secrets wouldn't be either.

GREGG

On Tuesday, less than eight hours before Strike Down began, I paced the marble tile lobby of the Grand Hotel Minneapolis next to a life-sized sculpture of a resting lion. Any minute I expected another lion to walk through the door, one who I was counting on to devour everything in her path.

The sumptuous space offered plenty of sleek couches and barstools, but relaxation was impossible. I'd spent the night at headquarters, tossing and turning on my office couch for a few pointless hours before showering in the locker rooms and starting on my opening day checklists at 3:00 a.m. I didn't relish being in the locker room, not alone at night, when the HVAC noises twisted into odd echoes within the travertine walls, but it was better than being at the penthouse. I wasn't sure what penalty I would face for telling Nora about Aaden and — out of the two choices — I took his ghost over Logan's corporeal fury.

The hotel was serving coffee and scones in the lobby, and I had to remind myself it was still morning. The rest of the city hadn't been working at a controlled frenzy for the past nine hours. Pacing the length of the lion sculpture, I scanned every person entering the hotel and scrolled through the emails, texts, and social notifications blowing up my phone. The director of events had emailed three times looking for Logan, who was due at the gym this afternoon for a VIP pre-party, and her tone was becoming increasingly unnerved. As I replied to her, someone at my shoulder softly cleared their throat.

"Is this a good time?"

I turned and fought a bubble of laughter. There was no such thing as a good time this week, not until the woman standing in front of me unearthed millions of dollars.

"Of course." I finished the email, then frowned. "How did you find me?"

"Your assistant." Nora glanced around and leaned her briefcase against the lion's flank. "She said you were waiting for someone, and to tell you that 'her flight is slightly delayed.' I hope that might give you a few minutes to chat."

"By all means, let's chat." I waved to a

nearby couch and forced myself to sit. Somehow it was easier with Nora Trier at my side.

After confirming no one was within earshot of us, she quickly summarized her team's progress before diving into specific questions.

"Payroll appears to be one area of abnormally high expense. In the beginning of the year, you paid at least five-figure bonuses to everyone on your management team."

"We have the best people, and we give them the best."

"Do you consider yourself and Logan to be the best, also?"

I tracked the guests streaming through the lobby, avoiding Nora's steady gaze. "That question sounds like a trap."

She pulled up some numbers on a tablet and passed it to me. "The two of you both took zero bonuses. Whose decision was that?"

"It was mutual."

"And contrary to every other company on the face of the planet, your salaries are less than your senior managers'. Even Darryl Nolan outearns you." Her tone was professional, but I sensed derision beneath the words. She must have spent some time with the accountant already. "Logan has an expense account for the kind of incidentals that come with being the face of the business — apparel, sports doctors, rehab, skin treatments. You, however, draw no fringe benefits beyond what the rest of the company enjoys."

I looked at her and couldn't help smiling. "Having trouble casting me as a Bernie Madoff or Kenneth Lay?"

She reclaimed her tablet. "You certainly don't appear to be reaping extravagant perks from your job."

"Oh, but I do."

I didn't even know if I could explain it, how it felt to have created an empire from nothing, to hustle and brand and market and position until I didn't even know who I was without this company. My name was meaningless, but every household in America knew Strike. We rose up by becoming the fuel for an entire country's rise. And we'd doubled down again and again, reinvesting every raise and bonus and profit for twenty years until our rise seemed unstoppable. If that wasn't extravagance, I didn't understand the meaning of the word.

Nora switched tactics. "Darryl indicates seeing a pattern of overspending. Beyond payroll, the anomalies appear to be new club construction and a newer vendor, Beta

Games, who has received millions in Strike payments this year."

"Strike is an urban experience and all of our clubs are built into existing buildings. That comes with increased costs — renovation, special codes, protections, and historical societies. A project as simple as plumbing or soundproofing can quickly cause unexpected delays and expenses."

"And Beta Games?"

The work Beta Games had done for us was one of the best-kept secrets of the tournament. I wasn't about to spoil it now, with only hours to go before we unveiled it to the world. "You said Parrish is coming to the opening events tonight?"

"Yes, we have a box."

"Then you'll see our investment in action. Look for an area called vStrike."

She made a note and then hesitated, checking again to make sure no one lingered nearby. "One final item and I'll let you get back to your day. At the meeting last Friday, you made an accusation." She let the reminder settle between us before lowering her voice further still. "Do you have any evidence to support your suspicions?"

I stared at the statue of the resting lion, guarding the entrance to the hotel. Did I have evidence Logan had sabotaged our company? That she wanted all of this to come crashing down on our heads?

"You saw the blog post where she introduced the tournament."

Nora nodded.

"We'd had Strike Down in the works for months already, but it was a standard event with prize money. No one ever suggested giving the company away. Not until Logan announced it to the world."

I remembered, with vicious clarity, exactly where I was when I'd read her post, my skin still burning from the island sun where we'd spent her fiftieth birthday. Phrases jumped off the screen. *I'm handing this company to you . . . to become the next face of Strike.* I'd gaped at my phone, caught mid-stride in the hallway outside my office, when several managers accosted me.

"What does she mean, hand the company over?"

"Gregg, what is this?"

I had no idea. We'd had differences of opinion over twenty years — she'd resisted the corporate affiliations of CEO TKO; I'd thought Strike Next would consume too many resources — but in the end we both recognized the value of the other person's vision, and we always made the ultimate decisions together with our team.

It was Logan who originally came up with the Strike Down concept, but I'd loved it immediately; it would give the media and entire global athletic community a ringside view of everything we'd become. The directors had thrown themselves into the planning with such dedication and enthusiasm that to award them less than five-figure bonuses was unthinkable, especially since, as more time passed, Logan participated less and less.

She'd made Aaden a trainer as soon as he'd graduated from college and had spent increasing amounts of time with him, coaching him between member sessions and sometimes late into the night. I'd called her more than once after midnight to hear Aaden's grunts and laughter in the background and then hung up afterward, trying not to imagine them sweating together, her fingers positioning his arms, rotating his hips. *Again. Harder.* When he began competing professionally, she accompanied him to prize fights across the country — just the two of them together — and gave vague answers whenever I asked about the fights. She deferred all the Strike Down decisions to the managers who were working their asses off, until the day she went rogue.

Giving the company away. She refused to

explain or defend her decision, saying it was done and she rebuffed any attempt to question her. Marketing tried to get on board with her "New Face of Strike" campaign and, to show their collaboration, came up with several options for new faces. They'd found some premier prospects: a Chilean fighter training to be the first two-sport Olympian from her country, an African-American woman out of Chicago who was putting all her brothers through college with her fight winnings, and several title-winning trainers we already had in place at various Strike locations.

But Logan wouldn't even look at the profiles. She took the presentation remote out of C.J.'s hand, dropped it with a bang on the table, and told us she didn't need any market polls to make her decision.

As the Marketing Director, C.J. tried to explain. "You don't understand the months of work that should go into a decision like this, how capricious a consumer can be about their supplement purchase, how every single nuance of our packaging design has to be perfect. The fighter we put on the label must simultaneously challenge and reward them, dare them to be better, and allow them to see themselves strapping on those gloves and kicking some ass."

159

"Why are you only showing me women?"

"Three quarters of our revenue is female-driven. The women's side of the tournament brackets are filling up twice as fast as the men's."

"Aaden just signed up." Logan's eyes seemed to glow as she pushed away from the table, effectively ending the meeting. "Now if you'll excuse me, I've got a sparring date."

And that's when it hit me. Time slowed as the pieces of the last few months and years slammed into place. I ran out of the conference room and caught up with Logan as she walked into the gym. Aaden was warming up in the ring. He bounced around the mat, shuffling and feinting, loosening up. When he caught sight of Logan, he started to smile and then — seeing me behind her — the smile died. He turned away, punching invisible foes into the ropes.

I grabbed Logan's arm before she could go to him.

"The entry fee is five thousand dollars. You told me he was using his salary to help support his mother."

She avoided my eyes. "He paid the fee."

My grip tightened. "Really."

She stopped trying to pull away and drew herself up, squaring her shoulders and daring me to keep speaking.

I took the dare.

Dropping my voice, I glanced at the ring where Aaden still threw jabs and crosses. "You can't pick him, Logan."

"The fuck I can't. I'll pick any winner I want. It's my company."

I drew in closer, within striking distance, and my next words came through clenched teeth.

"It's our company."

I wanted her to hit me then, to feel the shock of the blow in my gut and the waves of pain reverberating to every extremity. I wanted her to pummel me. *Me.* Not Aaden. The person who'd stood behind her for two decades, refining her edges, honing her message, molding her from a champion into an icon. But she didn't. She stared at me, wordless, until I released her arm and she walked away, vaulted through the ropes, and immediately fell into a boxer shuffle. She and Aaden began circling each other, their eyes glowing in the spotlights of the ring. Neither of them noticed when I left.

I took a breath, bringing myself back through the clot of memory to the Grand Hotel lobby and Nora Trier's quiet audience. The lion still rested in front of us, guarding the door.

161

"She pushed him hard. They trained day and night and she was determined that he was going to win, that no one could stop him. We argued about it frequently. I don't know what happened between them in the end, if they fought or the pressure became too much for him." I shook my head. "Wild speculations."

"Logan wouldn't talk to me and gradually I think she started to blame me. I hadn't wanted Aaden as the next face of Strike and I'd made no secret of it. Afterward, it was my idea to keep his suicide and the suspicious money in his account quiet, out of respect for him and his family — yes — but also for how the publicity would impact the company. And . . ."

My voice went flat and hard. "I wanted to forget him. I still do. I'm not proud of everything I've done." I looked Nora in the eye, owning my choices, the things I knew that made me less. "But I did it for Strike."

Before she could say anything, the noise level in the lobby rose and another woman's voice soared over the top of it.

"Sheee-ut. Look who it is."

We both looked up to see a tall, corn-fed blonde with a shoulder span that seemed to fill the room striding across the marble tile. She was surrounded by an entourage of trainers, family, and hotel staff, but her wide-set eyes were fixed on me and her mouth cocked into a lopsided grin. Her hair bounced and flowed around her, as sleek and shining as a lion's mane.

I stood up just as she caught me in a bone-crunching hug, and made the introductions.

"Nora Trier, meet Merritt Osborne."

Nora's expression seemed to click as she made the connection.

London 2012: Merritt had taken home the Olympic silver medal in Taekwondo. The same year Michael Phelps became the most decorated Olympian of all time and Usain Bolt was a human blur, Merritt had garnered more likes than any other single-word tweet on Twitter, with a picture of her being medaled and the caption, "Y'all!!!!!!!!!!"

"Merritt's competing in the pro welterweight bracket."

"Honey," Merritt's Deep South drawl was a hearth you wanted to curl up next to, and at least a dozen strangers' heads turned at the sound of it. She sidled up to Nora, dwarfing the accountant. "I owe this man. After I injured myself at the Rio qualifiers I thought I was out of martial arts for good. Then guess who shows up in Georgia like an early Valentine this February, telling me all about a kickboxing tournament in the great white North."

"You're from Atlanta?"

"Macon, originally, but I've lived in Atlanta for years now. You ever been?"

"Once." Nora's eyes flashed to mine before she picked up her briefcase. Then she excused herself, saying she had to find Logan.

I turned to Merritt, my lion in the tournament, and escorted her through the lobby. My mind, though, lingered with Nora Trier. I wanted to go with her, to follow her all the way back to Atlanta, before the money was gone, before Aaden had died, before all the things that happened to unmake a man.

NORA

As soon as she got into the skyway, Nora got a call from Mike, asking about their seats at the tournament and when she was coming home to get ready. She checked her watch. So much of the day was spent already and — after talking to Darryl Nolan and Gregg Abbott — she had more questions now than when the morning began.

"Why don't you meet me at the office and we'll go from there?"

He sighed and Nora knew she hadn't given the right answer.

"Okay." His tone was clipped. "Henry asked if you're coming to the Fourth of July parade with us this year."

"I have to work. This client . . . it's an emergency."

Mike didn't say anything. He didn't have to. As Nora crossed over 2nd Avenue, something on the street below caught her eye. She stopped short, making the person behind her exclaim. Nora threw an apology over her shoulder and hurried into the next building, down the escalator, and outside into the scalding sun.

A pop-up tent was set up on the corner, hawking red, white, and blue everything, an explosion of Chinese-made American paraphernalia. Nora looked through pinwheels, banners, streamers, hats, and flags, finally finding the thing she wanted — a box of sparklers. Mike was talking, but she had no idea about what. A memory had swamped her, one she hadn't even known she still possessed.

Summertime, some long ago, sticky Minnesota night, she'd brought sparklers to Sam White's house. She'd hidden them in her purse, waited until Sam and his wife left, then let the boys run up and down the driveway, waving fire gleefully at the sky. They'd written their names in the air and laughed when the burn in their retinas lingered long after the sparks had died. Later they hosed down the charred wires and stuffed them deep into the trash, faces glowing with the shared secret of their mischief. Nora wondered if they ever thought about that day or if, like her, they'd buried it beneath the pain of everything that came later.

"Tell Henry I'll be home for fireworks," she interrupted Mike, picking up the box and staring at it. "I promise."

When she arrived back at Strike headquarters, the office was swarming with people.

Nora's lead analyst met her at the door. "They're getting ready for some VIP pre-party at the gym. Logan will be there and she said you can interview her then."

"At a party?" Nora took in the preparations happening all around them, people carrying stacks of cartons and wheeling coolers through the hallways. They passed a cubicle with a woman bent over double, shaking out a mass of hair, and another with a man tucking and untucking his shirt. Logan Russo would undoubtedly be the centerpiece of this event, which meant Nora would have no chance to get her alone or speak candidly. The move was either incredibly obtuse or absolutely brilliant.

"I know, but that's the best we can do if you want her today."

"I want her today." They'd barely started the investigation and were already running out of time. If nothing else, she might be able to surprise Logan with an unexpected question. Even hostile executives could give themselves away without saying a word, and

167

one shifty look or stutter was all Nora needed to send her team searching in the right direction. Then she caught herself. She was planning to catch Logan Russo off her guard?

The analyst stopped when they reached the door of their conference room, preventing Nora from entering. She looked exceptionally uncomfortable.

"What?" Nora asked.

"There's one more thing."

Twenty minutes later, Nora sat in a studio the size of her entire house. One wall was completely lined with athletic clothes, and another fitted with lights, drop cloths, kickboxing equipment, and a green screen. A granite counter by Nora's chair held more tubes and bottles than she'd ever seen outside Sephora.

Moments after the analyst told her she'd have to "blend in at the party," a pair of black-clad, mocha-skinned twins named Daisy and Darius commandeered Nora and brought her to the advertising space. They whisked her behind a screen, stripped off Nora's suit, and held a blur of fabric up to her, frowning and murmuring half-word comments back and forth until they found one that made them both fall silent. After she was dressed in what felt like a rose-gold toga — she honestly couldn't say what it was, looking in a mirror seemed like a terrible idea — they sat Nora in front of the overflowing counter and went to work on her face and hair.

"Are you Logan's personal stylists?"

"We do Logan, we do all the models for the campaigns. We'll do the next face, too, whoever that is. Darius, look at this cheekbone."

"And her ears."

Nora fought the urge to shrink down, to cover her cheeks and ask what was wrong with her ears. Instead, she asked if the twins knew why they were styling her. Daisy shrugged.

"They said to make you look like somebody."

There was a mirror over the counter, but Nora kept her eyes down as Daisy and Darius grabbed product after product. She tuned out as much as she could, ignoring the quaking in her stomach while the twins had a conference about her hair. Sliding her phone underneath the oversized bib they'd draped over her, she escaped into the abyss of her emails and status updates from her team.

Outside the large bonuses, the group assigned to payroll hadn't found any unusual activity. No fake employees or fake gym locations, which were the two most popular spins on payroll fraud. Nora put a mental cross through payroll. No twenty-million-dollar hole there.

Beta Games was still their strongest lead on the tournament angle. Strike had paid them over five million dollars this year for a mysterious product called only vStrike. No one had found any detail beyond that and Gregg himself had acted cagey on the subject, but even if this vStrike thing was completely fraudulent, that was only five million. She still needed fifteen more.

The team assigned to new club construction were having even less luck. Strike's main contractor — Magers Construction — was closed for the entire Fourth of July week. Taking their children to parades, probably.

Daisy and Darius pulled sections of her hair through flat irons and chatted about something that could either be a dress or an inspirational memoir. Both possibilities seemed equally likely. Nora opened the document where she'd started compiling fraud profiles and scrolled through Strike employee names until she found the one she was looking for: Gregg Abbott.

She paused, her finger over the cursor.

What had she even learned this morning during their interview? He'd talked a lot, filling in some of the details about Aaden and how Logan's preoccupation with the young fighter had caused the rift in their marriage, but what did any of that have to do with the prize money? His disclosures had included everything except a straightforward answer.

Just as she did with Darryl Nolan, Nora had researched Gregg, trying to build a profile for the man. He traveled frequently, visiting Strike's network of clubs and suppliers, but his expenses were surprisingly trivial. He either drove or flew coach everywhere, stayed in budget hotels, and ate mostly at convenience and grocery stores, often listing competitor protein bars for the breakfasts on his expense reports, with sidenotes such as "causes bloat" or "peanut butter sawdust."

He had no criminal history, served on the Minneapolis chamber of commerce, and drove a ten-year-old SUV. His credit report showed a few revolving balances, nothing out of line, and the most debt he and Logan carried was on their riverfront penthouse overlooking the Mississippi. On paper, he was the exact opposite of the greedy CEOs like the Madoffs or the Lays, taking nothing from the company, not even recognition.

Darryl Nolan had accused Gregg of over-spending. He clearly didn't spend on himself, but costs for the company's sake were no less damaging. He'd been so proud of Strike's expansion, so oblivious to the risks involved in self-financing. Was it possible this whole case boiled down to mismanagement? Gregg had jumped to point a finger at Logan, but it was always easier to blame someone else for your own mistakes.

The other fact she knew about Gregg Abbott was one she couldn't write in the file: Atlanta. The pieces of their first encounter were starting to come together. Unhappy with Logan's choice, Gregg had gone to recruit his own candidate for the next face of Strike — a bubbly, blond, on-brand face — and while he was there, he'd found a distraction from his imploding marriage. If he'd kept that secret, what else could he be hiding?

"There."

Nora blinked as one of the twins whipped the bib off and prodded her to stand. They made her walk back and forth and turn in every direction, while they exchanged looks of pronounced satisfaction.

"Can I go now?"

"Honey, don't you want to see yourself?"

172

Her reply was a beeline for the studio door. Ducking into the skyway, she flattened a hand over her hair, which felt strangely liquid, and tried to ignore the looks people gave her as she passed. A Strike receptionist who'd checked Nora into class countless times over the past six months stood up straighter when she walked in and blushed while asking her name. When Nora gave it to her, her eyebrows creased slightly, as though confused she didn't recognize it, but she bowed and waved Nora inside.

Nora felt equally confused as she entered the main gym. The space had been completely transformed. Two columns of body bags flanked a red carpet that stretched from the ring on one side of the room to a bar on the other. Spotlights grazed over at least a hundred heads and a driving bass thumped underneath the threads of conversation and laughter. Waiters circulated with trays of appetizers and drinks while a photographer snapped shots of people striking their best kickboxing poses.

She immediately moved as far to the side of the room as possible, half hiding behind a body bag while she searched the crowd for Logan. It didn't take long to locate her. Surrounded by a group of people at the base of the ring, Logan's husky laugh cut through the music and seemed to vibrate in the back of Nora's own throat.

Nora stalled for a moment, and she told herself it wasn't because she was nervous. She tried to forget about the ridiculous dress and the bouquet of fragrances wafting from her own hair, focusing instead on the legend in front of her. Logan Russo matched neither the finance manager's nor her husband's fraud profile. As the face of the company, she received a thousand times more scrutiny than anyone else. Every eye in the room followed her, tracking her movements and facial expressions, and each Strike success or failure became a public assessment of Logan Russo. The pressure, to someone like Nora, was unimaginable.

Her phone buzzed, interrupting her fixation. Nora looked down to see a new text from the analyst who'd helped interview Darryl Nolan and had kindly — at Nora's direction — offered to take him out to lunch afterward.

DN exhibiting strong hallmarks of resentment. Citing gender discrimination. Says GA doesn't like him because he's a man.

174

Nora frowned as she replied,

Isn't GA a man, too?

He couldn't produce any examples, but admitted he always thought GA needed to be "taken down a few notches."

Nora told her to rerun every payment approved by Darryl Nolan in the last six months, then tried to put the phone away before realizing her dress had no pockets. She sighed. The finance manager clearly had a bone to pick with Gregg. And it was obvious to anyone with eyes that Logan had issues with her husband, too. Maybe Gregg was right to suspect her — she could easily have colluded with Darryl — but Nora wasn't going to find anything out by standing in a corner.

Taking a deep breath, Nora steeled herself and walked into the crowd. Everyone she passed took a step back, eyes widening and murmuring to each other. She ignored the stares and whispers, winding her way through the room and concentrating solely on the woman who held court at the end of the red carpet.

When she reached the inner circle, Logan — who wore a sparkling, wide-legged jumpsuit — angled toward her and offered a hand. "Welcome to the pregame."

"Thank you for inviting me."

Logan blinked as she tried to place Nora and when the realization finally dawned, her face broke into a mile-wide grin.

"My, my. The beautiful and talented Nora Trier."

Nora felt herself blush and hoped that between the chaotic lights and the fifteen layers of makeup, her embarrassment remained hidden.

"And what do you do, sweetheart?" asked a burly man to her left, sidling closer.

"She's a magician. She makes money appear out of thin air." Logan draped an arm around Nora's shoulders as the group laughed. "If you'll excuse us."

Logan steered them to the edge of the red carpet, leaving Nora with little choice but to match her pace. Several people moved to intercept them, but Logan turned inward, speaking directly into her ear, and the intimacy of the gesture created a bubble between them and the rest of the VIPs.

"Perfect timing. I was on my last joke."

People paused, openly staring and obviously trying to figure out who Logan Russo was consorting with. A photographer appeared and began snapping pictures.

"How many jokes do you know?"

"One. Or zero, if you don't think Mike Tyson is a joke."

"I've got one for you." Logan's arm was too comfortable against her bare shoulders, the warmth of it too distracting. Nora pulled away and, disregarding the silky fabric rippling around her, climbed into the ring. The ropes glittered with LEDs and a spotlight roamed the sparring area, but it was the only space in the room empty of partygoers. She turned and waited for Logan to join her before taking a breath and launching in.

"A man wanted to hire a manager and he asked every candidate the same question. What's two plus two?"

Logan listened to the whole routine without cracking a single smile, and combined with the sea of upturned faces, all of whom seemed to be laser-focused on the ring, Nora felt like a stand-up comic dying on stage. It took forever to get to the punch line and when she finally did, Logan didn't even offer a courtesy laugh. She just shook her head and said, "I'll never remember that."

"Do you remember hiring Darryl Nolan?" If small talk wasn't going to help, fine. She'd jump right to business.

"Sure."

"Do you work closely with him?"

"Not really."

"Has he asked you to approve anything recently? New vendors or special payments?"

"No."

Nora tried a different tack, one that made her pulse tick up. "Gregg took a trip to Atlanta recently."

"Gregg takes a lot of trips. He's happiest on the road, when he has the illusion of progress."

It was the most information Logan had volunteered since they'd sat in the steam room together, before she'd known who Nora was. Nora wished now that she'd made better use of her anonymity.

"What progress do you think he made in Atlanta?"

Logan stepped closer, staring Nora down with a look as lethal as any punch. Nora's arms tensed as she moved backward toward the ropes. The phone grew slick in her palm.

"I know he found a puppet."

"Who?" She waited for the name to form, dreading the possibility that it might be her own and she'd have to hear it like this — without her suit, without her briefcase, without any of the tools she used to distance herself. She fought to keep her breath steady, feeling a hundred times more naked than she had sitting in that steam room.

The seconds dragged out and Logan still didn't answer the question. Had she even asked it out loud? The music reverberated in her chest and the lights glinted off Logan's narrowed eyes until, unable to bear the intensity of the focus, Nora ran a hand nervously over her mouth.

Logan's lip twitched and then, without warning, she burst out laughing.

"What?"

"Daze and Dare are gonna be pissed."

It took Nora a second to realize she was talking about the stylist twins, and another second to register that she'd probably just ruined her face. "Oh."

"Come on."

Logan pulled her back through the glittering ropes and behind the column of body bags, leading her into a locker room and the giant mirrors by the sinks.

Nora blinked. The woman standing next to Logan was . . . not her. Everything about her gleamed, from the sleek curtain of hair to the golden eye shadow to the skin that shimmered beneath the flowing asymmetrical dress, everything, that is, except the smear of lipstick trailing down her cheek and chin.

Logan grabbed a towel and threw it at her, laughing.

"Not my usual look."

"It's hot."

"Right." Nora hid her face in the towel and scrubbed.

"It's a lot goddamn hotter than whatever Gregg thinks Merritt Osborne would bring to this company." Logan swiveled to lean against the counter, facing away, their shoulders almost brushing. "He told me about her as soon as he got back from Atlanta. He was all . . . excited, energized. I hadn't seen him like that in a long time."

Nora stopped scrubbing.

"He thought he'd found the perfect solution to the problem I'd made. And then . . ."

Nora followed Logan's eyes to a spot on the floor next to the lockers and she froze, realizing for the first time where they were. The police photos swarmed into her vision and the towel, now stained with blotches of red, felt like a dead thing in her hands.

Logan swallowed. She opened her mouth to speak, but nothing came out. The report on Aaden's death said that Logan had been one of the first people on scene. Had she stood in this exact spot, staring at the body of the fighter she'd spent so much time with? What else had died for her that day?

180

A noise from the party seemed to snap Logan back from whatever memory had swamped her. Standing, she walked to a door that looked like a storage closet, badged it open, then glanced at Nora before disappearing through it.

Nora didn't think. She dropped the towel and caught the door right before it slammed shut. On the other side she found herself in Strike headquarters with Logan's back receding down a far hallway. By the time she caught up to her, Logan had stopped outside a cubicle that looked no different than any of the others in the area.

Nora looked closer, scanning piles of magazines and a set of hand weights cluttering the papers on the desk. An empty cup was crusted over, its leftover liquid long evaporated. Dust covered the monitor and the badge hanging across it showed a dark, unsmiling face. Nora knew that face. She'd seen its last expression.

"I haven't let anyone touch this space since he died. I know it's stupid — he didn't even spend that much time at his desk — but it's all I have left of him." A muscle twitched in Logan's jaw and her eyes filled with unshed tears.

"Why did you bring me here?" Yesterday Logan hadn't even wanted to talk about

Aaden. She'd said he had nothing to do with the investigation.

"Someone told me you see things other people don't."

"Who said that?" After witnessing the scene between Logan and Gregg in his office yesterday, she couldn't imagine the two of them chatting about anything, let alone her.

Logan crossed her arms, staring at the empty chair. "Go ahead. Look around."

Nora hesitated, then slowly began to open drawers and sift through the files Aaden Warsame had accumulated in his brief career. Other than the badge hanging on the computer — which was another giant lapse of security to match the open server doors and unlocked computers — nothing here seemed inherently personal. Company memos, trainer tips. Nora found nothing that pointed to theft or suicide, much less the loss of twenty million dollars. What did Logan want her to see?

"Do you have children?"

Nora, kneeling now beside a low drawer, looked up in surprise.

"Yes, I have a son."

"I never wanted kids. All the fighters I knew who got pregnant had to quit for at least a year. Most of them never came back, and the ones who did were changed. Their jabs could be just as strong, their reaction times just as fast, but it was like their center of gravity had shifted and they couldn't quite figure out where it lived now."

"That's basically how it feels."

"Mine is gone. It's like I have no center left to find." Logan gripped her arms, legs braced wide as though worried she was going to be knocked over. The celebrity who'd laughed and paraded Nora around the party was nowhere to be seen. She swallowed and lifted her gaze. "Are you a good parent?"

Nora's hands fell into her lap. The professional answers, the jokes about parenthood, the quips and quotes she saved for interviewing clients all slipped away and the only thing she could see were Sam White's boys racing through the night with sparklers, laughing with the giddiness of kids whose father was strong and caring and alive. She couldn't remember the last time she'd made her own son laugh.

"I don't think so, no."

Logan stared at the badge hanging on the dusty computer. "Neither was I."

DAY ONE

July 2, 2019

Two days ago, a pilgrimage began. Fighters all over the world rose up with their gloves and wraps. They crossed continents on cracked and bleeding feet, making their way to the middle of North America where the last falls of the Mississippi die.

They're hungry.

And they're here.

For six months I've been talking about Strike Down and it begins tonight. Here's the rundown for anyone who doesn't know how this four-day tournament is going to roll.

- Day One: Opening Ceremonies and Preliminaries. Three rings of continuous fights will decide which amateur and professional fighters move on to the finals. In each category, fights are

184

organized by gender and weight classes from straw weight all the way to super heavyweight.

- Day Two: Amateur finals. Watch the best of the amateurs fight it out for thirty-six championship spots. The final three fighters in every weight class will receive purses to rival pro-MMA champions.
- Day Three: Exhibition. We're celebrating Independence Day by throwing the premier athletic and wellness convention of the decade. Freedom, baby, is why this event is free and open to the public. I'm talking vendor giveaways, samples, the hottest new gear, panel discussions on everything from debunking exercise fads and diet myths. (I'm fueled 100% by protein powder and avocados and I have no shame.) For tournament ticket holders, Strike's Minneapolis trainers will host demonstration classes all day long at our downtown gym.
- Day Four: Professional finals. The last day of competition will showcase the best of the best competing for the biggest kickboxing purses ever awarded. In addition to twenty million dollars in prize money, I'll be changing one

champion's life forever. One of the fighters who made a pilgrimage to the center of this country won't be going home again; they'll become the next face of Strike. On Friday night, history is going to be made.

Are you ready to fight?

Because

Strike Down. Is. Here.

GREGG

"We're broadcasting live from beautiful downtown Minneapolis here at the opening ceremonies of the record-smashing Strike Down tournament."

The announcer turned to where Logan and I flanked the view to the field, and god, what a view. Three rings rose from the massive space, the center elevated higher than those on either side, and beneath the rings people swarmed like bees in a hive. Geared-up fighters shifted through the walkways with fluid tails of coaches, friends, and family streaming behind them. Fans waved their countries' flags and took selfies. Lines for food and drink stretched across the concourses. Behind the cameras and the red velvet ropes holding back masses of onlookers, the five largest pivoting glass doors in the world were thrown wide. It looked as though the wall itself had opened up, like Logan had finally smashed through the glass ceiling and left the fallen remains for all to see. The sun blazed above the downtown skyline, illuminating the panels, wall, and the transparent roof with molten sunlight so bright it hurt the eyes.

Inside, the jumbotrons were blowing up with a different kind of light.

Finally here and ready to rumble.
#StrikeDown
omg,
@VenusWilliams sighting you guys.
#GrandSlam #faints #StrikeDown
Hell yeah, Funkytown! #StrikeDown

And, as soon as Logan walked into the stadium:

The Queen of Pain has arrived.
#MillCityMiracle #StrikeDown

The announcer — an ESPN commentator with neon white teeth — moved the mic immediately to Logan, where the camera lights bounced off her slicked-back hair. She wore an outfit I could barely describe. The top was a blazer with oversized gold sequin cuffs and a low-cut blouse, the bottom a black-and-gold asymmetrical skirt. It was like a suit had gotten into a fight with a prom dress, and the only obvious winner was Logan. She looked stunning. My wife, who never wore sleeves because she complained they were too confining and made her feel like a twelve-year-old boy, posed like some Hollywood screen goddess, owning every ounce of confidence the movie stars tried to project.

I wore a three-piece suit and together we looked like the couple you dream of becoming, wealthy, famous, and beautiful, standing at the precipice of the empire we'd created. I didn't let myself think about what this night could have been, if only we were what we seemed.

"Logan Russo, this is unarguably the crowning achievement in your company's meteoric rise in the athletic industry. How are you feeling right now?"

"Great." She flashed a smile across the crowd. "I haven't had to train for the past six months like the fighters who've come to compete this week."

"Contenders from eighteen different countries are here tonight, vying for not only the largest purse ever offered in the sport but also the chance to become the next face of Strike. I think it's safe to say the internet broke when you announced this tournament."

Logan laughed. "Well, I know our servers

crashed."

"The reaction wasn't all positive, though, was it?"

Logan's smile crystallized. She didn't twitch so much as a muscle in my direction, but the air between us changed as the announcer rushed to elaborate. "There aren't many female superstars in martial arts and even fewer older women. I think some fans are afraid that a new face of Strike means Logan Russo's voice and face will disappear."

"You guys know I don't do silent." Logan spoke to the watching crowd and a cheer went up from behind the velvet rope. After the cameras panned through their reactions, Logan continued, "As for erasing my image, I dare anyone to try to make me disappear. You're welcome to come to Minneapolis anytime and get a nice, close look from inside the ring. I'll be here. I'll leave a pair of gloves out for you."

She didn't look at me, didn't touch me, didn't make a single move in my direction, but she was speaking to me. My smile froze as the announcer laughed and said, "That's one invitation I won't be accepting."

Then he pivoted, sweeping a hand over the stadium floor. "I've been to hundreds of fights from Vegas to Dubai and let me tell everyone watching at home right now, Strike Down is something wholly new. You've taken sports competition to the next level."

"Here's the level-up master right here." Logan slid a hand over my shoulder, a caress for the camera, and gave me a saccharine smile. It was the first time she'd touched me since we'd been alone on the balcony the other night and it made my jaw clench. I wondered if her feet were still bleeding.

"Gregg Abbott. The man behind the woman."

I turned to the announcer. "Better behind than in front of her."

We all laughed before he got serious and asked one of the questions I'd written into the broadcast contract. "People have said kickboxing is dead, that American martial arts interest shifted to MMA a long time ago. What's your response to that?"

"MMA had a moment, a great moment, and I think we all enjoyed watching some of those matches. But that's all most of us could do — watch. MMA is inaccessible for, uh," I aimed a self-deprecating glance at Logan, "normal humans.

"Logan's vision for Strike was to bring martial arts into the urban community, where people really live and work and

191

hustle. And everyone has the ability to be a kickboxer. Women, men, adults, and children. We have seventy-year-old members who frankly terrify me" — the announcer chuckled — "and adolescent girls learning self-defense. That's one of the things that makes Strike Down so unique — our amateur competition. We've invited the entire world to get into the ring tonight and throw down. And in more ways than you might expect."

"You've got more surprises in store for us?" the announcer asked.

Logan leaned into the mic, her dark eyes gleaming. "There's always another surprise in store at Strike."

Crowds continued to flood through the gates, buying refreshments and programs, lining up for interactive demonstrations with the trainers, and taking thousands of selfies to flash overhead on the larger-than-life screens. Logan and I bounced from interview to interview, joking with reporters while greeting business owners, members, international fighters, and politicians. As the countdown clock ticked closer to zero, the seats began to fill, and the noise level rose.

When there was less than ten minutes on

the clock, Logan turned, her smile turning feral in the shadows. "Your puppy needs a walk."

My assistant Sara stood anxiously at the back of the reporters, eyes wide in silent appeal.

"Don't go anywhere," I said before moving through the throng. "We're on soon."

If she replied, I didn't hear it. I nodded, greeted, and shook hands until I reached Sara, who'd withdrawn even further behind a kiosk selling commemorative Strike Down apparel. An assistant to the core, she wore a sleek suit of all black that looked like a glossy full-body version of the yoga pants she sported daily.

"Anything today?"

"One of them was talking to Beta Games. Another took Darryl out to lunch and he didn't come back to the office afterward."

"Why not?" I frowned.

"He called in sick."

Darryl was "sick" twice as often as any other manager at the company. And he wondered why I would never promote him to CFO.

"Do you think Darryl was involved in . . ." She looked around, clearly not wanting to say anything out loud about the missing prize.

"At the very least, he didn't do anything to prevent it. After the tournament is over, we're going to have some turnover. Let HR know."

Sara nodded, her eyes continuously sweeping the perimeter of the crowd. Casually, I turned and helped her keep watch.

"Before they left for the day one of them was contacting other suppliers. Another questioned the IT manager about password security. And Nora Trier left the VIP party with Logan."

"Why?"

"They were looking through Aaden's desk together."

I stared at my wife in the crowd. She said something and laughter surrounded her, rippling out until it touched even us. Aaden Warsame would never have amassed the same charisma and I wondered if even Merritt stood a chance, if anyone would look as fierce and bright in this sun. The next face of Strike was waiting somewhere in this stadium right now. They wouldn't shine like Logan, but they wouldn't be obsessed with a dead man, either.

"No concrete leads on the money yet?" I asked, still staring at Logan. "That AI computer hasn't turned up anything?"

"No. Do you think they'll find it? In only

three more days?" Her voice rose and broke, betraying a hint of panic.

"She will." I had no choice except to believe that.

Sara shifted, said nothing. The best assistants didn't need to.

"Don't worry, Sara. Where are they now?" She pointed and I turned away from the pageantry of Logan, scanning the premium boxes in that general direction once, twice. Finally, on the third pass, I found it. The suite was semi-dark and empty except for her, even though I'd confirmed all of the partners and their guests on the reservation. Nora seemed invisible to the groups in the boxes around her, poised motionless at the edge of the balcony, surveying the scene with an unreadable expression. She showed no delight at the hundred wonders spread below her, nor boredom, censure, or disinterest, only silent absorption. What couldn't this woman see, if she looked long and deep enough? She would find the money — she had to, I couldn't even consider the possibility that she wouldn't — but I wanted her to know so much more, to unearth every secret from the last twenty years and trace their jagged edges to this place and time. I wanted her to understand what they had all cost.

As I watched, a man entered the suite and walked over to Nora. He wasn't one of the other partners I'd met at Parrish Forensics last Friday. He was shorter, with a round face and beard, and wore an untucked Hawaiian shirt. When he handed Nora a glass of wine, she grazed his cheek with an absent kiss, her eyes still fixed on the crowd below, and my entire body stiffened.

"Who's that?"

"No one. Just Nora's husband."

She hadn't worn a wedding ring in Atlanta. Of that I was sure.

He gestured animatedly with a bottle of beer, carrying on a one-sided conversation while Nora appeared to ignore him. She held the wineglass rigidly and her gaze moved to the crowd of reporters flocked around Logan. The longer I stared at them, the more familiar the space between them became, the hole in every marriage that gaped larger and larger until neither person knew how to cross it anymore.

"What now?" Sara asked, as the announcer began escorting Logan through the concourse toward center stage. The giant glass doors began swiveling shut, throwing blinding sunlight across the stadium, and for a moment Nora, her husband, and everyone else packed into the arena looked like they'd been set on fire.

"Now the fights begin."

NORA

Nora stood on the balcony of the suite next to Mike. She'd changed back into her suit for the tournament, but the costume wasn't helping. She'd never felt less professional in her life.

The money was everywhere, wafting off the chef-catered grills, lining the red carpet snaking through the vendor booths, and humming in the screens positioned at strategic angles that broadcast everything from press conferences with the elite international fighters to the trainer demonstrations happening live on the concourse. Standing in the shadows and holding a wineglass, Nora counted. Cost. Revenue. Risk. Reward.

She totaled the tournament expenses her team had compiled, spread it over the number of tickets sold, calculated the average spend of the heads milling below. Fixed overhead, variable costs, the factors that could spin an event like this into profit or loss. Projections had always soothed her, their steady columns and reliable results the one thing she could depend on. So why weren't the numbers doing their job?

Mike was talking. She couldn't bring his words into focus. She continued making calculations until the arena dimmed and the music swelled into a hard driving beat. The fights were about to start.

Thousands of people turned toward the jumbotrons where a montage of images illuminated the stadium. Logan, knocking out an opponent. Logan, holding a golden belt above her head as people flooded the ring. Logan, playfully waggling a protein bar like a fifties' mobster with a cigar. A ribbon-cutting in front of a club. More fighters. Students, seniors, dozens of women striking bags, and two exhausted, laughing people hugging each other in the ring, their sweat dripping together like raindrops to anoint the heads of the crowd below.

A microphone-laden table appeared on-screen and one of the Japanese fighters leaned toward the cameras.

"It's the largest purse in kickboxing history. I couldn't believe it when we got the news."

It cut to another fighter, another press

conference.

"This isn't just a fight. It's mind and body, giving back, rising up. Win or lose, I don't want to go home."

Then Merritt Osborne filled the screens, laughing. "It's definitely not the Olympics, y'all. It's better. So much better."

A few more clips aired, snippets from the elite fighters talking about becoming the next face of Strike. Their excitement was palpable; it seeped into the crowd, drawing attention to the giant banner that towered behind the last ring showing the signature Strike image of Logan's face partially covered by a boxing glove. A fifty-foot-tall eye glared at the crowd, dominating the thousands of heads swarming below it.

The press conference clips forced Nora to think of another face, the one she'd seen on a badge hanging over a dusty computer. How would Aaden Warsame have described what Strike Down meant to him?

Nora still didn't entirely understand what he and Logan had been to each other. Gregg had assumed they were intimate, but Logan's quiet admissions earlier sounded more like a grieving parent's. She couldn't ask Aaden. All she knew for certain was that he'd thought of Logan last. His suicide note had said *Logan, I'm sorry.* But was he apologizing to an employer, a mentor, a lover, or a friend?

After she'd gone through Aaden's cubicle, she'd instructed her lead analyst to have the computers search for the money that had mysteriously appeared in Aaden Warsame's bank account.

"You told us those amounts were negligible," the analyst said.

"Both of the owners keep circling back to him. It must have significance."

"Okay, maybe." The analyst looked skeptical. "But we don't have time to get distracted by a few thousand dollars."

"Just do it."

She knew she wasn't being rational, but Logan wanted her to see something. *Her.* A week ago she hadn't even known Nora existed and now, for some mysterious reason, she'd opened up and asked for Nora's help. Maybe Logan was playing her, but the sincerity of her words outside Aaden's cubicle reverberated in Nora's core.

So far the programs hadn't found a link from the company books to those deposits, but the computers were running even now. Inga didn't take breaks or sleep, and Nora could almost hear the buzz of the fans, feel the heat of the processors. If there was a connection between Aaden Warsame and twenty million dollars, she would find it.

The videos dissolved into the Strike logo and an emcee walked into the center ring.

"Welcome to the ladies and gentlemen who have traveled across the globe to join us in beautiful downtown Minneapolis tonight, and to all the fighters watching in Strike gyms across the country. Are you ready for the world's first Strike Down tournament?"

Cheers erupted throughout the stadium. Mike looked around, as if just now noticing the rest of the party wasn't in the suite, and told her he'd go find them. She nodded, but the majority of her attention was fixed on the middle of the stadium, where Logan and Gregg were walking onstage.

Nora drained her wine as Logan took the microphone and began working the crowd. Every person in every seat applauded her, laughed with her, followed each glittering movement as her dress flashed in the spotlights. Her scratchy alto, a voice that carried the scars of a lifetime in the ring, boomed through the stadium, reverberating deep in every spectator's chest. When she swore — "Can you fucking believe this night?" — the stadium erupted in cheers and screams.

Then the banner at the end of the arena dissolved, vanishing Logan's image into a shadow while keeping the raised glove in place. The real Logan pointed to it, declaring the next face of Strike would take her place in the banner by the tournament's end. The cheers, already deafening, doubled.

Five thousand for the banner. Two thousand more for contender photos, so any of the champions could be swapped seamlessly into the graphic. Design work, fifteen hundred. Nora grabbed random numbers, assigned probabilities, added all the components as the suite's air conditioner cycled on and her skin broke out in goose bumps. She was alone in the dark. She wasn't standing in the ring with Logan. She never had been.

The Parrish Forensics party had arrived half an hour ago, after meeting up at the office and walking over together. Corbett and his wife, Katie, showed up at the last minute, and spent most of the walk chatting with Rajesh and his wife. It wasn't until they were making the last turn in the skyway that Nora managed to get Corbett on his own.

"I need to talk to you."

"More dead men on the brain?"

"I'm serious. There's something going on with this case."

"Is it your man, Gregg?" He lowered his voice, glancing at the others to make sure no one was listening. "Is he trying to influence you?"

"No. Maybe. I don't know." She swiped a hand through the air. "I should be poring through financial statements, but instead I'm getting dolled up like Barbie and shown pictures of men with holes in their heads."

"Come again?"

"They're ready to tear each other apart and I can't find a safe place to stand." She swallowed. "The thing is . . . I don't even know if I want to."

"Ellie, your job is to find the money. That's all. Get the money and get out." As they joined the line to enter the stadium, Corbett's expression changed. He looked worried, but before he could say anything else, Jim came over and interrupted them.

"It's recklessness. Don't you agree, Nora?"

"What am I agreeing to?" She shifted a look back at Corbett, but Rajesh had moved into their circle, too. Whatever Corbett had been about to say was lost.

"Why wouldn't any prudent person maintain the twenty million in cash equivalents? That would be my first step in planning an event like this." Jim pulled out the tickets for the security guard to scan.

"He probably got in over his head." Rajesh smirked at Corbett, who didn't engage. "If he can't manage his books, how could he expect to execute a project like this? Especially considering it's a one-off. No standard work or budget template. All new vendors. I predict what we'll see is a mess, an absolute . . ." Rajesh trailed off as they moved through the giant glass doors and the scene opened up in front of them, a veritable wonderland of athletic entertainment.

"Wow," someone said, or maybe it was all of them, standing dumbfounded at the edge of the concourse.

A host in a Strike outfit complete with hand wraps showed them to their suite, pointing out the amenities along the way. They passed live fighting technique demonstrations, sampled the complimentary VIP smoothie bar, posed for pictures at the Instagram photo booth, where you could don gloves and choose from filters that included "Victory Glow" and "Black Eyed Glees."

After getting a round of drinks, they approached a strange sight. A uniformed attendant stood near the roped-off entrance of a huge steel-colored block, like a gigantic child's plaything gone astray. Nora, having never attended a football game, had no idea if this was a regular part of the tableau.

"Fighters." The man lifted his arms and spoke to the gathered people, all of whom sipped cocktails and chattered excitedly. "We've all played video games. We've seen what 3D and 4D has to offer. But this," he motioned to the pitch-black entrance to the cube, "this is a fight you have to experience in order to believe. Brought to you by Beta Games and Strike, may I present —"

"vStrike," Nora murmured.

The man's face lit up, finding her in the crowd. "I believe we have our first contender. Give it up for the lovely lady in black, about to step into a ring unlike any other."

Nora peered into the dark opening of the steel box as Mike slipped the drink out of her hand. She glanced at Corbett, who smiled and elbowed her in the side. "Are you scared, Ellie?"

The attendant drew the velvet rope back. Nora walked up the steps and inside the small room, which had dark gray walls and a springy floor. Other than a logo running along the ceiling, the space was a blank canvas. The attendant clipped a belt around Nora's waist that was suspended by thin gossamer strings from every wall, tethering her to the center of the room, then affixed a dozen small dots to her hands, arms, torso, legs, and the top of her shoes. They glowed neon in the semi-darkness and seemed to vibrate through her clothes and into her skin. Finally, he handed her a full mask with goggles and headphones that descended from the ceiling, asking her to put it on.

She glanced at the door, where all of the partners and their spouses stood grinning at her. Feeling distinctly like an animal in a zoo, she shook her head at Corbett, turned back toward the belly of the room, and donned the mask.

Darkness and silence engulfed her. She looked right and left, every muscle tense, wishing she'd taken a few minutes to read the program, so she might have any chance to prepare for what was coming. Was it a fight in complete darkness? Would blows start raining on her?

In the next second, she was blinded by stage lights. She turned in a complete circle, blinking at the exact scene on the field, only from an entirely different angle. U.S. Bank Stadium surrounded her, the giant Strike banner stretching practically to the glass ceiling that refracted a rainbow of sunset fire into every part of the arena. Thousands of people screamed from their seats, cheering and waving signs. She stood, not at the edge of the concourse but in the middle of the center ring, elevated, exposed, and completely alone. Silver gloves shimmered on her hands and when she threw an experimental jab, the material pulsed into the air surrounding it, sending ripples of glittering energy through the ring.

"If Henry could see this . . ." she breathed.

Then an announcer's voice boomed overhead. "Strike Down fans, get ready for the main event. In one corner we have . . ." The pause lengthened and Nora realized he was waiting for her.

"Nora Trier," she muttered as the crowd lights dimmed, throwing everything outside the ring into shadow.

"Nora Trier!" the voice repeated. "Facing off against . . ."

A half dozen faces materialized in front of her, bodiless heads staring her down. She recognized the two highest billed Japanese fighters and the Brazilian woman looking for the welterweight title. Merritt Osborne was also among the group. Nora's glove paused for a moment before moving to brush Logan's cheek. Instantly, the other faces vanished, but Logan's lingered a second longer, winking at her before disintegrating.

"The greatest kickboxer in history! Give it

up, ladies and gentlemen, for Logan Russo!"

On the other side of the ring, Logan's full, life-sized body appeared, pixel by pixel, until she looked as real and as imposing as an unbeaten prize fighter should. Every tendon stretched and recoiled. Every muscle gleamed like shards of glass. But there were tiny errors, too; the lines around her eyes and mouth were missing. When she started mouthing words — lost in the noise of the crowd — her lip didn't tug down at the left corner like it was supposed to. She was taller, more beautiful, and more menacing than the real-life Logan, and Nora felt like she'd been sucked into a painting or an idea. The painted Logan wore a glossy mesh shirt and her golden gloves left a trail of haze as she paced in the corner, eyes locked on her opponent. As she moved, the same neon dots winked on her body that the attendant had attached to Nora's.

"Watch that right hook. She'll double it up on your head before going for the body." A virtual coach had scuttled up next to her, looking suspiciously like the head of Strike marketing. "Block her blows and try to land as many as you can on the dots. The first fighter to land three unblocked hits takes the championship."

These weren't kickboxing rules. The fight

wasn't set up in rounds or even like Henry's game with energy and life bars at the top of the screen. A scoreboard hovered above them with three *X*'s and three *O*'s waiting to light up beneath each name.

When she blinked again, she'd been transported to the center of the ring, staring into Logan's implacable face. She was close enough to hear Logan's breath and should have been able to feel the heat rising off her. Neon flashed on either side of her temples.

"Aaaaannnnnddd GO!" A bell rang and Logan's fists became streaks of gold.

Nora startled back, automatically blocking the jabs. She twisted right and left, clamping her elbows to her ribs, and felt the belt tethering her to the center of the box bite into her waist. Pivoting, she kicked Logan's leg, making the dot on her thigh flash red and sending a buzz through her own foot and mask. The scoreboard lit up a green *O* under her name, but before she could celebrate or plan her next move, she was under siege. Logan threw a cascade of punches and roundhouses. Gold met silver, trails of light exploded into each other, surrounding them both in a cocoon of shimmering violence. One dot buzzed. Two. Nora stumbled back until she couldn't go any farther, ducking the double head hook the coach had warned her about.

She was outmatched. There was no winning this fight. Henry would tell her to jump in and attack, to "die big," the way he had in his fighting game, but Nora could only curl up and defend. It was all she could do to block the blur of gloves and feet. In a desperate move, she lunged into the painted Logan, pulling her into a grappling hold so that both of them were too close to land any blows.

Everything was surreal, both more and less than a dream. More because her brain was conscious, processing every cue — Logan's head pressed against hers, her breath stuttering in Nora's ear. Less because other, more vital data was missing. The sensors on Nora's body radiated heat and energy, but there was no resistance against her arms, no scent, no substance within the painting. The virtual reality was overpowering, and — Nora realized with a shock of clarity — it wasn't enough.

She wanted the real Logan.

Nora's arms fell, releasing the hold, and the virtual Logan drew back. She cocked her head to consider this unworthy opponent who had somehow blundered into her ring. The swelling noise of the crowd drowned out whatever the announcer shouted above them. Then the computer pivoted into a cross, the thousand glass shards of her pixelated body glittered in the stage lights, and the ball of her fist exploded the world into gold.

"I've never seen anything like it. No one's seen anything like it."

Mike, who'd also taken a turn at vStrike, was still gushing about the experience an hour later. The amateur preliminary rounds were in full swing, filling all three rings with ducking and kicking opponents while replays flashed overhead, but Nora barely noticed them. She was still replaying her own fight and trying to analyze what it meant.

She'd steadied herself by the time Mike had found the rest of the group, still finishing their turns at vStrike, and brought them back to the suite. Nora drank automatically, filling her hands with a new glass whenever the old one emptied. She discussed the progress of the case with Jim at one point, retaining absolutely nothing of the conversation, and debated most of the night about telling Mike what happened, but what would she say? This wasn't dating. It wasn't sex, this overwhelming desire to track Logan throughout the stadium, to replay every exchange, turn over each look and gesture to discover what, if anything, lay buried beneath.

By the end of the night, after the preliminary brackets had completed and the announcer wrapped up the fights, Nora was exhausted. She needed to talk to someone, someone who could understand that no matter how impartial she appeared, she wasn't independent, and that lack of independence was clawing at her throat.

"Where's Corbett?" she asked Katie, who was giggling and hiccupping as she and Mike collected their things.

"Got a message on his phone and said he had to run into work. You two want to share an Uber with me?"

Nora told them to go ahead, and fought her way through the crowds toward the skyway. Corbett would listen. He wouldn't judge. She'd already shocked him out of all expectations he might have had for her behavior or emotions. He would provide the guidance she so desperately needed right now.

She reached the skyway and was skirting the edge of the lingering groups of fans when a familiar figure caught her attention. One story below, on the plaza, Corbett's wiry-haired head moved through the crowd. Nora tried to go back, but the security guards weren't letting anyone return to the stadium; she was stuck in the glass-encased walkway. Following his progress, Nora started to frown. Corbett wasn't moving with the crowds toward the train or parking lots, and he wasn't walking toward the Parrish office, either. Instead, he skirted the edge of the stadium, checking his phone every few seconds.

Nora reached into her pocket to text him, but then fell still. Another figure joined him from the shadows of the stadium wall, someone wearing a long, dark coat. They put their hood up a split second after stepping into the light, but it was enough time for Nora to see the person's face.

Logan.

Corbett spoke to the hooded figure and they began to walk together, directly underneath the skyway.

Logan and Corbett?

Nora's mouth fell open. She backed up, bumping into a group of people, and rushed to the other side. They weren't there. She waited, her mind reeling, and by the time the pair came into sight again they were at least a hundred yards ahead of her and crossing an intersection. She broke into a run, but the amount of people leaving the stadium made it impossible to keep the street in view.

When she reached the intersection, they were gone. Nora checked either side of the glass, peering down each of the shadowy streets. She jogged another block, looking right and left. Nothing.

What the hell was Corbett doing with Logan?

Retracing her steps back toward the stadium, she pulled her phone out again. She was jabbing out the text, "Where are you?" to Corbett when she glanced into an alley and spotted movement in the shadows. Two people, half-hidden by a dumpster, seemed to be in the middle of an argument. She shook her head against the volume of alcohol she'd drunk tonight, and squinted into the darkness until the taller person came into focus.

It was Corbett.

As she watched, a flash shot out from the other person's arm — a haze of gold, like the vStrike gloves streaking through the virtual ring — then Corbett's body jerked and disappeared.

"Why would Corbett be standing around in an alley?"

"I don't know." Nora unzipped her dress pants and let them fall to the floor. Two hours later, she was still replaying the images she'd seen outside the stadium. Two people. A sudden movement. The person who looked like Corbett had fallen. And the other person, the flash of gold which must have been Logan, had followed him down. The skyway was well lit, making the alley seem twice as dark. It had been a struggle to make out anything at all. What exactly had she seen? To have witnessed it and still not know for sure was infuriating.

"He's not returning my calls."

"It's after midnight." Mike sat in bed scrolling on his phone. He'd still been chatting with the babysitter when she'd gotten home, the two of them laughing and trading anecdotes about Henry while Nora retreated immediately to the bedroom and called Corbett. His cell. His work line. He didn't answer voice or text. She debated calling Katie, but didn't want to worry her, not yet.

After she'd seen — whatever it was — Nora had raced through the skyway to a connected parking garage, ran down an escalator to street level, pushed through the tournament crowds still exiting the stadium, and jogged the block to the alley.

It was empty. Apart from a few dumpsters and some litter, the space was abandoned to graffitied cinder block. She'd turned around and stared at the groups strolling past before walking quickly to Parrish. Music pumped out of the bars lining the streets and a siren wailed a few blocks away. When she got to their building, Corbett's office was empty, but his minivan was still parked next to her car in their ramp.

"It had to be Corbett."

But the farther away she'd gotten from the alley, the less certain she was. She'd started drinking water and had taken a preemptive aspirin to un-fog her head.

"Is it so important that you talk to him tonight?" Mike tossed his phone on the nightstand and yawned. "Can't you just see him tomorrow?"

She'd be at Strike tomorrow, right where Corbett had told her to be. Get the money and get out, he'd said. He made everything sound so simple. But he hadn't told her he was late-night walking pals with Logan Russo.

Nora kept pacing, ordering and reordering the facts in her mind, trying to impose an arrangement that would make sense. Trying to make it simple. She knew three things for sure.

One. Corbett had gotten a call from someone and told his wife he had to work.

Two. He hadn't gone to work.

Three. He'd met Logan outside the stadium and they'd left together.

Everything beyond that was speculation and shadows, and the shadows were driving her insane.

Why wouldn't Corbett tell her that he knew Logan? He'd been required to disclose familiarity threats when the partners had vetted Strike. Any pre-existing friendship or relationship had to be evaluated, just as she'd disclosed her one-night stand with Gregg Abbott. That thought stopped Nora in the middle of her pacing. Were Corbett and Logan having an affair? Had she seen a lover's quarrel in the alley? It seemed ridiculous, but why else would he hide the association and risk his standing and credentials? The possibility made Nora's jaw clench. He'd acted so outraged when she'd explained the nature of her own marriage. And he had monogamous Katie along with a herd of children looking up to him, and . . . and it was Logan.

The feelings that had swamped her in the vStrike booth doubled into something darker and less controlled. She took deep breaths, reminding herself that she didn't know the context of what she'd seen. She didn't know anything right now.

"I'm sure he's fine. Whoever you saw in that alley got up and left, right?"

"You're not helping, Mike."

He rolled up to a sitting position and watched her with growing fascination. "You're really upset about this."

"I just saw Corbett being assaulted." She threw her arms wide, then qualified, "I think."

"It's not just that, though." He tracked her as she paced, and slowly a grin tipped up the corners of his mouth. "Well, what do you know?"

"What?" she bit out, even though she couldn't care less what Mike knew right now.

"Someone's gotten to you."

She stopped pacing and stared at her husband. The walls she'd built, her independence, her isolation, all of it was threatening to collapse. She opened her mouth, but nothing came out. Mike leaned forward and pointed to the phone she still gripped in one hand.

"He doesn't tell you everything. Do you tell him everything?" And then, after a pause in which his smile faded. "Do you tell anyone everything?"

Nora spun to the closet and pulled out workout clothes and her old running shoes.

"What are you doing?"

"I need to think."

"Funny, because it looks like you're running away."

Her head shot up from her laces. Mike sat in his rumpled T-shirt and nest of covers, watching her with the satisfaction of a guru who'd been waiting years for this moment, and suddenly she wanted to hit him. She wanted to take everything churning inside her right now, ball it into a fist, and punch him with it until this feeling was obliterated. But that made her think about Logan and the gravelly words filtering through clouds of steam: *You've never had to fight for your life.*

Shoving her phone into a pocket, she

stalked out of the bedroom.

"Be careful out there," Mike called after her. "You don't want to get hurt."

She wasn't sure about that anymore.

Grabbing a flashlight, Nora disappeared into the woods that — two days ago — she'd babbled about to Logan Russo, imagining meeting her on one of these trails, the things she would say to make Logan laugh, to make her notice. Now all she could see as the beam of light bobbed over the dirt and threw shadows in every direction was two figures walking away from her, and a golden strike that flashed and died.

As she came to a fork in the trail her phone buzzed, but it wasn't Corbett returning her calls; it was Inga. The computer had flagged some suspicious email content. Nora pulled up the document and started to read. Then she froze and the flashlight fell out of her hand and thudded to the ground.

The email was short, concise, but it punctured a hole big enough to swallow twenty million dollars.

And it was written by a dead man.

GREGG

On Wednesday morning, as the team ran through data from opening night and fired off orders and adjustments for round two, Nora appeared at my office door. I motioned for her to stay and wrapped up the meeting as soon as I could, sending the caffeinated troops back into battle.

Nora waited for everyone to leave before closing the door. "Inga found a lead in your email server last night."

Immediately, my pulse leapt and I stood, tossing aside reams of tournament data. Nora moved to the other side of my desk.

"Does Strike operate any other place of business within Minneapolis besides your headquarters and gym?"

"No."

"Are you sure? No other informal or unregistered locations?"

"Of course I'm sure." She glanced at her phone and I had to restrain myself from tearing it out of her hand. "What is it? What did you find?"

Her expression and body language were indecipherable.

"Let's take a walk."

The Stone Arch Bridge was a freeway of pedestrian and bike traffic. The entire city seemed to be basking on the sunbaked limestone that curved over the Mississippi, connecting downtown to the Northeast neighborhoods. I wished I had a single ounce of their calm. I'd already assaulted Nora with a dozen questions since we left my office, but she'd fallen silent, apparently subscribing to show-don't-tell investigative techniques. She walked briskly, single-mindedly, and I had to force myself to be patient.

As we passed our building, I glanced at the terrace on the top floor, then the ruins of the mill beneath it. I could still feel the bite of the railing into my back as Logan pressed me to the edge. I'd slept at the office again last night, which was more of a home than the penthouse at this point. I didn't know where home would be after the tournament was over, after the money was recovered or the other shoe dropped. It felt like no matter what happened next, in the end one of us would have to go over that edge.

I pointed out the ruins on the riverbank, the twisted shards of metal which were the only remains of the original giants of the city. "They said it shook buildings a mile away, the blast was so powerful."

"I didn't know flour dust was combustible."

"It's not intuitive, is it?" I glanced over at her. "That what feeds you can also destroy you."

Nora smoothed the strap of her briefcase, refusing to engage as we passed a family taking pictures of St. Anthony Falls and another couple leaning against the brick, lapping ice cream from rapidly melting cones. Her lack of attention seemed familiar, a replay of what I'd seen last night at the stadium.

"Why don't you wear your wedding ring?"

She let the question hover, growing and forming its own life between us. Just as I started to think she wouldn't answer at all, or merely deflect it as unprofessional, she stretched out her left hand and contemplated the bare fingers.

"It's an antiquated custom, signaling ownership. Rings tend to create unproductive assumptions." She paused. "They also hurt when you're kickboxing."

Logan had never worn her ring, either. She used to keep it on a necklace, but I couldn't remember the last time I'd seen her wear it.

"But you are married."

"Yes, to a former cook who sometimes finds me amusing. We live in Eagan. I'm a mother, too, but I don't have any pictures in my wallet to prove it."

Her tone threw me as much as the words. I didn't know what I'd expected by asking about her husband, but it wasn't this controlled fury, simmering underneath a veneer of etiquette. She had a child? Nora Trier seemed about as maternal as Logan. I couldn't imagine this woman changing diapers or playing patty-cake. As I searched for an appropriate response, she continued, and it sounded as though she'd carefully inventoried every word.

"Marriage can feed you — a good marriage. But trying to wring everything from it, expecting one person to fill your every need and anxiety and desire, then yes, I agree; it can easily destroy you. Maybe even before you realize it exploded."

We walked in silence for a minute, an entirely different silence than before.

"I don't want you to think that I sleep

with women outside my marriage."

"Why does it matter what I think?" She didn't glance over or change her pace, but I sensed her anger fading as the focus shifted back to me.

"Everything depends on what you think, doesn't it?"

"Everything depends on what I can substantiate. I can testify, for example, that you have slept with someone outside your marriage, but that's irrelevant to this investigation." There was no emotion anymore, not a hair out of place. She could have been calmly reciting a human resources policy, and I'd never been more attracted to her than I was at that moment.

It's amazing how parts of your life can only be read backward, and what you thought was impulse starts to align behind you in disturbingly obvious patterns. Logan had seemed unattainable in that ring at the MGM. And hadn't Nora — the seeming opposite of everything Logan Russo represented — been exactly the same? Out of my reach. Untouchable.

"Did you think about me at all . . . afterward?"

Nora looked at me for the first time since we'd left the office and suddenly I was back in Atlanta, remembering the whole thing.

I'd been drinking a scotch and working on a bullet-pointed list on a cocktail napkin. The hotel bar had been full of stranded Midwesterners, all of us delayed due to a Valentine's blizzard obliterating the Great Plains. I'd noticed a woman at the far end of the bar and asked the bartender what she was drinking.

"Hendrick's and tonic. No twist." He glanced down the mahogany at her profile. "Don't bother, man. She's all business."

I sipped Glenlivet. "So am I."

She'd been checking email. There was a fundamentally different energy from someone checking and replying to email than someone who was scrolling vacantly through social media. They sat taller and held their jaws tight, eyebrows down, sometimes even whispered drafts of their replies. This woman didn't give off the usual tells, but her feet were tucked under the barstool and she rotated one of her gray heels slowly from side to side, like a typewriter ball working its way across a page. No one else seemed to see her. She could've given the *Mona Lisa* lessons in subtlety, a woman so contained her very expressionlessness became a thing of beauty. When I had one finger of scotch left, I stretched and glanced over, but all I saw was a twenty-dollar bill tossed by an empty glass. Which was good, I told myself, looking over the list I'd made on the napkin. There wasn't room for any more bullet points on this plan.

As I left the bar, I tossed the napkin into the atrium fireplace and waited, watching it burn.

The next morning, I went to the gym. I loathed hotel gyms — they had a universal bouquet of zero-fucks-given in the air. The rooms were always strangely proportioned, full of outdated, bottom-shelf equipment and supplied with a sad stack of towels that managed to be simultaneously itchy and filmy. Meeting a fellow guest in the hotel gym was the easiest sell in the world; I always kept company cards in my phone case, because anyone who worked out in a hotel gym was *dedicated.* And dedication was the cornerstone of Strike.

When I found the fitness center, I stopped two feet inside the door. The woman from the bar ran on the last treadmill at the end of the otherwise empty room. Her calves stretched long and lean, muscles bunching in sharp lines under the kind of skin that would flush with excitement or stress. I tamped down my excitement and took the treadmill two machines away from her, nodding a perfunctory, harmless-stranger smile

— the smile every man has to perfect these days — when she glanced over to assess the intrusion.

I tapped my machine up to a brisk walk on an incline, checking my iWatch heart rate (Noticeably higher than resting. Thanks, Apple) while she flipped a page on a magazine, some kind of professional journal but I couldn't read it without her seeing I was reading it. After a few minutes of silence punctuated only by pages turning, I turned and pointed to the TV in the corner.

"Is there a remote?"

She didn't bother looking up. "I don't know."

Midwestern accent. Not frozen-throated, deep woods Minnesota, but still laced with prairie-flat vowels. She must have been stranded by the storm, too.

"Sorry, you must prefer it off. I just wanted to check the weather. My flight's been delayed for a blizzard."

"I know."

I'd had our next six exchanges lined up in my head, nonchalant, casual, a slow build of conversation that wouldn't look like it was going anywhere. Her reply, though, jerked me out of the setup and fast-forwarded straight to the end. My feet landed hard and clumsy on the treadmill belt as I studied her. She didn't elaborate, didn't slow her pace, but seemed to expect my stare. Flipping a page, she kept running and reading. A trickle of sweat dripped down her temple and slid into the hollow of her throat.

"What else do you know?" A smile tugged at my mouth.

"That Minneapolis is set to reopen around noon, our flight is tentatively scheduled to board at three o'clock Eastern, and you're not wearing the Atticus glasses that you had on in the airport yesterday."

"They're Armani."

"Atticus Finch." She threw me a condescending glance and my veins automatically dilated, pumping a surge of blood to all the places the treadmill hadn't woken up. Jesus Christ, I wanted this woman to talk down to me while straddled on top of me.

"Do you know who that is?" She couldn't resist asking.

"Not an eyewear designer." I played dumb just to watch her mouth pinch, then bumped the treadmill up to a brisk jog. "He's the guy from *Moby Dick,* right?"

She shook her head and turned another page on her magazine. This time I caught the title: *Fraud.*

We chatted for a while, her maybe out of

a default Minnesota politeness, me while I processed that magazine, and neither of us getting close to winded. When she hit five miles, she slowed her pace and closed the magazine. She wouldn't take long to cool down.

"What will you do with our bonus day? See the sights of the Atlanta airport?" I nodded to the magazine. "Learn how to commit fraud?"

She smiled. "I know all the ways."

"Maybe you could teach me, then."

"I assumed you'd rather have sex for a few hours."

It took a superhuman effort not to pull the emergency cord, not to give her the reaction she was expecting. Casually, I punched my pace down to a walk and cocked an eyebrow at her. "I'm an excellent multitasker."

She stepped across to the open treadmill between us. Her face was glistening and flushed red from her run as she pointed her phone at me. "Smile."

I hit the cool-down button as she opened an app. "Checking predator databases?"

"I'm sending your picture to my husband. Should I," she narrated as she typed, "have sex with this man?"

I swallowed a grin and kept walking. She

was either bluffing or texting a girlfriend, but before I could suggest grabbing a smoothie together, a beep from her phone signaled someone's reply.

"He says, 'Nail that silver fox.' "

I burst out laughing. "Tell your friend I'm flattered."

"Silver fox is blushing," she narrated again.

"Am I?" I murmured, hitting the stop button on the treadmill. "That would be a first. As would this."

The truth always sounded like a lie. I was fifty years old and had never been unfaithful. I'd wondered about it, lately, what it meant to cross that line, if it had meant anything to Logan when she had. I'd sat in plenty of hotel bars in the last year, trying not to think about Logan and Aaden together, and considered what would happen if a friendly chat over drinks turned friendlier. A few months ago I'd even danced with a woman, somewhere in California, turning circles to a slow, throbbing song in a dark room, but the more she clung to me, limp and happy, the more I lost all interest. The sad fact was that I didn't know what to do with a docile female. That made me sound like a fucking rapist, but I was married to a prizefighter who used to beat the shit out of me every night, bruising me until I begged for more. I didn't understand desire without pain.

I'd been married to Logan for twenty years and I'd been committed the entire time, even after she lost any interest in bruising me and started spending all her time with a man half her age. Strike was the only thing keeping us together now. It was the child neither of us could abandon.

And now, in another gym on the other side of the country, here was a woman who seemed like the opposite of Logan — tightly wrapped, so perfectly contained her beauty was almost invisible — blazing into a hard-breathing, laser-eyed, rose-cheeked boss. Every word she spoke was stripped, flayed, and measured. She wasted nothing. With any other woman I would assume this text game was all a taunt, some trap designed to make me fall flat on my would-be-cheating face, but I'd bet everything in my wallet that wasn't the case. She was utterly sincere.

"What's your name?" I had to know.

"Nora." She turned her phone off and picked up the magazine, getting ready to leave.

A name meant to be moaned. I repeated it and held out a hand, waiting for her to shake it. When she did, I noticed a faint purple shadow cresting her knuckles. I paused, staring at the mark, before remembering my manners.

"I'm —"

She pulled her hand quickly out of mine.

"Your name" — she placed a single finger over my mouth, and it took every ounce of my willpower not to bite down on it — "is Atticus."

She brushed my lip, examining it, and smiled.

"I'm in room 412. Give me a half an hour and bring your glasses."

Four months later, crossing the Mississippi, I wondered if I'd had the slightest effect on her. I'd relived that morning so many times, but what had I been to her? A placeholder. A pair of glasses and a smile. Maybe I'd never been in bed with this woman. I'd only imagined I was there because of the mundane fact of our bodies unraveling inside each other.

She didn't answer my question, but as we reached the end of the bridge asked one of her own. "Have you talked to Logan?"

"About Atlanta?"

"No." For the first time, she looked unsure. "I saw . . . something . . . last night." Her next question caught me by surprise. "Does Logan know any of my partners at

Parrish?"

"I don't think so. Why? What did you see?"

"An explosion."

We were back in time again, but now with the present superimposed. Nora and I stood in front of Logan's old apartment building, the place she'd refused to give up after we'd bought the penthouse. The neighborhood had changed, gentrified by an influx of artisans, craft brewers, and endless baby boomers downsizing on the north bank, but the brick twelve-plex looked as dirty and neglected as I remembered it.

"What are we doing here?"

"Following an email. Can you let us in?"

I pulled out my keys and found the one Logan had given me twenty years ago, after I'd moved here from Chicago, our young selves bursting with plans for a future people had called delusional, impossible. That future seemed almost quaint now. Inside, the entryway had the musty odor of disuse. I started up the stairs, but Nora stopped me and made me check the mailbox. Dozens of letters fell out when I opened it, all of them identical. I caught one before it spilled to the floor and stared at the envelope. The return address said Magers Construction, the company contracted to build all our new clubs, and the letter was addressed to Strike.

"What the hell?"

GREGG

I unlocked Logan's old apartment door and went straight to the table, dropping the pile of letters on it. Nora reached for the top one.

"Who is Magers Construction?"

"They're a premier architectural, engineering, and construction firm, specializing in historical preservation of existing buildings. They've built every Strike club across North America."

Nora showed no reaction to this information and I got the feeling she already knew the answer. She must have known about the letters, too, since she brought me here. Did she already know what was inside of them?

As if on cue, she set her briefcase down and opened the one she was holding, pulling out a single sheet of paper. It looked like a check stub without the check. The header said "Deposit Confirmation," and the description section contained only a single phrase: "Retainer refund — Dallas." The deposit amount was almost six hundred thousand dollars.

Our Dallas club had been completed two weeks ago; I'd personally flown there for the final walk-through.

After a silence that seemed to last five minutes, Nora set the paper down. "If Magers Construction is working for Strike, you should be paying them. Why are they sending money to you?"

"The retainer." I swallowed, still staring at the ink. "Magers typically requires a letter of credit from their clients, a financial guarantee for costs that tend to arise with their type of construction. Unexpected plumbing or electrical problems, creative ways to design around historical register restrictions, that kind of thing. It's supposed to be ten percent of the total cost of the project, but since Strike is self-funded —" I looked up.

"You don't have access to a line of credit." Her eyes flashed. "You paid a cash deposit."

"Yes, but we expected the majority of the funds back. We've always received the refunds of the unused retainer amounts upon completion of the clubs, since the beginning."

Nora pulled out her computer, checked a

document, and tapped the last four digits of the deposit account that appeared at the bottom of the slip. "This isn't one of Strike's bank accounts."

We looked at each other, a moment's pause, before we both turned and began tearing open the envelopes. Baltimore, $732,000. San Diego, $911,000. Denver, $859,000. Slip after slip of endless zeroes. Money sent to Strike. Money that Strike — or the majority of Strike — never received.

By the time we got to the last slip, there was paper everywhere. Shreds of envelopes littered the table, chairs, and floor and the stack of deposits crowded Nora's laptop. Her fingers flew across the keyboard while I paced the narrow strip of linoleum that made up the kitchen.

"Goddamn Darryl. I asked. I asked him about the retainers when . . . when . . ." I couldn't name an exact date. The tournament had consumed so much of my life in the last months. All the conference calls about vStrike, the logistics, liaising with fighters across the globe, not to mention visiting the new clubs and checking construction progress. The project managers had assured me the remaining retainer balances were being refunded. They'd given me reports, which I'd filed, and we'd all moved on to the next club.

"None of these amounts have been received in any Strike bank account." Nora's keyboard stopped clicking and she angled toward me. "Magers is closed this week, but we tracked down their payables supervisor and asked for a total list of refunds in the last six months. Her reply matches the slips, except for one. This is twenty-seven deposits and there should be twenty-eight. There's one missing."

"How much is it altogether?"

Nora didn't answer. She stood up and began walking through the efficiency, the half kitchen that bled into a living area and ended in a bed shoved under the wall-length windows, searching every inch of it.

"Nora? How much?"

She ignored me and opened cupboards and drawers, looking through the bathroom and utility closet. Finally, she went to the trash can, turning it over on the table and going through it with the tip of a pen, lingering on a few receipts and an old take-out carton. At the bottom of the can, she found another envelope and a balled-up piece of paper. Flattening it, she breathed out a low puff of air. "Bingo."

I grabbed the paper out of her hands, staring at the network of lines and smear of ink.

Philadelphia, $743,000. The edge of the slip had grease stains on it. Someone had looked at this, had perused it while food dripped fat over their evidence of embezzlement. Everything in me went cold.

At my side, Nora quietly took the paper back and laid it on top of the others. "Twenty-eight deposits. A little over nineteen million dollars."

Almost the entire missing prize money. She'd found it, but there was no relief, no exhale of tension like I'd expected. I stared at those stains on the paper, the indisputable evidence that Logan had been here, and struggled to check my emotions. "What did you find that brought us here? You said Inga flagged something in the email server?"

Nora unfolded one of the thrown away receipts from a sandwich shop, darkened with greasy finger splotches, and frowned. She didn't want to tell me.

"Nora." I fought to keep my voice calm. "You knew this was Logan's old apartment when you came to my office this morning. You knew she . . . that it was her, before you even brought me here." It came out sounding like an accusation, then I repeated it to myself, forcing the words into the air, feeling for the truth in them. "It was her, wasn't it?"

Nora typed a few final things on her computer before closing it. "The investigation isn't done yet. We have more work to do before I can confirm that. Do you know where Logan is?"

No. I had no idea where Logan was anymore. I shook my head, fists balling.

"I'll need to speak with her . . . about a few things . . . but my immediate priority is to start tracking the funds. At least we can see where they initially went."

"What do you mean? The money's right here."

"These are only deposit verifications."

"So you find the account and you find the money. Done."

Nora gave me a look she probably saved for her son, patient and unbearably patronizing. "I told you, Gregg, that if this was a case of fraud we might catch the thief, but the money itself could be anywhere in the world, hidden in jurisdictions we can't even touch. This slip," she lifted the top grease-stained paper, "is just the starting line. Cash moves at the speed of data, again and again. We have no idea where this chase will lead."

I backed away from the table, and the possibility that twenty million dollars could be lost. Nora had found this much; she would find the money, too. I couldn't entertain

242

any other scenarios, not now, with the end of the tournament only two days away.

Nora tracked my reaction with an expression I couldn't name. "You've said that Logan had a close relationship with Aaden Warsame."

"She did."

"Do you think Aaden would have done anything questionable for her? If she'd asked him to?"

Without intending to, my eyes found the spot on the living room floor, the circle bleached forever lighter than the dirty rust-colored carpet surrounding it. Eighteen years later I could still see, with absolute clarity, that rat-faced intruder who'd broken into this apartment, and his expression when Logan knocked him to the ground. It was all he'd wanted in life, to feel her wrath. And then he'd tried to end it, before her attention wavered. The knife itself was mostly hidden in his hand, the dark seep of blood through his shirt strangely unaffecting, but his face — I understood that look.

"A man Logan never met before tried to kill himself," I forced myself to move away from the spot, nodding behind me, "right there. At her feet. For her.

"I've had to file restraining orders against fans who wanted to be too close, who deluded themselves that they knew Logan, and tried to become whatever might earn her attention. She gets tweeted at a thousand times a day and they all say the same thing: look at me."

I walked to the area where a normal person would put a couch or a coffee table and glanced at the hooks in the ceiling where the punching bag used to hang, always covered in duct tape because she'd broken it so many times.

"I know how they feel. In or out of the ring, there's a burning in Logan's gaze, an intensity. When you have her attention, you have every shred of it. You feel yourself come alive. No one in my life ever looked at me like that before.

"I used to train with her right here. I'd strap on the pads and step into her sights, waiting for her to knock me down." Slowly, I made the same circuit around an invisible punching bag, hearing the thump of Logan's gloves, driving and incessant.

"When she hit me, I became someone else, someone more than just another suit hawking products and chasing sales. I became someone worth beating."

I stopped circling and looked at Nora. She wanted to know if Aaden Warsame would have done something questionable for

Logan. Like enter a tournament he wasn't qualified for, or train sixty hours a week to prove himself? What wouldn't he have done if she'd asked?

"Aaden had been a fan of Logan's since the day he walked into the after-school program, and he had her attention. I'm sure he would've wanted to keep it."

I tried to breathe, to steady myself and get control of the situation, but my mind was on a loop, bouncing between the grease-stained deposit slip and the rat-faced crazy fan. Logan, sitting at that table eating a sandwich over stolen millions. The pathetic need of that stalker, starving for Logan's touch, for any scrap of her. My stomach began to turn. Sweat broke out on my forehead. I needed a distraction. I needed to become someone else.

I raised my arms, palms open, like I'd strapped the pads on already. Nora tilted her head in surprise. Her chest rose and fell, rippling the silk of her shirt.

"Jab, cross."

I took a step toward her. Nora's eyes flashed with something beyond this case, beyond Atlanta, a simmering need I didn't understand, but that's always the unknowable part: what compels each of us into the ring.

Slowly, miraculously, she fisted her hands and raised them to an on-guard position. I braced my legs, anticipating the blow; I'd never wanted to be bruised more than I wanted Nora's fury at that moment. I wanted her to take everything, to see more with that penetrating gaze than Logan had ever been capable of seeing, to hit me until we both forgot why we'd started.

"Please."

Nora jabbed, a scissor of fist and elbow, striking me in the opposite palm.

"Harder."

She sent a cross into my other hand, slapping flesh against flesh, then pivoted back into a jab. We began to circle each other as her punches beat steadily faster, knocking my arms back. I coached her, taunted her, said anything I could think of to make her drive into me. Then, without warning, she delivered a front kick to my thigh that sent me into the wall.

"Again." I pushed away, shaking out the bright blooming numbness in my hands, desperate to feel it everywhere.

But she didn't. She lowered her arms, stepping back. "I can't. I need to . . ." she trailed off, until what she needed to do contracted in her blazing eyes.

Without considering the consequences, I

stepped forward and wound my hand through her hair, the damp strands coming loose from the knot, and kissed her.

NORA

When Gregg raised his arms and told her to hit him, something inside Nora flared.

All morning, she'd been ignoring her anger, keeping herself and her team working at lightning speed to uncover everything they could find about Magers Construction — the company that had been tricked into diverting almost twenty million dollars of Strike's money — but she couldn't completely bury the emotions from last night. Her surreal vStrike fight had already brought up more issues than she could handle, but it paled in comparison to what she'd seen afterward.

Mike kept insisting, even as she was getting ready this morning, that it might not have been Corbett in the alley.

"It was dark. You'd had a few drinks, and you were — apparently — upset." Her husband's amusement at her emotional turmoil did nothing to calm her down, and

Corbett's phone was going straight to voice mail now, making it impossible to find out what had actually happened.

She left the house without a word and accelerated too fast out of the neighborhood, almost not braking in time when Henry and his friend biked over to wave goodbye. They both swerved to the sidewalk, narrowly missing her bumper as she screeched to a halt.

Adrenaline flooded her chest, but she forced a smile and a wave, trying to act normal, as though she hadn't almost run over her own child. The boys hesitantly turned around and returned to wherever they'd been playing, Henry looking back over his shoulder like he was scared she would try to follow them.

She needed Strike. All morning, as her team dove into the company's headquarters records, her muscles had twitched from lack of use. They'd demanded to be on the other side of the wall, in the gym, driving her fists and feet into the bag. So strange, for someone who'd spent her life running, to feel this craving for the fight.

Which was why, when Gregg raised his hands in the Northeast neighborhood apartment and said "please" in that quiet, desperate voice, her pulse leapt, her hands clenched in anticipation, and she'd let loose every bit of confusion and rage from the past twenty-four hours.

He took it, each punch, each shot of violence, and urged her for more. Her knuckles burned as his palms turned raw and red. His eyes glowed as she pushed him back, advancing.

"Faster, Nora. You can do better than that. Hit me harder. Hit me like you mean it. Hit me —"

She drew back, shifted her weight, and kicked him into the wall. His back thudded against the plaster, sending a surge of triumph through her entire body. It was almost like being Logan.

The thought stopped her cold. "I can't. I need to . . ."

She was standing in Logan's old apartment, inhabiting the space of the woman she'd been mesmerized by for months. Before she could process anything beyond that, Logan's husband stepped in and kissed her.

He drew her up, hard and tight, inviting her to bruise him in every way possible, and for one mindless moment she did. She let herself go, slipping further into the fantasy. She breathed him in with Logan's nose, bit him with Logan's teeth, but when he said her name — "Nora" — the illusion ended. She broke away.

"No. It's not me."

Breathing heavily, Gregg ran a hand over his mouth and stepped back, leaning against the wall.

Nora went to the table and put her laptop away. She picked up the stack of deposit slips, straightening them until the edges cut into her hands.

"Do you have any evidence that Logan and Aaden had an inappropriate relationship? Or that she might have had undue influence over him?"

"Other than his suicide note?" Gregg's voice was uneven.

Nora turned. Halfway between them was the strange circle in the carpet, bleached and blotchy, the place where a crazed fan had intruded on their lives. How many people had thrown themselves at Logan's feet over the years, all of them delusional, yearning for some imagined connection? How close was Nora coming to that circle?

Swallowing, she said she'd be in touch with her progress, and left Gregg alone in the musty dark.

Nora walked back downtown as fast as she could, crossing the bustling Stone Arch

Bridge with the case-clinching evidence of a nineteen-million-dollar fraud tucked neatly in her briefcase. She should have been skipping, fist-pumping, and texting the entire team with the good news. Instead, she wanted to vomit.

She'd just hit a client and then kissed him while imagining herself as another client. Her personal and professional lives, which she'd kept rigidly separate since the day Sam White put a bullet in his head, were careening into each other with breathless velocity. She never should have taken this investigation. Her independence, her entire career, felt on the verge of exploding.

When she reached the south bank where the flour mill graves rusted in the shadow of the bridge, she reached into her briefcase and pulled out the email Inga flagged last night, the key document that unearthed the crime. She had to focus. If she could forget everything that just happened — ignore it, bury it — maybe she could still make it through this case. There were only two days left in the tournament. Win or lose, by the end of the week it would be over.

Nora read the email again, concentrating her entire being on its content.

From: Accounts Payable, Magers
    Construction
To: Logan Russo
Subject: RE: RE: RE: New Instructions

Dear Ms. Russo,
Great!! We'll make this change right
away!

Regards,
Maggie Smythe
AP Supervisor
Magers Construction
"Make it a great day!"

From: Logan
Russo To: Accounts Payable, Magers
    Construction
Subject: RE: RE: New Instructions

Hi Maggie,
Yes, thank you for confirming. The new
bank info is correct for reimbursements
only. All contracts and administrative
communication should continue to be
routed to the 3rd Avenue address and
your regular contacts.

Logan Russo
Strike

From: Accounts Payable, Magers
    Construction
To: Logan Russo
Subject: RE: New Instructions

Dear Ms. Russo,
We received the below email requesting
a change in your remit to information.
Please confirm these instructions so we
can make the change to your customer
profile.

Regards,
Maggie Smythe
AP Supervisor
Magers Construction
"Make it a great day!"

From: Aaden Maxamed Warsame
To: Accounts Payable, Magers
    Construction
Cc: Logan Russo
Subject: New Instructions

To Whom It May Concern,
Please note the new electronic transfer
instructions for all future payments and
refunds to be processed to Strike.

Strike Inc.
315 University Avenue SE
Box 0010
Minneapolis, MN 55414
Bank Account 058088438
Routing Number 091900533

These instructions can be confirmed with Logan Russo, General Partner of Strike Inc., copied here.

Best Regards,
Aaden Warsame
Strike

Less than a hundred words total.

A hundred words to net almost twenty million dollars.

Logan's confirming reply was what had triggered Inga last night, but it wasn't signs of stress or pressure that the computer had detected in the content of Logan's email. It was the opposite. After processing hundreds of Logan's blog posts and direct messages to trainers, Inga had learned the kickboxer's curse-laden, abrupt, declarative sense of normal. Logan's typical communication was exactly what Inga would flag as high-risk material in any other investigation, but not here. In this upside-down world, Inga had found the one email that sounded as cool and professional as Nora herself, and flagged it as a glaring anomaly.

Thank you for confirming. The new address is correct.

Nora stared at the signatures. Logan Russo. Aaden Warsame.

At the beginning of the week, if Nora had been told Logan embezzled money with someone's help, she would have bet on Darryl Nolan. Darryl was the financial expert, the one with the required knowledge to commit fraud, who understood all the ways cash could be diverted, funneled, and hidden. But they'd checked the IP addresses of the emails. Both messages were sent from Strike headquarters while Darryl had been sunning himself on a beach in Florida. The controller, it seemed, was off the suspect list.

But Aaden? Aaden Warsame hadn't even seemed like a possibility. How had a young fighter, with no business background outside of his mother's grocery store, written this email?

It was the details, the tiny details that bothered her most.

Box 0010.

It was an apartment building. The appropriate address would be Apt. 10, Unit 10, or even just #10. "Box 0010" skirted the razor-thin line between accurate and misleading. It was close enough to the truth that the postal carrier would know where to deliver the letters, yet presented as infinitely more professional than what the tarnished yellow boxes in the building's entryway deserved. It carried the tone of a P.O. Box or even a bank lockbox.

He'd also known not to specify the address was for refunds only, which could have raised red flags. He'd left that clarification for Logan to deliver, a substantiated and trusted business owner whose instructions would be taken by a vendor without question.

The whole email was too smooth, and at the same time too blatant. This was a giant middle finger of a scheme, a fraud that begged to be found. No one in their right mind would think they could get away with this.

Nora's team hadn't been disturbed by any of these points this morning. They were too busy celebrating.

"Oh my gosh, you were completely right about the Aaden connection." The lead analyst went on to apologize profusely for questioning Nora's judgment the day before.

"I'm not sure," Nora hedged, but no one

was listening to her, not when they had a lead.

"The money in his checking account makes sense now." The analyst jotted each one on the whiteboard, making notes as she went.

$5,000. January. Sweetener. Introducing scheme.

$9,500. February. 50% down payment for agreement to help commit fraud.

$9,500. March. Final payment for services rendered.

"The computers never found any matching withdrawals from Strike's books. They must have come from a personal account." The analyst wrote on the side of the board,

LR Account?

"Speculation. There could be a dozen alternate explanations for that money." Nora argued, even though the analyst's logic was compelling. The timeline matched. The last deposit had credited to his account just days before he killed himself. And if Aaden had been an honest person, a hard worker and dedicated fighter, the guilt from something like this might have put him over the edge. It wouldn't be the first time she'd seen it happen.

When Nora reached downtown, she walked into the closest building and made her way through the maze of hallways and bridges connecting the skyscrapers. The skyway lunch counters weren't even open yet, their day still waiting to begin.

Nora tucked the email away, suspicious of the evidence staring right at her. If Logan Russo had organized this fraud, why had she taken Nora to Aaden's cubicle yesterday? Why would she ask Nora to look through the dead fighter's things? Maybe that had all been a distraction and Nora was just too infatuated with Logan, too busy kissing her husband, to see it.

Her phone buzzed and Nora pulled it blindly out of her briefcase, still wrapped up in the two simple emails that had stolen almost the entire tournament prize, the lure of a few well-placed words.

"Hello?"

"Nora!"

She checked the caller ID quickly to confirm the voice on the other end of the line. There was crying in the background, a child's belligerent wail, but more than that — the hitching lungs and wheezing of someone truly panicked.

"What is it, Katie? What happened?"

"It's Corbett," his wife sobbed into the phone. "Oh god, I think he's dead."

NORA

Nora raced to Hennepin County Medical Center, a hospital located only a few blocks from Strike Down and the alley where she thought she'd seen Corbett last night.

Katie fell into her arms as soon as she arrived in the flag-festooned intensive care waiting room.

"Was he mugged? Or hit by a car?" Nora had gotten only garbled information from her on the phone and the two things she'd caught didn't make any sense together.

"They don't know if he's going to make it." Katie sobbed into her shoulder. "He's in surgery now and no one will tell me what's going on."

Nora understood how she felt. Corbett's kids huddled in the corner, sitting listlessly near a duffel bag full of untouched games and electronics. They watched their mother cry while silent tears streamed down their own faces.

The next few hours passed in a blur. Mike showed up and went straight to Katie, offering the comfort Nora didn't know how to dispense. The Parrish office called at regular intervals, asking for updates she didn't have. She couldn't see Corbett. The intensive care unit only allowed family inside and even those visits were doled out in tiny increments by nurses who understood what the doctors wouldn't say. The facts they did divulge — organs stitched back together, blood pumped in, cranium fractured, brain swelling — kept reducing into a bald and unmistakable summary: Corbett could die. He might die before she ever got to grill him about last night. He might die without knowing how furious she was with him. He might die and never unwind at Ike's, arguing over pints and making her dissolve into laughter again. Her best friend might die.

Nora needed information. While everyone else sat around hugging each other, Nora found out what she could. According to his intake record, Corbett had been brought in just before midnight last night, a John Doe without any identification, and had barely survived the initial emergency surgeries, flatlining once before they'd stabilized him. The fact that he'd made it this far, everyone said, was supposed to be encouraging, but a

261

strangling fear convulsed around Nora's throat every time someone exited the ICU.

When the police arrived, Nora hovered in the background as they pieced together the timeline from a distraught Katie.

Corbett had left the tournament somewhere between 10:30 and 11:00 p.m. This, Nora had already known. Had, in fact, watched him walk away from the stadium in Logan Russo's company.

"He had some emergency," Katie tearfully confirmed. "He said to grab an Uber and not to wait up. So I didn't. Mike and I shared a ride and I went straight to bed. But when I woke up this morning and he still wasn't home, I started to worry. He didn't answer his phone and he wasn't at Parrish. Finally, I started calling local hospitals. I thought I was overreacting, but then . . ." She broke down, and Mike stepped in to put an arm around her.

The detectives filled in the blanks. At 11:07 p.m. on Tuesday night, they reported, Minneapolis emergency response received several calls reporting a hit-and-run accident in the Mill District. A few witnesses saw a man running around the corner of a building and directly into the path of an oncoming car. One witness claimed the car swerved onto the sidewalk. Another said the man stumbled into the street first. The exact place of impact couldn't be determined because there were no tire marks on the street.

"The car didn't brake?" Katie choked on the question, horror filling her already overflowing eyes.

Witnesses and forensics had agreed. Someone driving a dark sedan crashed into Corbett, threw his body over the top of the hood, and sped around a corner without slowing down. Based on the extent of his injuries, they estimated the vehicle must have been going around thirty-five to forty miles per hour, over the speed limit for downtown but not fast enough to draw attention before or after the impact.

"The driver hasn't been identified." One of the detectives answered the unspoken question. He assured them that all precincts were on the lookout for a car matching the eyewitnesses' descriptions, and they were reviewing surveillance footage to try to ID the vehicle, but were backed up with all the holiday events going on around town. Nora read between the lines: no one was pulling overtime for this.

"What happened to his wallet and phone?" she asked.

"We found them." The detective produced

a clear plastic bag with the items inside and handed it to Katie. "We tracked his phone to a garbage can less than a block away from the scene. Wallet, too, empty of cash. Not sure why they took the phone and just dumped it, unless they were looking for better models."

"You think he was robbed and then ran into the street?"

"It's the most plausible scenario based on what we know. Someone holds him up, he gives them what they want, then runs from the gun and straight into a windshield."

Katie made a strangled noise and Mike glared at the cops, but Nora appreciated their efficiency. She kept her questions equally succinct.

"No leads at all on the vehicle?"

"Nothing. Off the record, it's likely a drunk or distracted driver who's scared shitless right now. We usually bag these ones off a license plate or when they take the car in to get it fixed."

Meaning they were already closing the case file. A petty robbery leading to a hit-and-run accident. Tragic but unintentional. Nora wished she felt the same certainty, but some of the facts weren't lying obediently in line with the others. The car hadn't slowed down. It may even have swerved onto the sidewalk, according to at least one eyewitness. Then there was the issue of what she had seen from the skyway that night, two dark figures she thought she knew. Maybe one of them actually had been Corbett. Maybe he wasn't running from a mugger at all.

She glanced at Mike, but he was already leading Katie back to the chairs by her kids. Nora hesitated, debating. She couldn't be at all sure of what she'd seen. The only person she trusted to confirm or deny was lying unconscious in a hospital bed. As the detectives turned to leave, the TV mounted in the corner of the ICU waiting room aired a commercial for Strike Down and Logan's face filled the screen, her unflinching gaze daring Nora to speak.

"Wait," she stopped the detectives. "I need to make a statement."

Two hours later, Nora sat in the basement of the hospital next to the other Parrish partners, Jim and Rajesh, as blood was siphoned out of them, wondering if she'd done the right thing.

The detectives had been skeptical, to say the least, when Nora asked to speak with them privately, but they escorted her to an empty office and listened with growing credulity as she provided carefully selected facts. She told them about spotting Corbett and Logan Russo from the skyway, and following their progress across the plaza. She admitted losing track of them in the crowd, but then glimpsing what she believed was her partner's silhouette in the alley, arguing with someone, then the sudden movement and glint of gold, followed by the disappearance of the taller person.

"And you think he was in this alley with Logan Russo?"

Nora swallowed. The line between reality and fantasy had become uncomfortably distorted in the apartment with Gregg. What if her instincts were wrong? What would Logan and Corbett even be doing in an alley together? All her suspicions would sound ludicrous spoken aloud.

"Logan Russo was wearing a black and gold outfit last night, and this person's height and build seemed to match Ms. Russo." Her unwillingness to speak in absolutes or provide a positive ID clearly irritated the detectives. One of them pushed his chair away from the desk and left the room. The other, a jeans-clad man of Asian descent with a hard jaw and tired eyes, crossed his arms and stared at her.

"Do you know Logan Russo?" he asked,

and the familiarity in his tone piqued Nora's memory. She glanced at the card he'd given her. It was the same detective whose name had appeared on Aaden Warsame's case file.

"Not well," Nora replied, sitting up straighter.

"But you know her height and build."

Nora remained quiet.

"What's your connection to Strike?" Detective Li tried again.

"I could ask you the same thing."

They'd circled each other for a while. Unless she was subpoenaed, Parrish's work for Strike remained a confidential matter, and while Aaden's email indisputably linked him to the fraud, it wasn't the case in question. She couldn't produce a credible link between the missing twenty million dollars and Corbett's accident, so when Detective Li pressed her she gave scant information. Her firm had been engaged by Strike. No, Corbett was not assigned to the matter. No, she couldn't provide further details.

By the time she returned to the ICU waiting room, the other partners and their wives had arrived, and she, Jim, and Rajesh had gone together to donate blood.

Nora sat in the basement room, staring at the dark coil of tubes sucking from their arms while the three of them tersely divided

Corbett's assignments.

"At least it's a holiday weekend," Rajesh commented at one point. "Less deliverables."

Nora stared at his mouth as they formed the words, then to the bag of blood steadily filling beneath him. Mike and the wives all acted like this was strictly a hand-holding, back-patting occasion. The partners were moving ahead as though it was an unfortunate, although not unplanned-for, business predicament. Everyone seemed to have been given a guide in pointless etiquette except Nora, but they didn't know what she did. They hadn't seen Corbett with Logan. If anyone was going to find out the truth, it had to be her.

Before she could figure out how to do that, she got a call from her team with an update on their progress.

The account information Aaden had given to Magers in the email wasn't a normal bank account. It was an online platform, an account designed specifically to transfer money internationally. In the last few years, these kinds of web companies had popped up with increasing popularity, offering customers lower fees and less red tape to send money abroad. With a few pieces of identifying information and no oversight at all, anyone could get an account and routing number with all the appearance of a legitimate business. Even though it was exactly what she'd expected, Nora felt her stomach drop.

"Have you confirmed the account details?"

"We sent a request, but haven't received an answer yet, and with the holiday tomorrow . . ." Her analyst trailed off. Neither of them said it aloud. The day after the Fourth of July was Friday, their deadline. They couldn't wait around for a confirmation on an account they both knew was going to be empty. The money was gone.

"Where's Logan?"

Logan was the unknown variable, the last still-conscious person who might be able to link all of this together. And this time, when Nora talked to her, she wouldn't be distracted by red carpets or empty cubicles.

"She hasn't been in the office. No one's seen her since yesterday."

Nora told the analyst to wrap up for the day as the nurse pulled the needle out, and then stared at her phone as the screen went dark. The phone — Corbett had been checking his phone outside the stadium. And Katie had said he'd received a call from someone before he'd left the tournament.

Maybe she could piece together more of the night from his phone records.

When Nora got back to the ICU waiting room, she went straight to Katie and asked to see Corbett's phone. Katie motioned to the duffel bag where the kids' toys and games still sat untouched. Nora dug around until she found the evidence bag from the detectives, and then plugged the phone into her own charger, waiting for it to come to life and hoping Katie knew her husband's password.

Corbett's wallet was still in the bag, too. Nora hesitated and then glanced around the waiting room, making sure no one was watching.

Keeping the wallet inside the cover of the duffel bag, she flipped it open and looked through its contents. Credit cards, insurance information, an old lottery ticket, a few pictures. It felt wrong, sifting through his most private things, and she wasn't even sure what she was looking for.

"Nora." Someone called her from across the room and she startled, closing the wallet and stuffing it away.

"Just a second." Guilt flooded her as she pushed the duffel bag off her lap, feeling like the worst friend in the world. Then something caught her eye.

The tag affixed to the inside of the bag was barely visible, but she could make out a few faded letters someone had printed over the care instructions. "WAR"

She reached into the bag and stretched out the tag until the entire word came into view.

WARSAME

Notice from Strike Communications Team

July 3, 2019

A story aired tonight on the Twin Cities NBC affiliate network about a serious accident outside U.S. Bank Stadium. On the evening of July 2nd, a man attending the opening night of Strike Down was struck by a car in a seeming hit-and-run. Emergency services immediately brought him to Hennepin County Medical Center, where he remains in critical condition. Any information about the accident, which occurred around 11:00 p.m. on July 2nd in the area of 4th Avenue and 3rd Street, should be reported to the Minneapolis police. We are deeply saddened by the event and ask our community of fighters and fans to help identify anyone involved. Strike has engaged extra security and police to help direct crowds tonight and for the rest of the tournament.

Now back to the MAIN EVENT!!

GREGG

"What the hell was it doing in a subscriber email?" I demanded.

C.J., the Marketing Director who was long past done with this conversation, folded her arms as the elevator door opened to the stadium press box. Sara waited on the other side holding a laptop and a breakfast shake. Feigning deafness to the argument in progress, she handed me the cup and fell into step behind us.

"It's our largest, most engaged community —"

"Who live ninety-two percent outside Minneapolis." I gestured to the world at large, as if anyone out there was capable of helping me in here.

We were among the last to arrive at the meeting. This morning's tournament update was being held on-site for the Fourth of July exhibition, which was already underway. The rest of the management team stood at the panoramic edge of the press box, talking and pointing at things beyond our view.

"It's the quickest way to reach the most people." C.J. hammered her point home. "We have an eighty-eight percent open rate on the subscriber campaigns and the detective said urgency was critical, that eyewitnesses might forget what they saw if —"

"I doubt *anyone* is going to forget, now, that we had a violent incident at our inaugural Strike Down."

"An accident. Don't say incident; it's evasive and makes people want more information." She paused at the edge of the room, away from the chatter at the windows. "And it didn't happen at Strike Down. It happened outside the stadium, which the email — you might note — makes perfectly clear. Relax, Gregg, and let me handle it. We're out in front of it now. People aren't getting hearsay through back channels; they're getting the news direct from us and we appear more committed than ever to protecting our community. The message is that we fight for each other at Strike. We'll fight for them, too."

Two more managers filed past us toward the people lining the window. I shook my head and muscled down the warnings still firing in my gut. "God, we could've sold tickets just to watch you work."

She tipped her head and gave a graceful magician's flourish. "You're the only one who can afford the seats."

We joined the rest of the team where the exhibition sprawled into view and the roiling in my intestines momentarily froze. I'd just come through the stadium floor but it looked completely different from up here. Thousands of heads became a sea of pixels, moving and shifting through the rings of vendor booths and demonstration areas. Giant lines snaked out of the concourses by the virtual reality booths, waiting to fight. According to the contractors, vStrike had been operating nonstop since opening night, with never less than a thirty-minute wait. It was our highest-trending hashtag for the last twenty-four hours, surpassing even Logan, and the buzz was only growing, filling the back of my head with a whisper of promise.

On the field, a tightly coiled queue of people waited to meet their favorite athletes, who shook hands and posed for selfies against red carpet backdrops. Swarms of teenagers surrounded the three rings, where Strike Next athletes, paired with trainers, were teaching self-defense basics. The kid in the middle ring doubled over, jerking the trainer over her back and throwing him onto the floor. The onlookers jumped and cheered.

Still, there were bare areas — great patches of grass, undisturbed by the pixels, void and empty. Exhibition day, the penultimate day of the tournament, should have been pure spectacle, a siege of fans and enthusiasts. There shouldn't have been room to breathe.

"It's not even noon yet." C.J. rebuked the thought before I could voice it.

"It's the Fourth of July. Blue sky, seventy-four degrees. No one's working and we've thrown open the doors of the premier venue to the premier event of the summer. We should've seen a surge by now."

"They're sleeping in. Fireworks aren't until ten. Get your mind off the notice."

The notice was only part of the problem, the tiny fraction of it I could vocalize. I stared at the lower sections of mostly empty seats, where sporadic groups of people lounged, taking a break or having a snack. Above them, the suites lay dark and dormant, including the one Parrish Forensics had bought for opening night. My attention had risen with helium force throughout that night, subconsciously searching for Nora's husband, my perverse, piss-marking need to see what he looked like, how he acted. I hadn't noticed Corbett MacDermott at all. I hadn't realized how much one man's broken body was going to matter.

It had been twenty-three hours since I'd last seen Nora. Twenty-three hours since I'd kissed her and twenty-three hours since she'd discovered the path to the missing millions. And now, nearly a full day later, nothing. No money. No Nora. Her analysts assured me they were working through the holiday and would update me "as soon as we have verifiable information to impart," but Nora herself hadn't been back to Strike since she'd left me standing in Logan's old apartment — aroused, empty-handed, and alone. She'd been at the hospital, at the bedside of her near-dead partner. The shadows were creeping closer, covering the tournament itself. We couldn't afford bad publicity or questions, not when we'd already stretched ourselves to the breaking point. Strike Down had to be perfect. It had to —

"Let's get this over with. I've got fifteen million signatures waiting to cramp the shit out of my hand."

Everyone at the window turned as Logan walked into the room. She wore gym clothes, an artfully cross-ripped tank top with shimmering leggings and high-tops that she stacked on top of the table, leaning back and gazing expectantly at us over the dark slash of her mouth. I took it in — the lipstick, the celebrity-gone-grocery-shopping outfit, the oiled biceps ready to angle into a thousand Instagram stories — as I moved to the opposite end of the room and gestured for everyone else to sit.

"Sara?"

Nodding mutely, Sara booted up the projector, but the Events Coordinator held up her hands and seemed to be taking a quick attendance. "Wait. Who's at the office?"

"The trainers are running the show at the gym today for all the sample intro classes."

"No, I mean with the accounting people and their creepy computer. Are they all with Darryl?"

Everyone looked at me and I cleared my throat. "The Parrish team found something yesterday that could lead to the bulk of the money."

The room erupted in exclamations and questions. They all wanted to know details, whether it was oversight or deliberate, if someone had purposely sabotaged our company, and I found myself channeling Nora's calm and caution.

"There's still work to do and they can't

divulge much until the investigation is complete. It's a good sign, I agree, and I'll update everyone as soon as I know more," I said, looking at Logan, where a small smile lay like a gauntlet on her face.

After the room settled down again, we reviewed yesterday's data. Attendance. Sales by category, time, and location. Social assets and feedback. Logan's face smoothed over until any trace of emotion had submerged under a gleaming, immaculate mask. Although her feet remained propped on the table, she watched the screen as attentively as a summer intern, occasionally interrupting to clarify a point and once to ask the exact follow-up question I was going to address.

She'd displayed a caricature of herself these last two days, brighter and filed down at the edges, as if doing a softball impression of the persona we'd created together. I wasn't an idiot. The woman who'd threatened to kill me on our balcony, who'd walked over broken glass rather than spend another minute in my company, was here in this room. She was waiting to make her move, and I couldn't risk a single blink.

"vStrike is a runaway hit." Logan interrupted the presentation again. "It looks like we've got Chris Pine trapped in those boxes."

C.J. grinned. "I'd want a different kind of virtual encounter with Chris Pine."

"New division!" Logan banged on the table and everyone laughed. She leaned over her legs, stretching out her tendons before rising to survey the stadium floor.

The Events Director covered the rest of the updates and then glanced in my direction before moving on to her last point.

"There were no incidents around the stadium last night and we've got increased security again today, including three dedicated squads to direct traffic." The mood in the room changed, and there was a moment of silence before Logan spoke. She didn't turn, but asked the question while facing the exhibition with her hands on her hips and legs braced wide.

"What about the man?"

"The last we heard he hadn't woken up yet," C.J. replied.

"And the investigation?"

"They still haven't found the driver, as far as we know."

"There was no footage, no security cameras?" Logan fired each question without pause, still facing away from the room, showing us only the perfect arc of her trapezius.

"I — I don't know, Logan." For the first time all morning, the Events Director faltered, checking her phone as if a notification holding all the answers might have popped up. She glanced around the table, eyes falling on C.J., who cut in.

"We aren't given that level of information from the police, but it's not like it happened in a Warehouse District back alley. This is the Mill District. There are restaurants and hotels everywhere."

"Did you see anything that night, Logan?" I don't know why I asked, other than the odd direction of her questions, how she was searching for information that should have only been of trivial concern. It was my first comment since discussing the missing twenty million dollars, and it made the room fall quiet. Even the music and loudspeakers from the exhibition below faded into distant, meaningless noise. Everyone at the table looked up from their screens and notes, caught between my face and Logan's back, trying to process what exactly I was asking my wife.

The moment drew out and my pulse began pounding in my ears, the blood rush of anticipation for a reply I didn't know if I

281

wanted. I made myself breathe, made my face impassive.

Finally, Logan turned, and we might have been the only two people in the room. She gazed at me and the dark glint of her lips tipped neither up nor down.

"If I had, I would've called the police, like the notice instructed."

"We certainly appreciate that, ma'am."

The entire room turned to see two men standing in the doorway. The first flashed a badge, and I recognized the other. From the sudden silence across the table, I knew Logan did, too.

It was the same detective who'd investigated Aaden's death.

Nora

Nora rarely visited Cedar-Riverside. What she remembered from her undergraduate days was a transitional neighborhood of thrift shops and storefront restaurants crowded into the shadow of the University's west bank campus, but that was twenty years ago and long before the streets were rebranded as Little Mogadishu. Immigrants had dominated this part of Minneapolis since the Scandinavians in the late 1800s, and it was currently home to the largest Somali population in North America.

On the morning of the country's birthday, the sidewalks of Little Mogadishu were bustling. The summer sun magnified the bright colors of women's hijabs, kids chased each other around with U.S. flags, and men stood chatting and laughing outside coffee shops. Feeling absolutely none of their relaxation, Nora took a deep breath, straightened her blazer, and walked into

Halal Grocery.

The store was housed in an old brick building. A woman at the cash register, wearing a black hijab, nodded at her while she helped a customer bag their purchases. To occupy herself, Nora counted inventory and found that the store carried everything from cuts of meat to souvenir Minnesota postcards.

"Do you need help finding anything?"

Nora startled; she hadn't heard the woman approach, but saw they were now alone in the store.

"Bilan Warsame?"

"Yes?" The woman did a quick scan of Nora from head to toe, probably guessing — accurately — that she was some kind of auditor.

Nora introduced herself and told Bilan she was conducting an investigation, using the fewest and vaguest words possible.

"What are you investigating?"

"I need to ask you a few questions." Nora pulled out her phone and held it up, showing Bilan the stock photo of Corbett from the Parrish website. "Do you know this man?"

Bilan shook her head as she moved back to the counter. "Are you the police?"

"No, it's a private matter. I'm trying to

understand —"

More customers came in, filling the store with noise, and Nora backed off to let Bilan assist them. She had no idea if she was ready for the answer to her next question.

Last night, when she'd seen the name "Warsame" written on the inside of the MacDermotts' duffel bag in the hospital waiting room, she'd gone immediately to Katie.

"That?" Corbett's wife shook her head at the bag like it was a fly buzzing near her face. "I don't know. It was in the closet one day. I gave it to the kids to put their car trip things in, because" — she started to well up again — "we were supposed to be driving to the North Shore this weekend."

Mike gave Nora a look that told her she wasn't helping, but she wasn't interested in Katie's emotional well-being at the moment. She moved to the kids and asked a few of the oldest ones. None of them knew where the duffel bag had come from. It wasn't one of theirs.

Warsame, she'd briefly hoped, might be a more common word than she thought. When she Googled it, though, the only hit was the one she already knew — Warsame was a Somali surname, meaning "good news."

Good news was in short supply this morning. No one had been able to corner Logan at the tournament last night; the online account where Magers Construction transferred the refunds hadn't responded; and Corbett remained unconscious. He couldn't tell her anything about Logan, the alley, or that duffel bag. The number of questions she had for him kept multiplying, but as she sped into the city, she realized there might be another way to get the answers she needed.

The Parrish Forensics office was closed for the holiday and although she'd been there alone hundreds of times, working through the night on countless investigations, in the past she'd always been the one chasing the thieves. Now, walking through the dark corridors toward her best friend's office, she felt dangerously close to becoming one.

Inside Corbett's office, the only light was a blinking voice mail button. Nora took a deep breath, turned her phone flashlight on, and closed the door. His computer was secured and she couldn't begin to guess his password, but it didn't matter. Corbett — the inventor of Inga — knew better than to keep anything incriminating in electronic form.

Nora lifted a framed family photo off the wall and flipped it over, shaking the key to his filing cabinets out of a hidden pocket. Her hands shook as she unlocked and opened every drawer, scanning each file and folder. She skimmed through billions of dollars in cases, confidential information she had no right to look at, her pulse racing with every noise and creak in the building. None of the files mentioned Logan Russo or Strike or even Aaden Warsame.

She was on the verge of giving up when she found it. In the very back of his lower desk drawer, behind a pile of kids' drawings and stuffed in a take-out bag, Nora pulled out several stacks of bank-wrapped bills. The top seal had been ripped, as if some cash had been taken from that stack, but the rest remained intact. Nora counted quickly, totaling the stash up to well over twenty-five thousand dollars. What the hell?

She sat back on the floor, staring at the bills on top of the greasy take-out bag, her mind reeling. Nothing was adding up. For her entire career, she'd relied on her ability to build a trail of solid evidence to uncover the crime, but the more information she found in this case, the less she knew. Had she even known Corbett at all? Quickly, she put everything away and left his office as fast as she could, calling her lead analyst to see if Logan had turned up yet.

"She's not here at Strike headquarters and she's not answering her phone. The exhibition at the stadium should begin soon and she's due for an appearance there."

"I'll find her." She had to. But in the meantime, she went to the only other place where she might find answers, the place she knew she'd have to visit as soon as she read the email from Aaden Warsame: Little Mogadishu. His home address had been listed in the employee files, and both the second-floor residence and store were registered in his mother's name.

It took another twenty minutes before Halal Grocery emptied of customers again, but this time Bilan seemed in no rush to help her. Nora picked up an item at random and brought it to the counter.

"You're sure you haven't seen that man before? Maybe your son knew him?"

Bilan stepped back from the cash register as though it had burst into flames. Her eyes flashed. "What do you know of my son?"

"Very little." Moving carefully, Nora flipped to another picture on her phone and held it up.

"Do you recognize this bag?"

The older woman pressed her lips together, then looked back at Nora with resignation. "So you know Logan Russo."

After flipping the closed sign and locking the front door, Bilan led Nora up the back stairs to her apartment. They walked through a cluster of sunny well-kept rooms until they reached a closed door at the end of a hallway. Bilan's hand faltered on the knob, an unbearable pause before she squared her shoulders and opened it, moving inside.

Nora hesitated in the doorway, reluctant to cross the threshold. Where the rest of the home was decorated in tasteful African prints and colors, everything in this bedroom screamed American. A punching bag hung in one corner and ripped magazine photos were taped on the walls. Nora saw Muhammad Ali, Joe Louis, and even a few pictures of Bruce Lee, but the person whose image dominated the room was Logan Russo.

"I immigrated here when Aaden was just a baby. His father was a fighter. He died in the war, and I vowed afterward that I would raise my son in a place where he wouldn't have to fight." Bilan sat on the neatly made bed and ran a hand over the bedspread.

"We had family in Minnesota already, and

they told us of the *martisoor* here. Hospitality. Warm people in a harsh land."

Slowly, she opened the nightstand and
pulled out a long winding cloth that Nora
recognized as hand wraps, the first hand
wraps Strike always gave to new members.

"He was thirteen when he first went to
the gym. I didn't know who she was. I was
just thinking, okay, he'll get some energy
out. He always had so much energy. And I
hoped it would keep him out of trouble."

She pressed her lips together, fighting a
well of emotion as she laid the hand wraps
gently on the pillow. Then she took a folded
piece of paper out of the nightstand and
stared at it. From where she stood in the
doorway, Nora couldn't see what it was.

"He became a fighter, just like his father.
And now he's dead, just like his father, but
I can't blame a war this time."

Bilan stood and looked around the room,
the slip of paper still in her hand.

"Logan Russo came here, a month after
Aaden's death. She wanted to know the
name of his bank."

"His bank?" Nora instantly straightened,
pushing away from the door.

"She kept bothering me about it until I
finally took her there and we talked to the
manager. She wanted to see the security

camera footage from when the deposits were made, the money everyone thought my son had stolen."

Nora recalled the three amounts her analyst had written on the whiteboard, and their own theories about the money.

"The bank wouldn't show us anything," Bilan continued. "They said it was confidential unless requested as part of a legal investigation. We asked the tellers, too, but none of them remembered taking any of the deposits.

"I already knew where at least one came from, though. She did, too." Bilan held out the paper in her hand and Nora unfolded it. It was a letter wrapped around a deposit slip for five thousand dollars, the January deposit her analyst thought was a sweetener. Nora glanced up and Bilan nodded, giving her permission to read the letter.

Dear Aaden,
I know you don't want to take this. You've had your say and I get it. But before you turn this five grand into confetti, hear me out. I'm only going to say it once.
A lot of people are telling me this tournament is crazy, that the prize money is too much, that I'm insane for

wanting to give my company away. The thing is I'm not giving away shit. They don't know that. They can't see what we're about to do.

My mom wasn't a fighter. She grounded me every time I got into a brawl and locked me in my room with a copy of Shakespeare's greatest works. (Like that guy didn't have a hard-on for a good fight.) She reminded me a lot of your mom, actually. It was my dad who saw something good in my fists. He made me jog through the neighborhood every morning before dawn. He had me lifting weights next to the oil cans in the garage. We drove across two states for my first professional fight and as soon as we got there, Dad found a guy who was taking bets and handed him our car keys. I freaked out and said something like, "What are we going to tell Mom?" And he replied, steady as a fucking rock, "We're not telling her shit because you're gonna win."

And I did. I refused to go down because he knew I wouldn't.

I always wondered how Dad was so certain, what he saw in me. I thought maybe it was some biological, paternal pride thing, but it goes deeper than that.

I feel it now. It rings in my bones every time I watch you fight. It fills my stomach and brings tears to my eyes. You're the one, Aaden. You will fucking do this and no one is going to see you coming. I don't need anyone else to understand what I'm doing and frankly I'm glad they don't. It makes me feel smarter, to know what I know, to be the one standing on the sidelines and betting it all.

I've handed over the car keys.

It's up to you to get us home.

L

"Five thousand was the entry fee for the tournament. She gave it to him. She admitted that to me. But she claimed she didn't know where the other amounts had come from."

Bilan wiped her eyes. "I think now she must have been telling the truth. Why else would she have come and convinced me to go to the bank with her? But at the time, I couldn't see that. I needed to blame someone for my son's death. For taking him from me. I'd lost him so many times. To fighting. To manhood. To American culture."

Bilan sat down again and slowly began replacing the hand wraps in the drawer. Nora couldn't fathom it. She couldn't see the bottom of Bilan's grief and something deep in her gut clenched at the thought of holding Henry's clothes in an empty room, of having nothing left of him but fabric and memories. She'd never written him a letter like this, telling him how much she believed in him. She'd never told him she kept her distance because she hadn't wanted him to hurt like she'd been hurt, but maybe she'd just hurt him in other ways.

Bilan closed the drawer and stood, blinking. "I made Logan wait outside the bank while I closed Aaden's account. He had almost twenty-seven thousand dollars saved. It wasn't just the strange deposits. He'd planned to buy a new cooler for the store."

She wiped her eyes and moved back into the hallway, shutting the door to his room. "I put the money in one of Aaden's duffel bags, the first one I'd bought him when he began going to Strike, and I gave it to Logan. I wanted it all to go away, the money, the accusations and rumors, and her, too — everything she'd brought into our lives."

"You put twenty-seven thousand dollars in cash in a duffel bag and handed it to Logan Russo?"

"Yes, the one you showed me in the picture. That was Aaden's. If I hadn't bought him that bag, if I hadn't let him go to Strike that first time . . ."

She couldn't finish the sentence and Nora didn't know how to finish it for her. She tried to give Bilan the deposit slip and letter back, but the older woman shook her head as she locked up the apartment.

Once she was back on the street, Nora looked at the scrawled handwriting and then turned toward the downtown skyline.

She needed to find Logan Russo.

The stadium was ringed with crowds, people flowing in and out of the giant glass entrance to the Strike Down exhibition.

"Logan is here." One of Nora's analysts met her at the doors. "She's in the press box with the rest of the managers. We should be able to intercept her between that and her fan meet and greet, unless you want to interrupt their meeting?"

"No. That's fine. Let me know as soon as they adjourn." Nora melted into the crowd on the stadium floor. She needed time to process everything she'd just learned.

The duffel bag had belonged to Aaden. Bilan gave it to Logan, stuffed with cash, and somehow the bag had turned up in her partner's closet, while stacks of bills were hidden in his desk drawer.

She hadn't known how Corbett could be connected to Logan. Her knee-jerk response — in all her shortsightedness and jealousy — had been to imagine an affair, but it was money. Of course. Everything boiled down to money. Money was why Sam White had killed himself. Money was why her parents disowned her. Money was the reason Mike put up with an unfeeling wife. People killed for money. People died for it. Love might hurt, but money would strike you down forever.

Logan had paid Corbett, had given him a bag full of Aaden's money, but why? Had he helped Logan commit the fraud? Logan couldn't have passed the duffel bag on until after Aaden was dead, when the refunds were already pouring into the fake account. The timeline didn't make sense.

Then there was the problem of Logan asking Bilan to go to the bank. Why would she be checking security camera footage if she'd given Aaden the bribes in the first place? To make sure she hadn't appeared on camera? Why go to all that trouble when the email itself hadn't even been deleted off the server? It didn't add up, and maybe Nora was awful at everything else in her life, but she knew how to add.

Even the letter to Aaden was maddeningly

ambiguous. In the moment it had sounded like a message from a proud parent, but now certain lines bubbled back up, shifting with hidden meanings.

I'm not giving away shit. They don't know that. They can't see what we're about to do. Was she talking about Aaden winning the tournament or the two of them stealing the prize?

Nora walked faster, weaving through the laughing, posturing, shadow-boxing crowd, dodging limbs and the hawkish swoop of vendors. Perspiration dripped down her back and her breath became jerky. The only person who knew what really happened, the only person alive and conscious — Nora swallowed — was Logan Russo.

She looked up at the press box and stopped cold.

Logan stood at the window, staring right at her.

Nora was too far away to make out her expression or even, in fact, if Logan had picked her out of the crowd, but her skin prickled with a bodily awareness. She felt like a bug being surveyed by a callous god. Before she could decide what to do, someone bumped her from behind and began profusely apologizing, momentarily distracting her. When she looked up again, Logan was gone.

Nora pushed through the crowd, working her way back to the concourse. She grabbed her phone and it immediately lit up with a call from her analyst.

"We can't talk to Logan right now."

"Why not? I just saw her. She's up there." Nora cut through a massive line for vStrike and, once she'd gotten clear, started jogging toward a bank of elevators.

"Yes, but so are the police."

She looked up again but didn't have a view of the press box anymore. "What do they want?"

"We don't know."

Nora swore and hung up. The analyst found her less than five minutes later, pacing outside the stadium. She clearly had no idea how to handle her unraveling boss.

"Anything?" Nora bit out.

"No." The analyst watched her, open-mouthed, and then began babbling about the rest of the team's lack of progress, trying to fill the silence. "We're haven't gotten any hits with our resource at FinCEN."

The Financial Crimes Enforcement Network maintained a vast database of bank deposit information across the country, assisting law enforcement with uncovering and prosecuting money laundering and fraud. All of the Magers Construction refunds were multiple hundreds of thousands of dollars. If they were transferred within the United States, FinCEN would have records of them.

"Obviously." Nora couldn't stop moving. "The money's offshore. Our only hope is that the online account will be in Strike's name so Gregg Abbott can access it. Beyond that we have no idea where to look."

"We can't do anything with the online account today. Everything's closed for the holiday."

The word tugged at the back of Nora's mind. Holiday. An offshore holiday.

The memory jerked into focus and she pulled up short, almost dropping her briefcase. "The blogs."

"What?"

"The Strike blogs. Oh my god."

Shouting at the analyst to stay where she was, Nora ran into the skyway.

GREGG

Every marriage is different. Good marriage, bad marriage — if you're that binary — young marriage, lifelong marriage, multicultural marriage, marriages of convenience, love, or economics; no two functioned the same. Still, there are commonalities, like being in a unique position to observe your spouse, knowing things the outside world would never see. Even in a marriage like mine, a marriage some people might've called a merger, I'd learned things about Logan no one else in the world would've dared guess.

Logan doesn't lie. She doesn't beat around the bush. She doesn't mince words and she sure as hell won't pull a punch. She'll gut you but she'll be honest about it, or at least that's the image Logan Russo has cultivated. I know. I helped her trademark it.

Logan's lies were hard to spot because she believed them. She was the ultimate salesman, the one who'd already sold herself and could then sell anyone. But I'd lived in the legend's shadow for two decades. I'd been her partner for so long that, if I didn't stand in her way and make myself an opponent, she forgot I was even there. That's when you learned the most about someone — when they thought they were alone.

Let me tell you a story about Logan lying.

I was adopted by a couple who lived in suburban Chicago, the husband a computer programmer and the wife a Mary Kay skin care salesman. My biological parents were from Ohio, the agency said. That was all. Ohio. An entire state I avoided because I refused to see someone with my face in a gas station, looking horrified by the echo of some long-ago half-drunk mistake. Strike has no clubs in Ohio, and Logan has never once asked why.

When I was two, my parents divorced and I rarely saw the computer programmer again. He sent child support, apparently, which my mother invested in her Mary Kay business. She held parties at our house and took me along when she visited customers. She taught me to say, "Wow, you look pretty" after she'd finished applying product to the women's faces. How to say it right, and sometimes reach out a hand like I wanted to touch their cheeks but knew better. Then I'd run back to my toys in the corner, grinning because if she got a sale there was a sucker for me in the glove box. She was gunning for the pink car, and she knew every trick.

"You have to live your brand, sweetheart," she'd say as she slathered some new lotion on our faces at night, examining our skin in the mirror. She took notes, developed custom talking points, showed up at every school event with business cards and samples in her cotton candy–colored purse. When we watched TV, we'd dissect the commercials together, and when we went shopping she pointed out every strategy — color, graphics, copy, all the elements that combined into a flawless appeal for every consumer dollar. I don't know who those people in Ohio were, whether it was in my blood or not, but by the time we were driving around in her pink car and I was president of my high school's young entrepreneurs' society, there was no stopping me. I was a salesman.

I worked at various companies in college and afterward. I sold everything from vitamins to vacuum cleaners, and found a niche in athletic supplements right when action movies were exploding and everyone wanted

Van Damme pecs and Linda Hamilton arms, but by the time I got my MBA I was ready for more. I opened my own brand management business and consulted with hundreds of companies, designing logos and taglines, building mailing lists (actual, physical mail for the dark ages), and convincing them that the internet was a growth channel. I created identities without knowing my own. And I didn't know it until I went to Vegas and got tickets to the Russo-Palicka fight at the MGM.

It was all there in that night, my entire world shifted and I saw Strike in all its naked, gorgeous ferocity. I saw my purpose, the brand I was born to live.

A few weeks later, I flew Logan to Chicago to meet my mom, who was in hospice, bald and decorated with breast cancer ribbons to match her car. She sat in that bed, assessed Logan's skin, and told her she had sun damage, then wrote out a detailed regimen, in wavy, broken cursive, on the back of a business card. I was touched and surprised at how much, seeing their two heads bowed together, one covered in glossy, black hair, the other bare and dull as Mom described each item's formula and benefits before pressing the card into Logan's hand. That is what commitment looks like. That is living your brand.

At the end of the visit, Logan embraced my mom, looked her straight in the eye, and told her how much she was looking forward to trying the products. "Or my skin is, anyway."

Then she laughed, and we left. I still had my apartment in Chicago then and Logan stayed the night before flying back to Minneapolis. It wasn't until a few days later, after she'd gone home, that I found my mother's business card in the bathroom trash. The shaky lines of her instructions were wet and smeared, illegible.

Mom lost the fight not long after. No Mary Kay products ever showed up in Logan's medicine cabinet, and neither of us mentioned it. She probably thought it was a kindness, indulging an old, dying woman, but it was the first time I saw Logan with the gloves and ring stripped away, the Logan who thought no one was watching.

Twenty years. Twenty years of marriage made me the only person in the room who knew Logan was lying to the detective.

When he and the other officer interrupted our Day Three kickoff meeting, everyone appeared unruffled. A flashed badge wouldn't make anyone on the Strike management team clutch their pearls, except maybe Darryl, but he wasn't here.

"I apologize for interrupting." Detective Li didn't bother with introductions or smiles. "But I was hoping to have a quick word with Ms. Russo."

Several of the directors glanced at Logan, who merely lifted an eyebrow.

"Regarding?"

"Regarding the hit-and-run near this location a few nights ago."

"And you just happened to be assigned to the case?"

"I handle a lot of cases in the first precinct."

Various looks of confusion and understanding were exchanged. The Events Director moved to wrap the meeting, but I stood.

"Stay and finish up here. We'll find another space for Logan to talk to the officers."

"That'd be great, Mr. Abbott." The detective waited for Logan and me to lead the way out. "We have some questions for you, too."

After we found an empty suite and went through the usual preliminaries, Li got to his point.

"What's your relationship with the victim of the hit-and-run, Corbett MacDermott?"

"None." I answered for both of us.

"He's a partner in an accounting firm that you're actively working with, correct?"

"How do you know that?" C.J. had been dealing with the police on this, but I doubted even she knew the connection. She would have had no reason to link MacDermott to Parrish unless she'd Googled him, and she would've mentioned it in the meeting if she had. Google searches were a time-honored marketing bullet point.

"Is it true?" Detective Li pressed.

"It's a private matter."

"Not if it's relevant to this case."

Logan hadn't said a word yet. She'd staked out a chair in the corner of the suite and was watching me talk to the cops like it was mildly interesting reality TV, something you watched at the dentist's office when you didn't have control of the remote. I sighed.

"Yes, we hired Parrish Forensics last week to help us with a cash flow issue."

"And Mr. MacDermott?"

"Was in the room when I met with the partners. I believe I shook his hand, but that was the only time I met him. It's Nora, Nora Trier from Parrish, who's been working with us."

"And you, Ms. Russo?"

Logan gave the detective a cool look, but

I cut in. "She wasn't at that meeting."

Detective Li wasn't swayed. "Had you met Mr. MacDermott elsewhere?"

And before I could interject again, Logan answered, as calmly as if she were ordering coffee. "Yes, a few times."

I blinked and before I could recover, Logan launched into a brief description of meeting Nora's partner during a promotion at the club last winter, how he seemed to be there more out of friendship than any desire for fitness.

Then she said she saw him again on Tuesday night, the night of the accident.

"We were leaving the stadium at the same time and he congratulated me on the tournament. Introduced himself and mentioned the class he'd attended."

"Was anyone else with you at the time?"

"No."

"What about the security guards?" I asked, turning on her.

"I was tired of them."

Before I could say anything else, Detective Li cut in. "Where was this?"

"Just outside." She thumbed in the direction of the glass doors. "I was heading back to the condo and we walked in the same direction for a while, until another fan interrupted us."

"Did Corbett keep walking with you?"

"He wasn't there after I passed the parking ramp."

My mom taught me how to recognize when a sale wouldn't happen while she drove to and from her house calls. Some kids learned manners. I learned how to spot the lie hiding beneath the manners. There are almost zero physical cues to Logan's lies. She has none of the classic tells. She doesn't glance up or down, blink too much or too little. She doesn't curl her lip or add flourishes to her "no's." Her hips don't turn to the side, the body's tendency to shy its core away from the fiction. Her stories don't waver in detail or consistency largely because she doesn't tell stories. Most of her verbal communication has been groomed down to a grab bag of motivational sound bites and veiled threats. When someone shouts at you to punch them like you mean it, you don't question their honesty.

Back in January, a millennium ago, when Logan gut punched all of us with her announcement about handing off the company, I accused her of wanting Aaden to fill her shoes.

"It's not fair to the other contenders if you're walking into this tournament with someone already handpicked as your heir apparent."

"You're lecturing me on ethics?"

"Then tell me I'm wrong."

She turned to me, squaring first her jaw, then her shoulders and on down until her entire frame was a study in right angles. If it were possible, even her pupils would've had corners.

"I haven't picked Aaden Warsame to take over the company."

The truth was there, cowering beneath the edge. Maybe she even half believed what she said, but the words had flattened. Her voice lost a fraction of depth from the top and bottom of her range and her eyes seemed to crystallize. She saw me but I wasn't there. I was only an obstacle in her and Aaden's path.

Now Detective Li was making her replay her last encounter with Corbett MacDermott. He asked for more details about the conversation, anything she could remember, and I couldn't shake the feeling that something about this entire interview was off. Why had this case been assigned to the man who'd investigated a trainer's suicide? Wasn't a hit-and-run accident even more clear-cut than a corpse with a gun and a note? He paced in front of Logan after she said she couldn't recall any more details, both his posture and face blank, giving nothing away.

"Why were you leaving the tournament so early? Aren't you the face of the company?"

"No, not anymore. And I was never the brains, right, Gregg?" She gave me a hard, glittering smile. I didn't answer.

"I was tired," she shrugged, turning back to the detective. "It had been a long day."

"And you didn't hear the accident at all? It must have happened when you were still walking."

She shook her head. Her voice had tightened. It wasn't completely flat, not a monotone, but she'd lost a sliver of her range. The wavelength of Logan's tells. My stomach dropped as I remembered her questions at the meeting, asking if there had been any cameras, any recording of the accident. Suddenly her presence — in full Logan Russo costume and makeup, dangerously on-brand — made perfect, horrible sense.

Logan.

An accountant, one who worked with Nora.

My mouth went dry as Detective Li handed her a card. "If you think of anything else, Ms. Russo, anything at all that might be helpful."

She took it, nodding, even as she shifted a glance at me. "I'll call you."

Red, White, and Boom

July 4, 2019

Today's the day, guys, and it's not about hot dogs or sparklers or watching parades under a boiling sun.

It's about the fight.

Imagine, for a second, a 168-year-old marriage that is so shitty it's not enough to dump the other person's stuff into the ocean or squeeze them for more money than they own. No one is right or good and it's not about that anyway. It's about physically hurting them to show them who's in charge. You strike and they strike back. You fight until everyone's bleeding and freezing and starving and eventually even the neighbors get involved to try to settle things. The British thought we were upstart colonists, a cash cow to be crushed back into submission. And we showed them what revolution looks like. We lost a lot of battles, but we never stopped getting back to our feet. We survived traitors and mutiny. We dropped surprise attacks. We were ready to die, to throw it all away, before ever climbing back into that marriage bed again.

Eight years. This country was born in an eight-year bloodbath and, for better or worse, we've never lost our taste for the fight. We celebrate with *explosions,* people. So tonight, while you're oohing and aahing at all the gunpowder decorating the spacious skies, remember:

If you're being used.

If you're being underestimated.

If you can't fucking take it anymore.

Don't.

Show them you're ready to blow the whole thing up, that you'll die before letting them win. Whether your ancestors fought in the Battle of Bunker Hill or they clawed their way out of a civil war to find refuge in this country, you're a child of blood and you're not afraid of it. When I say God bless America, I mean God bless the fighter who lives in you.

NORA

Henry disappeared and reappeared along the winding trail circling the lake. Woods and reeds crept in on all sides of the dirt path and as the trail veered onto a bridge over the shallows of the water or ducked around a clump of trees, Nora lost sight of her son's figure before the path opened up and she saw him again.

"Catch up, Mom."

He wasn't even out of breath. A two-mile circuit used to exhaust him. He would run in spurts and sprints, his little legs pounding the dirt until he got winded moments later, although he pretended he wanted to stop and look at a turtle sunning itself on a partially submerged log or one of the egrets striding gracefully through the shallows. Now, only a decade into life, his body was already evolving into a man's. His legs stretched long and unfamiliar, his sneakers gliding like chunky boats on his feet. He ran with ease, darting into the growing shadows. As he turned off on a lesser used path that led deeper into the woods, he paused, crouching inward, and then a ball of light crackled to life in his hand.

"Henry, no!" She sprinted toward him, her heart rate accelerating, but he took off before she could catch up. The artificial fire of the sparkler sizzled and hissed, dodging in and out of the shadows of the trees ahead of her. The forest still stood lush with spring rain, green in every direction, but it only took one stray spark. One dead tree.

Laughing, he trailed the sparkler behind him, an unmoored child on holiday.

Offshore. Holiday. The words pounded in her head. It was still the Fourth of July. Corbett still lay unconscious in the hospital, caught somewhere between dead and alive, between friend and foe. And while she chased her son into the trees, her team was chasing twenty million dollars across the Caribbean.

She couldn't believe she hadn't made the connection before. It wasn't until pacing outside U.S. Bank Stadium while Logan was being questioned by the police that the memory came into focus.

"Where are you going?" her analyst had yelled after her, but Nora had no patience for explanations. She needed action. She needed to be moving forward.

"Stay there!" she shouted before disappearing into the skyway. "Call me when you have Logan!"

Nora had subscribed to the Strike blog when she'd first signed up at the gym for the same reason she subscribed to everything else — as a potential conversation starter for reluctant witnesses. She might have to interview a weight-lifting junior accountant or a finance intern who happened to be a black belt. She hadn't expected to enjoy the blogs and she certainly didn't anticipate she'd be checking her inbox the moment she woke up every day.

Logan's voice became her companion in the predawn mornings when the house was quiet, Mike and Henry still flushed with sleep and oblivious in their beds. She read them over breakfast, in the bathroom, and while letting her car warm up in the wood-shrouded cul-de-sac. Seeing Logan Russo's name in her unread mail sent a surge of excitement bubbling in her throat, anticipating Logan's energy, Logan's anecdotes and humor. The emails were the antithesis of Nora's day, a brazen blast before she moved on to hours of case files, financials, and court documents. On Nora's business trips,

Logan's blog was the voice of home. And when Logan traveled, Nora felt like she was with her — even when she went on holiday, like for her fiftieth birthday.

Nora had known, even as her team tried to get confirmation about the online account where Magers Construction had transferred the refunds, that the prize was already gone. She'd thought the only way to follow the money trail was through that online platform, but maybe she didn't need it at all. Maybe she could already guess where the millions had been sent.

"Did you find it?" Nora had called ahead to the rest of the team still at the Strike office, and burst into the conference room after having run the last few blocks from the stadium. One analyst was scanning two different monitors, while another had pulled up a giant map on a wall screen. All of them seemed distracted, a few red-eyed, and it took Nora a moment to realize they were upset about Corbett. No one knew what she did about her partner.

" 'I woke up a few days ago as a fifty-year-old woman in a villa in paradise. That's not a metaphor. I thought fifty deserved a holiday.' " The analyst wiped her face with a Kleenex as she read Logan's blog entry from January, then frowned at her computer. "Where was she?"

"The Bahamas." Nora leaned over her shoulder, pointing out the next few lines. "See? 'Bahama Mamas.' 'Pastel tributes to colonialism.' "

"That could be virtually any Caribbean island. How do we know we're not dealing with Nevis?"

"Bite your tongue." Nora walked over to the map on the smart board. The team had zoomed in to the Caribbean region, the southern hot spots of offshore banking from the United States, far past U.S. jurisdiction. Each island had their own laws and regulations. Some were respectably transparent. Others dwelled in the shadows. Nevis, the country that was barely more than a dot next to the island of St. Kitts, was a bottom feeder in the shadow banking world. They'd have an easier time locating a body on the ocean floor than finding money in Nevis, and Corbett — if he'd somehow become involved in this — knew that.

"The articles of incorporation specify that either of the shareholders has the power to open and close accounts independently. She could have easily and legally opened a local bank account while they were on holiday. Should I set up an interview with Mr. Abbott?"

Nora's last encounter with Gregg flashed to mind, along with the smell of the dingy Northeast apartment. He'd seemed precariously close to his limits, replaying violent memories of his wife with the managing partner of a proven fraud investigation. She exhaled slowly, steadily.

"Not yet. Until we have enough evidence to support a scenario, we're keeping this channel of investigation confidential. To everyone." If Corbett could be compromised, anyone could be. Right now, Nora didn't trust a single person outside this room.

She moved to the spray of islands tracing the north side of Cuba. The Bahamas had become less attractive to money launderers in recent years, but it still offered plenty of wiggle room for run-of-the-mill tax evasion or a multimillion-dollar divorce. She had to believe, based on the references in Logan's blog, the money had gone to The Bahamas.

"There's nothing in either of their expense reports from that time. No plane tickets, hotel receipts, or car rentals. I can't tell where they went," another analyst piped up, flipping through multiple windows of data.

"No, it was a personal trip. Or it was supposed to look like one." Nora leaned in, squinting at the islands. Someone, sensing her next order, zoomed in further so that Nassau, the major banking hub in The Bahamas, stretched over the center of the screen. Nora blinked and saw it immediately.

"There."

Right above the banking center — a bridge to an even smaller island.

"Paradise?" One of the analysts squinted as she read.

"Paradise." Nora flipped back to the blog entry and read, feeling her excitement mount. " 'I woke up a few days ago as a fifty-year-old woman *in a villa in paradise. That's not a metaphor.*' That's where they were, Paradise Island in The Bahamas!"

"Okay . . . maybe." The analysts glanced at each other, clearly not convinced, but then another spark fired, a shock of lightning to her brain.

"Pull the Aaden Warsame police report!"

Rushing to another computer, she opened Strike's banking files. "Read the account number from the piece of paper that was found in his wallet."

One of the analysts recited the digits, while Nora scanned the known Strike accounts. The number in Aaden Warsame's wallet didn't match any of them.

"This could potentially be it." Her mind

raced ahead. "This could be the offshore account. He sent the email initiating the fraud. He may have been privy to the next destination of the funds."

"Or it could be his own bank account. He had unexplained deposits."

Nora dug through her briefcase until she found the deposit slip Bilan had given her.

"No!" The last four digits on the slip didn't match the piece of paper from his wallet.

"Where did you get that?" one of the analysts asked, but Nora had already blazed ahead. On the smart board, she shrank the map of The Bahamas down to half size and put the note from Aaden Warsame's wallet next to it. She pulled up a list of every international bank with a branch in Nassau and they began pinging them one by one, sending account verification requests listing the Strike name and the account number from Aaden's wallet. All they needed was one match.

When they finished the Nassau bank requests, Nora had everyone keep working. Covering their bases, in case she was wrong about The Bahamas, they moved on to the British Virgin Islands, Barbados, St. Kitts, even Nevis, all the places U.S. money liked to hide. If they were lucky, they'd receive responses on a quarter of their requests. The only sure way to confirm an account was to send it money, nominal transfers of a few dollars, but the risk was too high — a deposit notification would tip their hand and increase the odds that whoever had stolen twenty million would transfer it instantly to another ghost account on another shadowy island. The money trail, Nora knew, could be endless.

The longer they worked, the more Nora's euphoria drained and reality set in again. Despite her hunches, they were no further along than they had been this morning, and there was only one day left in the tournament. Twenty-four more hours of frantic searching, but now with the weight of Corbett's deceit. He'd lied to her and he might die before she could even confront him about it. As her team continued to fire off electronic requests, Nora got a call from her analyst at the stadium.

"Logan left."

"What?"

"She had to go directly to the meet and greet after the police talked to her. They said I could grab her afterward, but now she's gone. Even her bodyguards don't know where she went. She left the stadium and she's not —"

"Answering her phone." Nora finished the sentence and swore, startling everyone in the conference room. Everything in this case circled back to Logan. How had she thought pinning Logan Russo out of the ring would be any easier than inside it?

The entire drive home, she saw nothing but Logan, every untouchable line of her body, her glossy, slicked-back hair, her smirking mouth, her dark eyes shining with the intractable force of her personality. Nora had spent a year of her life fixated on this woman, because — she realized, ironically — it had been safe. She couldn't be hurt, standing in a corner, watching a celebrity from a distance. A fantasy would never accuse or abandon her. A fantasy asked for nothing in return. The fantasy of Logan had filled all the places she'd kept empty, the caverns she'd carved to hold herself apart. This case had shattered the safety of her fantasies, had brought the real Logan into dangerous proximity. The real Logan had taken her independence, her best friend, and, if Nora wasn't more careful than Aaden or Corbett, she might destroy her entire life.

When Nora got home, she needed to run. The urge to disappear into the trails the way she used to, before she'd ever known Strike

323

or Logan Russo, overwhelmed her, but Henry had been waiting in the driveway for her as soon as she pulled up.

"Only three more hours until fireworks." He was practically bouncing, a sudden reminder this was a day most people enjoyed, a day for relaxation and sun-soaked barbecues. Mike had mentioned a parade, hadn't he?

"Here." Remembering, she reached into her console and pulled out the box of sparklers she'd bought downtown. "These should keep you busy until then."

He accepted them grudgingly. "Those are for babies."

"The package warnings, not to mention all available logic, point to the contrary. I'm going for a run."

"Can I come?"

How long had it been since they'd hiked the trails together? Since he'd asked to spend time with her? Maybe it was the thought of Sam White's boys and their long-lost innocence, or maybe it was the image of Bilan sitting in an empty bedroom, but Nora blinked away tears and told him to change into tennis shoes.

Almost as soon as they got on the trails, though, he kept a suspicious lead, stretching the distance between them until he made that turn into the deep woods, the ten-mile loop where few people ventured, and his ten-year-old boy motives became clear. He lit the firework and ran straight into the forest, heedless of the consequences.

He barreled up a hill, waving the sparkler in the air as his too-long legs flashed white before disappearing over the ridge. She lengthened her stride, feeling the unused muscles burn into life. Piles of dead leaves hid under boughs on either side of the trail — brown, dry, and flammable. She pushed herself faster, reaching the summit of the hill in time to see him disappear around another bend.

Calling his name again and hearing only receding laughter, she sprinted down the trail. She'd lost sight of him completely; even the hissing ball of light had vanished. She pushed around curves and up more rocky inclines, expecting to spot him at every turn but finding nothing except more forest. Her breath shortened, coming in pants now as the adrenaline met resistance in her body. She passed a used sparkler wire, still smoking on the ground, and grabbed it before it could ignite. An ugly feeling broke over her skin. It was like chasing the Strike money, the prize just out of reach, evident but untouchable. How could she expect to find twenty million in the Caribbean if she couldn't even find a child setting an entire forest ablaze?

Finally, as she crested another hill at the top of a large open valley, Henry came into view. He'd stopped at the mouth of a meadow, sunlit and secluded, the long grasses waving toward another burned-out sparkler wire in his hand. He didn't see her. He was talking to a woman leaning against a wooden bench whose dark hair gleamed in the setting sun.

Logan.

Nora stopped, gasped, and clutched a stitch in her side. At the noise, both of them looked up the trail. Henry's face was hesitant, but Logan smiled, her eyes tracing down to Nora's braced hand. Instinctively she dropped it, not giving away any weaknesses. As she walked down the hill, she forced her breath back to a facsimile of normal.

"Hey, Mom." Henry's voice was suddenly young and unsure. "This lady just asked if I knew you."

"He is the spitting image of you, Nora Trier." But Logan stared at Nora as she said it.

Without taking her eyes off Logan, Nora

reached in Henry's direction, palm up, and waited. He kicked a rock, putting off the inevitable.

"You told me I could play with them."

"Not here. It's dangerous and illegal."

"That sounds like half the fun," Logan said, her mouth crooking up as she held Nora's stare. She still hadn't moved from her spot against the bench, and didn't seem at all interested in explaining what she was doing in the middle of Nora's woods.

When Henry finally produced the box of sparklers and the lighter, though, Logan's hand shot out and grabbed the contraband with catlike reflexes, making him jump.

She shook one of the sticks out of the box and lit it, watching the wire hiss to life. "I haven't done one of these since I was a kid."

Nora stepped forward, putting herself between Logan and her son, and took the box and lighter. Henry wasn't content to be protected, though. He edged around her elbow, drawn like a moth to the fire.

Logan jabbed the sparkler around, writing secret messages in the air. "Just because something's dangerous doesn't mean it's not worth doing."

Running an involuntary hand over Henry's hair, Nora pulled him closer. She tried to calculate the best way to proceed, to find a way out of the woods. She chanced a glance at the darkening path on either side. They were miles from everything and she had no idea what Logan Russo wanted badly enough to bring her here, to this unmistakably deliberate nowhere. What dangerous things did she think were worth doing?

Logan looked up from the sparkler, her eyes burning with the same intensity Nora had seen on a thousand billboards, packages, and screens. The stare that had haunted Nora the entire way home, not an invitation but a dare. Take me, if you think you can.

And Nora realized, all at once, that the person who needed to disappear wasn't her. It had never been her. It was Logan Russo.

"Henry, go on ahead. I'll meet you at home."

"Are you mad at me, Mom? Can we still go see the fireworks tonight?"

"Go."

She waited until he made it to the other side of the meadow, which seemed to take an age, until his taffy-stretched legs and chunky shoes were swallowed safely back up in the shadows of the trees.

The sparkler sputtered and died.

"Why are you here?" she asked.

"You said you ran in this park. I came last night, too, but I didn't find you."

She'd been at the hospital last night, reconstructing Corbett's accident and trying to figure out what had brought him to a dark alley, how her best friend could possibly be connected to a dead young trainer. The answer, to that question and so many more, was right in front of her. Her pulse raced, there was no way to control it, but the investigator in her needed to know everything. "I have some questions for you."

"What a coincidence."

Logan pushed away from the bench, rising to her full height. Nora could smell the UV on her skin, could see a trickle of perspiration gathering in the hollow of her collarbones, and she wondered how long this kickboxing god had been prowling the woods looking for her.

Run, Henry, she thought. Keep running.

RATIONALIZATION

GREGG

Friday.

The final championship. I'd visualized it for months, maybe longer. Years? The germ of it went all the way back to that first night at the MGM in Las Vegas, as I inhaled the dazzle of lights, the violence and victory, the sex and bright, flexing feats of power. For two decades I'd worked to build an empire big enough to house that colosseum and here it was. Finally.

Sleep had been impossible last night. I'd obsessively devoured news coverage on two different laptops in my office, tweeting, reposting, emailing into the morning hours from the couch where I'd spent every night of the past week. I composed at least five messages to Nora and deleted them before sending. It didn't take a computer programmer to know what her artificial intelligence program would say about emails delivered at three in the morning, regardless of syntax. It would say I was desperate, and it would be right. I needed to know she'd found the money, but now — after that interview with the police yesterday — I also needed to know if her partner had woken up. If he'd said anything about Logan.

Why had she lied to Detective Li about knowing this accountant? There was only one explanation. A twenty-million-dollar explanation. I kept flashing back to the deposit slips in her old apartment, specifically the one Nora had found in the garbage, covered in grease stains. Had Logan and Corbett MacDermott been there together? Were they having casual lunch meetings to discuss fraud? If so, why admit she knew him? Why claim to have seen him on Tuesday night, right before a mysterious accident, unless she was afraid someone would place her at the scene and wanted to get ahead of the story. Controlling the message, just the way I'd taught her.

A braver man would have investigated, would have confronted his wife without regard to the fear of being thrown off his own balcony or tossed in front of an oncoming car. I was not that man. I'd left the stadium last night during a thunder of detonation and Technicolor flashes reflecting off the skyscrapers of downtown, as

334

Logan's unscheduled, unscripted blog filtered through my head. *No one is right or good and it's not about that anyway. It's about physically hurting them to show them who's in charge.* I walked past our building and imagined the penthouse terrace covered in a shroud of ash, while Logan watched the sky burn. God bless the fighter in me, I thought grimly, the one who would live to fight another day.

The office today was deserted. Every Strike employee had migrated to the stadium by this point in the tournament, except Darryl — who'd taken another sick day and was, if he had a single goddamn brain in his head, working on his résumé right now — and the Parrish team had apparently left last night. According to Sara, they'd "processed all necessary on-site information" and retreated back to their own office tower.

By midday, I broke down and emailed the lead analyst, requesting an update, and received an infuriatingly political reply. They were "aggressively pursuing all avenues of opportunity" which meant they didn't have the money yet. The deposit slips we'd found in Logan's old apartment were nothing, just pieces of paper. They wouldn't cover the thirty-six giant cardboard checks waiting to be awarded to tonight's winners.

One of those winners had to be Merritt Osborne. At least twenty percent of my tweets last night were dedicated to highlighting some aspect of Merritt's preliminary fights, where she'd dominated every opponent in the ring. Her blond braid, streaked red and blue for Independence Day, had lit up Instagram and already become a viral gif. I stopped at her hotel to check in on the way to the stadium, and she met me with another bone-crunching hug.

"How are you feeling about the Brazilian tonight?" Merritt's final round opponent was a highly decorated fighter who'd broken a Russian woman's jaw in the ring earlier this year.

"Honey, this bitch is going down."

It was all I needed to hear.

Less than an hour before the great glass doors opened, I stood alone on the concourse of U.S. Bank Stadium. The interior lights were on, but the spotlights hadn't been booted up, leaving the center ring in shadows. The jumbotrons remained dark, all their slow-motion moments of glory and despair still locked in an unknown future, waiting to be relived at a hundred times their size. Soon tens of thousands of people would flood through these gates and watch a champion ascend, bringing a new face, a new age in the life of Strike. I ignored the buzz of my watch and phone and stared at the vast, empty world I'd created. That's where Nora found me.

"I didn't expect to see you here." The analyst who'd replied to my email told me "they" would be in contact, which I assumed meant any of the underlings, one of the ubiquitous suited people who'd prowled headquarters all week, but the sight of Nora left me physically weak. They must have found the money. It was back in Strike's account. Why else would she be here in person?

"Forgive me for intruding, but I do need a few minutes of your time. Somewhere private, if possible." She glanced at Sara, who must have escorted her into the stadium and was standing at my shoulder, waiting for instructions.

"Of course." My face smooth, smile benign, betraying no hint of the blood that had just significantly picked up its pace. I swept an arm upstairs, inviting Nora to proceed. "Sara, I'll be in the press box if you need me."

She nodded and walked us as far as the elevators. "Have you heard from Logan yet? We're still trying to get ahold of her to go over the night's itinerary."

Logan hadn't shown up for the morning status meeting, and it had been someone's action item to track her down and brief her. Obviously that person hadn't been successful.

"No." A shadow passed over Nora's face as I said it, there and gone.

"Okay, no worries." Even though her voice registered several octaves of worry, Sara flashed a shaky smile. "We'll track her down."

Nora and I stepped into the elevator and were enveloped in quiet as soon as the doors shut. I resisted the urge to move closer, to take the undeserved comfort I desperately needed and invoke a familiarity we didn't, in fact, have. I'd been inside this woman, I'd tasted her two days ago, but every intimacy moved us farther apart. She could have been riding the elevator with a stranger. There was no body language I could read, no indications, no tells beyond the fact that she was, as always, prepared. She faced the doors, giving nothing away.

"I'm sorry about the other day," I offered, with a quarter turn to face her, riding the nebulous edge between confrontational and dismissive.

"We've located the account where the

Magers Construction refunds were sent."

I nodded, relieved and simultaneously rebuked. We weren't going to be speaking of personal lives, much less living them.

"The account details were basically listed on the deposit slips, right? You confirmed them with Magers?"

"No. That was an intermediary account, a holding area to stage international transfers. We've located where the money went after that."

The elevator stopped and somehow I made my feet move out of it, feeling my rage at Logan deflating, knocked aside by the enormity of this news.

"Where?"

A trace of satisfaction crossed her features. "Nassau."

"That's where we went for Logan's birthday."

"I know."

A smile broke over my face, the first genuine dawn of happiness I'd felt in days. Everything was finally falling into place.

"You actually did it. You found twenty million dollars in less than a week."

The compliment drew no smiles. "Let's not get ahead of ourselves, Mr. Abbott. We're going to take the next step and see where it leads. Since Strike is the listed owner of the account, you have the right to inquire on and transact the funds."

The next step took longer than I thought. Banking, it turned out, was tedious as hell and Nora had the patience of a saint, asking for us to be transferred, waiting on hold, producing account numbers and confirming information. All I did was sit next to her in the press box, checking email and social media blasts, stifling yawns, and saying, "Yes, this is Mr. Gregory Abbott. I authorize the information to be released," from time to time. At one point I asked about her partner and whether he'd regained consciousness yet, but Nora just shook her head, refusing to even look at me.

During the fourth round of telephone banker questioning, Sara came into the room with two other Strike employees. All of them were panicking.

"We still can't find her," Sara stage-whispered over the speaker.

One of the other admins jumped in. "We've been calling her cell phone every twenty minutes. It goes straight to voice mail and the voice mail is full. No one's seen her at the office or gym. They said she hasn't been in all day."

"There's no reason for her to be at the gym today. There's no classes this week."

Then, louder, toward the phone. "Yes, this is Mr. Gregory Abbott. I authorize the information to be released."

Sara nodded to a trainer, who spoke up. "Last week she made plans with her Friday class to go for a run along the river, since the normal session was canceled. They were all there at noon, waiting, but she didn't show. I . . . I took them instead."

All three of them exchanged looks, anxiety riding high on their cheekbones, tightening their shoulders.

"Is she with the twins?" Daisy and Darius sometimes commandeered Logan for hours at a time, styling her into whatever look they'd invented for the occasion.

Sara shook her head, almost in tears now. "She missed her appointment with them, too."

I heaved a sigh, trying to control the flare of anger. "She's probably at the house, getting ready. I'll go and bring her. How much time do we have?"

"Logan is due onstage in seventy-two minutes," Sara answered immediately, not even needing to check her phone.

"Okay, let me —" But before I could finish the thought, Nora's voice cut through my consciousness.

"And when was the date of cancellation?"

As I spun around, time slowed down into the jumbotron moment, the slow-motion point of impact just before everything went dark.

"Monday, okay. And you can confirm the entire nineteen-million-dollar balance was transferred out?"

"That's correct, ma'am." The voice on the line affirmed in a flat, bored accent. "The account is at a zero balance and has been closed."

Logan. Fucking Logan.

Everything in me vibrated on the way to our building, an anger too large for one person's skin. I didn't see the throngs of people pushing their way into the stadium; I only felt their heat, absorbing their enthusiasm and transmuting it into a dark, blinding rage. The downtown noise receded to nothing. The corner where a man's body had been flipped over a car, gone. The only thing that existed at that moment was my wife, my stealing, cheating, probably murdering wife. If she was at the apartment, balconies be damned. I was going to kill her or die trying.

Nora had watched me with dispassion after requesting the transfer details and ending the call. "The next account will likely be in the transferor's name only" — she avoided any names in front of the employees in the room — "which would mean we can't access the funds without a judgment in whatever jurisdiction it's been opened in."

I didn't reply. Sara and the others still hovered in the background, listening, their fears compounding. They were waiting for me to speak, to illuminate the path forward, but the world had gone black in the space of a phone call.

"Mr. Abbott," she paused. "Gregg. This is the point in the investigation where we could discuss the possibility of legal action. My team will continue to gather evidence and we'll provide you some scenarios to raise capital based on our prior assessments this week."

A rumbling swell filled the stadium below us. The doors had opened. Music began pumping out of the audio system as the screens blazed to life with the image we'd unveiled on opening night — the signature Strike glove with a shadow behind it. A space only big enough for one champion.

I must have said something, I had no idea what. An acknowledgment to Nora. An encouragement to the Strike staff. The world had distilled to the single task of finding and confronting my wife.

Outside our building, a dark sedan pulled up to the curb and Detective Li climbed out of the car with the officer from yesterday in tow.

"Can this wait?" I didn't slow down.

"We're actually here to talk to your wife."

"It's not a good time. The championship finals are about to begin."

They flashed their badges at the doorman and followed me into the elevator, as though I hadn't said a word.

"Ms. Russo made an appointment for this day and time. She contacted us yesterday, saying she had some additional information regarding Corbett MacDermott's accident as well as Aaden Warsame's suicide." The detective let that settle for a moment. "Do you have any idea what she wants to tell us?"

I knew what I wanted to tell them — that Logan Russo was a ruthless, bloodless criminal — but I still didn't know how far those crimes extended, or why she'd called the police here, now.

"I have no idea."

I reached the penthouse with less than an hour to find Logan, get rid of the police, and get back to the tournament, but when I unlocked the door and waved them in ahead of me they stopped short, blocking me from crossing the threshold.

"What is it?" I craned my neck around them, braced for some horrible scene.

"Did something happen here?" Detective Li asked.

"I haven't been home in almost a week. How would I know?" I shouldered past them and into the condo. The kitchen was a disaster, dishes and half-eaten takeout littered everywhere, but it was the mess beyond that which had gotten the officers' attention. The terrace door, where Logan had thrown my scotch on Sunday night, was still shattered. She hadn't even cleaned up the glass. It littered the terrace and dining room floor, glinting like a minefield. I still had my shoes on, though, and strode over the shards as I shouted for her, straining to keep the rage from leaking into my voice. I checked the bedroom first, the master bath and closet, then back downstairs to the workout room. She wasn't anywhere.

When I came back to the great room, the other officer was leaning over an area next to the balcony door, his hands gloved, a plastic bag in one hand. Detective Li straightened up and approached me.

"Are you saying you had no idea your house was in this state?"

"I've been at the tournament and the office."

"You haven't even been home to sleep?" He raised an eyebrow. Sidestepping the crouched officer, I opened the broken door to the terrace. "Logan?"

She wasn't outside and the ash from this morning, the firework debris, had been blown into unreadable patterns by the wind. I stood for a moment at the edge of the balcony, facing the mill ruins and breathing deep, trying to clear my mind. Where the hell was she?

"Mr. Abbott, can you explain this?"

Forcing my hands not to fist, my face to remain smooth, I turned. The kneeling officer held up the plastic bag, now filled with brown-stained shards. In front of him stretched the trail of Logan's blood from five days ago, when she'd walked barefoot across glass after threatening me against this exact railing.

I explained it. Not all of it. Not the entire fight word for word, but the more I said, the more I saw how it all looked through their eyes. The broken glass. The bloodstains.

"Where is your wife now?" they asked. They kept asking the same question with different words.

I didn't know. I had no idea where Logan was. Just like I had no idea where she'd hidden twenty million dollars. Or what she'd done to Corbett MacDermott. The hour was almost up. I had to get back to the stadium.

"She did this," I repeated over and over, but the truth sounded like a lie, even in my own ears.

NORA

As Nora confirmed the Nassau account had been emptied and closed, she watched Gregg's face drain of all color. The possibility that the money might be irretrievably gone obviously hadn't occurred to him until that moment. He was a salesman, perpetually focused on achieving the endgame, regardless of the odds or cost. Losing was never an option for a salesman.

For an accountant, though, losses were where things got interesting. Nora kept her expression impassive as she asked the Nassau bank to send her records of the outgoing transfers. She needed evidence of the routing information to track the money to the next account, the next shadowy island. As soon as she hung up she got a message from Mike.

Corbett awake. Wants to see you.

Good. She wanted to see him, too.

She fired off a quick reply and told Gregg

it was time to look at alternate scenarios to raise cash, but the co-owner of Strike had more problems at the moment than missing money. He rushed out of the stadium to look for Logan, leaving a wake of increasingly upset Strike employees murmuring to themselves.

"She's not at their house. I already went there and no one answered the buzzer."

"Has anyone seen her since the meeting yesterday when the police came?"

"She went down for a meet and greet, and then she posted that crazy revolution blog, I guess, but after that . . ."

Nora wove her way unnoticed around their fringes and slipped out of the room, knowing she was the only person capable of adding the last sighting, the final point on the Logan Russo timeline. It still burned in her mind, sparkler bright, with only the trees and the dying sun for witnesses. It hadn't been in a ring. No virtual or magnified reality. The end of her Logan fantasy had come differently than she'd expected, if one could assign expectations to these things. Two women had gone into the woods. One came out.

Henry had been waiting for her like a good son, hovering at the edge of their neighborhood with concern squeezing his face.

"Mom, where were you? We're going to miss the fireworks."

"I must have lost track of time."

He drew a breath, the next complaint already bubbling up his throat, then stopped when she reached him and lost the benefit of shadows. "You're all dirty. What happened?"

"I fell on one of the trails. I'm fine." Nora didn't glance down, didn't stop walking. If she paused to think about what happened in the woods, the tremors would take over and she doubted her power to make them stop. She moved past him and gestured — a wave to usher him back to the house and wipe away everything he'd seen and was seeing now. Explosions. She needed to fill his mind with fire and light. "You and Dad get ready. I'll meet you at the car in three minutes."

They'd made it in time, barely. Standing on the roof of the hospital, where the administration gave families and patients a privileged spot to absorb the spectacle of the Minneapolis Independence Day fireworks, Nora watched Henry ooh and aah alongside Corbett's children while soft serve cones leaked down their arms. He giggled with them, pointed at his favorites, and she could actually see all thought of his mother with the strange woman fading from his memory. No one would ask him about it. The only risk would be if he mentioned it in front of the wrong person, and that risk became more controlled by the minute. What were the dealings of adults, after all, next to fireworks and ice cream?

There were no treats when she arrived today in the now familiar waiting room, but Nora took care of that. Handing Henry a twenty-dollar bill, she sent him and Corbett's children off to the vending machines to plunder for sugar. Aaden Warsame's duffel bag sat open on the floor as they thundered past, unnoticed by anyone but her.

Her phone buzzed again and she saw an email from the Nassau bank with the record of nineteen million dollars leaving The Bahamas. Nora scanned the routing information and smiled; the money had been sent to Tortola in the British Virgin Islands on Monday — exactly as Logan had confessed in the woods last night. But testimony under duress from a now missing woman didn't exactly qualify as strong evidence. The email from the bank presented a cleaner story, connecting the dots, one island at a time.

Mike and Katie updated her on the news from the surgeon, who had assured them everything had gone as planned. They'd grafted a new section of bone to Corbett's right femur and repaired the rest of the leg with screws, pins, and rods.

"Leg surgery is a good sign," Nora nodded, her gaze still drifting to the duffel bag. "Like moving on to the statement of stockholder's equity. They've already covered the critical accounts."

Corbett's wife gave her a blank, sleep-starved look. Mike shook his head, almost imperceptibly, and then the nurse came out and told them Corbett was still awake, coherent, and asking for Nora.

Dozens of machines and monitors lined the hospital room, surrounding a single patient. At first Nora thought she'd been led to the wrong person because this man wasn't Corbett. This was a grotesque wreck of a human. A metal exoskeleton ran the length of the bed, seemingly holding the body together, and every piece of exposed skin flamed in garish color. Roiling purple. Meat red. One side of his face looked raw, like it had been flayed with a knife. Or skinned off on pavement. A cast covered his nose and both of his eyelids bulged shut like a frog's. It was only the sight of the patient's leg, in traction with fresh post-surgery sutures running down the blotched and bloated skin, that assured Nora she was in the right room.

"Ten minutes," the nurse said as she checked a few readings. A heart monitor blipped an unstable rhythm in the foreground. "And don't touch him."

"It's okay if she pours the whiskey straight into my mouth, though." Corbett's voice sounded disembodied. His eyes didn't open and his lips barely moved.

"Sweetie, I got you. Just say the word and I'll have the feeding tube put in," the nurse shot back without a hitch in her stride.

"Single malt."

"You know it." She passed by Nora on her way out, with a warning arch of eyebrow and a murmured "Nine and a half minutes."

The machines continued to bleep. Nora swallowed and went to the door, shutting it silently and turning the lock until it clicked. Then she approached the bed, weaving her way between the cords and metal, as invisible now as she had been at the stadium. The nurses' station was right outside the windows, but nobody saw her reach for Corbett's tube-laden hand. A weak pressure depressed her fingers as she slid them under his.

"Ellie."

She stared at the face, or what used to be a face, the one she'd made laugh over a pint, that had looked for her countless times from the end of a mahogany bar, that plowed obliviously through skyway crowds while she submissively darted and dodged. The same face that had the audacity to judge her life choices last week even as he'd pushed her to take the Strike case. He'd known the exact depth of this snake hole, and he'd convinced her to enter it anyway. Everything she'd known about Corbett had changed, to the point where she might not recognize him even if he stood before her healthy and whole. Then she wondered — if he knew what she had done in the last few days — whether he would recognize her, either.

Deliberately, she tapped down the row of his exposed knuckles — the only part of him that still seemed flesh-colored — with the index finger of her free hand, whispering as she went. A chant, a nursery rhyme only he knew the ending to.

"From Magers Construction to the online account."

"From the online account to Nassau."

"From Nassau to Tortola."

Light taps, skipping a stone over the

water, twenty million stones crisscrossing a sea.

"From Tortola to . . ."

She hovered above the last knuckle, waiting. Even Logan hadn't known the final destination of the stolen money, but her story in the woods had started in a familiar place.

She'd met Corbett when Nora had brought him to the trial "bring-a-friend-for-free" class. She'd picked on him that day, calling him Ben Affleck from the movie *The Accountant* and Nora had thought that was the end of it, but she didn't know the two of them had spoken again after class. While Corbett was waiting for Nora in the lobby, he and Logan began chatting. Logan asked if he really set up tax shelters and protected his clients from evil corporate assassins. He'd laughed and handed her a business card, telling her to call him if she ever needed any accounting or bodyguard services.

To Corbett's surprise, Logan did.

"She took me to some crap apartment in Northeast and showed me an email she'd found in her sent files." Corbett's voice barely carried over the noise of the machines. "She said she'd never written it. The other person on the email couldn't confirm or deny anything because —"

"They were dead."

Corbett nodded once, a small jerk of his bandaged head. "Then she showed me a deposit confirmation. Said her husband must have done it. He was the only one who had the access. He was framing her for embezzlement."

"She alleged." It was the second time Nora had heard this story in the last twenty-four hours. "Did she have proof?"

Corbett shook his head. "I told her to hire us outright and get a lawyer, that we could try to uncover how Gregg had framed her, but she refused. Said she wanted to beat him at his own game. She handed me a duffel bag full of cash. No strings. No records. I knew it was wrong, but Katie wants all these vacations and the kids have one bloody camp after another . . . so I took the money. I set up some bank accounts and called it done. I didn't expect to ever see her again."

"That's why you were so quiet when Gregg Abbott accused his wife of stealing twenty million dollars," Nora said. "Because you helped her steal it."

The heart monitor blipped faster. Too fast. She made a shushing noise and circled his palm, calming the witness to extract his testimony.

"When we went to our last happy hour, you made sure I was the one who took this assignment. Why, Corbett? Did you think I wasn't good enough to figure out what you did? Or did you assume I would be more willing to excuse you?"

"No. Ellie. That's not . . ." His hand convulsed on hers and his eyes flew open, but they didn't seem able to focus on anything. She shushed him again, made soothing sounds to bring his heart rate down. She couldn't have the nurses coming back, not yet.

He swallowed again and the pain of even that simple action was audible. "I thought I could get her to return it. That she would listen to reason."

"But she didn't, so you moved the money again. It's not in The Bahamas. It's not in Tortola. You moved it to another account where no one could find it."

"I told her we had to come clean and tell you everything. That I wouldn't give her the account until she agreed." He made a noise that sounded like a half laugh, half groan. "She landed the punch before I ever saw it coming. She knocked me on my ass, demanding the money, and I ran. I ran right into the street and the car. My own goddamn fault. I'm sorry, Ellie. Ellie?" He blinked one eye open, which was flooded red and clouded with drugs. The other seemed sealed shut. It puffed and trembled, filling with liquid. He struggled to locate her.

One minute left. The seconds ticked down. A tear leaked out of his open eye and wound a path down the raw flesh of his cheek. She felt an answering well in her own eyes.

"You know, I realized something this week; you were right. I never let Sam White go. I never stopped blaming myself. That's why I talked Mike into the open marriage and why I keep Henry at a distance. I thought if no one got too close, I could bear it when they left.

"But I put up all those walls for nothing. You saw right through them and became my friend anyway. And Logan — she was everything I wished I could be. Strong. Warm. Whole. When I saw you two together that night, I was furious. You'd both drawn me in, you'd made me care despite all my efforts not to, and then you left me behind. So irrational." She traced the underside of his palm. "I guess love always is."

A noise jerked her head up. The nurse stood outside the door, shaking the handle.

She mouthed an order through the window and pointed down. Nora turned away and the noise grew louder, then a hand slapped the glass.

"I'm done, Corbett. I'm done putting up walls. I'm done hiding behind my job. I'm not letting anyone cast me aside and make me believe I deserve it." There was a clamor outside the room, a rise of angry voices. "Where's the bank?"

He told her, breathing numbers as she tapped the last knuckle on his hand. A key was jammed into the lock and the door flew open, followed by the nurse and a security guard.

As they pulled her away, he said, "One of them's lying, Ellie. Find the truth. You're the only one who can."

GREGG

I'd wanted her gone for so many months, had fantasized about it, dreamed of a world that didn't revolve around Logan, a world where I could meet a normal, competent professional like Nora Trier and have the right to ask her out to dinner. And the company. There were so many things Strike could do, so many channels where we could expand. We had the tournament publicity, the vStrike experience, the new gyms, so much opportunity on our horizon. The thought of removing Logan Russo from my life was powerful, liberating, orgasmic.

It was one day too early.

Detective Li and his partner searched the entire penthouse, every closet and drawer, with my permission, while I texted everyone at the stadium variations of what my sleep-starved brain was screaming. *Pivot. Pivot.*

"Normally we don't file missing persons reports on adults until seventy-two hours have passed," the detective interrupted my furious messaging, "unless we receive evidence to indicate the person is in imminent danger."

She was in imminent danger. From me.

"We're talking about the woman who once fractured an opponent's collarbone and then complained when the fight was called early."

The detective nodded, surveying the great room that showed zero evidence of a happy marriage. No pictures. No dents in the couch cushions showing customary sitting places. Just a set of boxing gloves tossed on the coffee table and a trail of blood droplets along the floor. He asked me to recount the last time I'd seen my wife, and seemed incredulous that I hadn't physically laid eyes on her since he'd interviewed us together at the stadium yesterday.

I pulled up social media and followed the #LoganRusso and #MillCityMiracle pictures across platforms: Logan, posing with a half dozen bubbling millennials at one o'clock. Logan, leaning into an Arnold press with three meatheads wearing wife beaters twenty minutes later. I took him through a cascade of her Strike Down exhibition selfies until late yesterday afternoon, when she disappeared, and how I'd monitored tournament coverage all night from my office couch.

"Did anyone see you there?"

"No."

"Why didn't you go home last night?"

"I haven't been home all week." The truth, again, was clearly the wrong thing to say.

"Have you had some sort of disagreement with your wife? Business problems? Personal?"

All of the above.

"My time has been consumed by Strike Down. A lot depends on the outcome of this week." My watch buzzed and I checked it. Sara. Still no sign of Logan at the tournament.

"You don't seem worried about your wife's whereabouts, Mr. Abbott."

"Logan's not missing, not like that."

"Then where is she?"

She's rolling in a pile of money somewhere, laughing her ass off.

I made a snap decision. If things progressed the way they were going, I'd have to involve the authorities at some point. It wasn't the time and place I would choose, but you can't always control these things. "We've had some . . . theft . . . at the company. This is highly confidential. I can't have it leaking onto any social media. But they — the accountants we've hired to find the stolen money — they've tracked it to Logan."

The interview took a sharp turn after that. I explained the events of the last week, Nora's findings, the diverted refunds and empty accounts, while Detective Li and his partner exchanged increasingly meaningful glances.

"So, you believe your wife stole twenty million dollars from her own company —"

"Our company."

"— jeopardizing this tournament of yours and then just took off into the sunset?"

Pivot. "She's punishing me. It's about me, not the company."

He asked why and I told him "marital problems." I wasn't bringing Aaden Warsame into this conversation.

Detective Li picked up the evidence bag lying on the counter, the blood-crusted shards of glass.

"Where are you planning to be tonight, Mr. Abbott?"

"At the tournament, obviously. I should have been there twenty minutes ago." To clean up Logan's messes, for — I hoped to God — the last time.

"Contact us if you hear from your wife" — he handed me a card — "and I'm going

363

to ask you to stick around the city until this matter is resolved."

I raced back through the Mill District and arrived in time to see the lights dim and hear the cheers rip through the crowd. Logan was supposed to be onstage with the emcee, who instead took the mic alone and moved through opening announcements, doing his best to work the crowd into a fever pitch.

Poor Sara was losing her mind. While the police had been questioning me and poring through my home, she'd seized upon every Strike employee in her path and grilled them about Logan's whereabouts, leaving hysteria in her wake. By the time I arrived and reined her in, the damage was already done. I was met with questions and stricken faces, trainers who dogged me through the concession and vStrike crowds to recount in mind-numbing detail the last moment they'd spotted Logan.

"It's fine. Don't worry." I methodically soothed and dismissed. "She wanted to hand off the company anyway, remember? We're just getting a little preview. We'll get through this."

But I didn't know how. None of us did. As the emcee handed things over to the commentators and people flooded the rings, preparing their fighters for the bell, suspicions began landing like dark uppercuts to my gut. I'd wondered why she'd been so visible this week, why she'd planted herself in front of every camera and phone, given a hundred interviews and hugged a thousand fans. Her giant presence chiseled a place into this tournament we couldn't fill without her, and then it wasn't enough for her to disappear quietly with twenty million dollars. She'd called the authorities to broadcast her absence. It had to be deliberate. Nothing about Logan happened by chance. She'd never intended to talk to them, to give any information about Aaden or Corbett MacDermott; she'd wanted them to discover she was missing, and incriminate me.

She'd taken the prize. She'd taken the whole goddamn show. She held all the cards and, wherever she was at this moment, she knew it.

The lack of sleep, the frustration and fury threatened to undo me, and I latched on to the one positive voice in my head, the whisper that propelled me through every back-patting, bolstering conversation. Merritt.

I hadn't known if I could convince Logan

to pick Merritt Osborne as the next face of Strike. Aaden's death, rather than clearing Logan's tunnel vision, had shut her down completely. Whenever I'd tried to bring Merritt into the conversation, she'd refused to respond. On my last attempt she'd just lifted a single eyebrow and said, "A silver fucking medalist?"

As though being the second best in the world was shameful.

But now, if Logan was gone . . . the thought suspended, unfinished. I didn't know how to navigate this night, how to spin what we were going to have to spin, but maybe there was hope. Nora mentioned raising capital. She would get us through this, patch the twenty-million-dollar hole, while Merritt smiled and waved from out front. There *was* a path forward, there had to be. After the Washburn Mill exploded, killing everyone inside, the owners rebuilt without hesitation. They won awards, launched Gold Mill Flour, and orchestrated a series of mergers to become General Mills, an empire worth more than seven billion. Strike would thrive, too. We were a phoenix waiting to be born from the ashes.

The fights began, and the blood started to flow. The fighters — scenting millions in the air, the promise of those giant, cardboard checks — assaulted each other with everything they had. The combos blurred together, each punch and kick more punishing than the last. They went for ribs and jaws, they attacked the soft flesh of stomachs and breasts, they beat each other into the ropes. Noses broke, spraying the mats with blood, which was replayed on the jumbotron to a deafening soundtrack of yells and groans. Medics waited on the sidelines, stretchers and ambulances at the ready, but no one was throwing this fight. They staggered and weaved, coming back with hooks and roundhouses on flesh turning to pulp, giving it all for the stakes of their lives.

Booming commentary filled the stadium. The crowd turned thunderous. They shouted with every slow-motion hit on the giant screens, where the continuous Twitter feeds scrolled through reactions, pictures, and excitement. A hashtag began emerging, though, filtering through the noise.

"Haven't seen the queen??!! #StrikeDown #WheresLogan"

"Umm . . . looking for the original face of Strike."

"I drove from #Utah for this and I need me some #LoganRusso!!!"

"Waiting for the Mill City Miracle up in here!! Where is she????"

The #WheresLogan hashtag started trending, taking over. Signs popped up across the sections and pictures of the shadow figure behind the Strike glove were posting everywhere. C.J. had the PR team begin monitoring the feed, weeding out as many mentions of Logan as they could and replacing them with round updates. Their fingers flew, trying desperately to influence the content, but the demands for Logan would not be drowned out.

Three hours later, Merritt's fight with the Brazilian was due to begin in the center ring and she appeared on the floor with her intricate braids now shimmering in a full spectrum of red, white, and blue, drawing cheers and fist pumps as she waved into the flashing lights.

The shirt under my jacket was soaked in a cold sweat. I made myself breathe. "How are we going to spin this?"

"Spin? Gregg, where is she? We don't have a contingency plan for Logan Russo vanishing into thin air." C.J. was furiously texting, following me to the press box where a dozen sports reporters expected to interview Logan about her anticipated pick for the next face of Strike.

"We'll make a contingency plan. I am not letting her fucking win."

I felt C.J. looking at me, but she said nothing. She understood. She had to. Logan was sabotaging her company, too. She didn't say another word until we got to the box, and then affixed a smile on her face, greeting every reporter by name and deflecting the barrage of questions about Logan. Just before we sat down, I got a call from Detective Li.

"We've received some new information."

"Where is she?" I spoke through a clenched jaw, nodding at no one through the forest of ESPN cameras.

"We put out an APB on her plates and got a hit right away. Local officers identified her car abandoned in a suburban parking lot. Lebanon Hills Regional Park."

"Where?" Turning as casually as I could away from the reporters, each of whom seemed to have grown six extra ears, I paced to an empty corner of the room.

"Do you know the area?" he asked.

I was more familiar with Beirut. "I have no idea where that is. Is she there? Did you find her?"

"No. It's almost two thousand wooded acres. We've got people canvassing the trails, but we're losing the sun. Do you have any idea what your wife would be doing in Eagan?"

369

The name was vaguely familiar, part of the ring of nondescript suburbs where they housed cheap twenty-four-hour gyms in strip malls. He asked me a few more things, routine questions that seemed anything but routine as I struggled to place Logan in an obscure, wooded park. Had she decided to bury the money? Burn it?

After the call, C.J. and I went through the motions with the press. Logan was indisposed. *Pivot.* She was incredibly grateful to every fan and fighter, and wished she could be here tonight to make the announcement about the next face of Strike. Unfortunately, I would have to do it in her place. *Pivot.* No, the police presence was totally normal. After the terrible hit-and-run accident, we wanted everyone to enjoy the tournament safely. No, we didn't have any more details on the accident. No, Logan was unfortunately not available to make any comment.

Covering for my wife, again, and how was it possible within the physical laws of the universe that she'd become more onerous when she was gone? This wasn't how I'd envisioned a Logan-free Strike. C.J. backed me up where she could, taking my prompts and adding her own flourish, but the more we said, the more they wanted to know. I was actually relieved when the announcer boomed overhead.

"Ooh, that was brutal! That landed hard. Head hook, followed by a roundhouse to the head and she's down. She's on the mat, ladies and gentlemen, and she is not getting up!"

Each word became louder and more intense. Abandoning the press conference table, the reporters rushed to the edge of the balcony with C.J. hot on their heels. I took longer, breathing deep, trying to compose the next ten minutes. Then the ten after that. Logan was not going to break this company. A new face. A new life. The rebirth would begin tonight.

"Medics are in the ring."

By the time I reached the balcony, a crowd of people blocked any view of the prone fighter. The Brazilian paced the opposite side of the ring, waving off the coaches and trainers who hovered at the ropes. "Let's watch that replay while they make sure Osborne is okay."

Osborne.

My eyes snapped to the jumbotron, where a slow-motion pan showed the Brazilian's glove sneaking over Merritt's guard and slamming into her skull. She ducked away, straight into a kick coming from the opposite side. A trail of blood shot from her mouth. Her eyes bulged and rolled before she went down, dropping like dead weight to the ground.

Looking like — Logan's voice taunted in my head — a silver fucking medalist.

NORA

One of the first things Jim Parrish had taught her, after he'd recruited Nora outside the courthouse all those years ago, was that a good investigator was unpredictable. They exploited overlooked data, showed up at unexpected times, changed focus quickly. They created no patterns, worked to no discernible rhythm. In certain cases, a good investigator could look, to the untrained eye, like a very bad investigator.

Nora had walked into this investigation assuming she could handle it like any other case, looking for the intersection of opportunity, pressure, and rationalization. She'd been thorough, resourceful, charting every possible outlet for Strike's hemorrhaged millions, but she hadn't been unpredictable, not where it mattered. Someone had laid out a path long before she ever accepted this engagement, and she'd followed it like a perfectly trained retriever. She'd been the bad investigator who appeared to be good.

Gregg Abbott had accused his wife of stealing twenty million dollars. Logan Russo said her husband was framing her. One of them was lying. Maybe they both were. In order to figure out who, Nora would have to conduct the interview of her life.

The security guard didn't stop at the entrance to the ICU ward after he dragged Nora out of Corbett's hospital room, but she was too busy typing the account number into her phone to struggle.

"Nora?" Mike sprung out of his chair as the guard hauled her straight through the waiting room and into the corridor. The kids, thankfully, were still at the vending machines. Mike chased them down the hall, making every head turn as he shouted, "What are you doing? That's my wife."

"Your wife endangered a critically ill patient. She's leaving the premises now and if she tries to come back," the guard's grip on her forearm tightened, "we'll have the police give her a free tour of a jail cell."

"No, there's some mistake. Nora would never — she —"

Nora saved the account information and turned to look over her shoulder. Mike's shirt was the same one he'd worn to the fireworks yesterday, stained with ice cream and puffed over his belly. His beard had grown even thicker after days of neglect.

"It's fine," she shook her head.

"But this is crazy."

The crazy part was that her husband had no idea what she was capable of. She'd never let him close enough to see.

"I'm sorry, Mike, for everything. You deserve so much better." She shook the guard off long enough to pull Mike into an embrace. He stiffened, surprised by her hug, and she felt another wave of guilt for what she hadn't been to him. The guard pulled them apart and dragged her into the elevator.

"Stay with Henry. I'll explain later."

The door closed as Mike shifted from foot to foot, mouth gaping, and before she knew it, the guard was depositing her at the curb. "I hope you got what you came for."

"And then some."

Ignoring the texts now flooding in from both Mike and Katie, Nora looked up the name of the bank where Corbett had confessed to hiding the money and dialed the number.

"Hi, this is Logan Russo." A man walking into the hospital did a double take, and Nora winked at him. "I'd like to check my balance."

She rattled off the information requested. Account number and personal data, not even blinking at how readily she had the details at hand. Of course she knew Logan's birthdate, her address, the last four digits of her social. It took less than a minute. Sixty seconds to confirm nineteen million dollars were safe in Nevis. The last dot on the map, the end of the chase, but it wasn't over yet.

Nora turned to the stadium rising above the cityscape, where the tournament lights flashed against the transparent ceiling. The championships were almost done, but there was still time for one last interview.

By the time she flashed her temporary Strike badge to the security guards posted at the gates, the fights seemed to be over, except no one was leaving. It only took a few inquiries to learn Merritt Osborne had been injured in the final match. Dead, one vendor said. No, just knocked out, corrected another. The champions milled around the rings, surrounded by cameras and coaches, waiting for the big announcement Logan wouldn't be making.

She found Merritt on a stretcher in the locker room, being prepped for removal to an ambulance. Tears leaked down the corners of her eyes into the brace holding her neck and head in alignment, while her entourage hovered uselessly nearby.

"I'm so sorry," she kept repeating. "I let you down. I'm so sorry."

Gregg, standing just outside the ring of EMTs, mumbled a reply and lifted a hand, where it hovered stiffly in the air before dropping back to his side. He didn't seem to know what to do. Nora spotted the Marketing Director at the fringes of the group, fixated on her phone, and moved over to her.

"Is it serious?"

C.J. shrugged, not looking up as she continued to type. "Concussion. Maybe some internal bleeding."

"That's too bad. Gregg wanted her, didn't he?"

"He thought Merritt would represent empowerment and energy, the next phase of Strike." C.J. retracted the phone and frowned at the stretcher being wheeled out to the ambulance.

Nora shook her head. "Why did he think Logan would have picked her?"

"You want to know the secret?" C.J. glanced over. "It never mattered who she picked. White, black, trans female, cis male. She gave so much prestige to this brand we could turn a pebble into a star. Aaden would have been fine — a great immigrant story — we just would've had to shift away from our female-centric message. Broaden the base. Gregg never liked him, but between you and me it's too bad he's not in the running."

"Too bad he's dead, you mean."

She made a noise of agreement, her attention pulled back to the magnet of the phone. "Now Merritt's out, Logan is missing, there's no money, and who the fuck knows what's going to happen next. I should've started working on my résumé as soon as he turned down the vStrike offer."

"Excuse me?"

"You could've found five billion in those virtual-reality simulators. Everyone was pushing Gregg to go commercial and enter the gaming market. Twenty million would have been a joke. But he refused. He was obsessed with finishing all the new clubs. Then it was all about filling the seats, practically giving them away just so we could say we'd sold out. And now look where we are."

"Five billion?"

"That was the initial offer from the gaming company. We could've negotiated up. Way up. But Gregg said the timing wasn't right. He wanted to debut vStrike at the tournament first."

"Why?"

C.J. shrugged.

Gregg had turned down a multibillion-dollar sale? They'd already sunk all the research and development costs for vStrike. That five billion would have been pure profit. What was he playing at?

With Merritt, her entourage, and the medics gone, Gregg stood alone in the middle of the room. She took a step forward, intent on getting him alone, but C.J. cut in front of her — "nope, save it" — and pulled Gregg back to the stadium floor.

Nora shadowed them, listening as C.J. listed attributes — the Brazilian champion's flair, the Japanese champion's intensity, as well as fan picks and pans over the course of the week. Her synopses were quick and calculated, riding underneath the noise of the crowd, but Nora still heard the echo of their previous conversation. Five billion turned away. Could the next face of Strike be more important than that? She followed them all the way to the stage, where the emcee was awarding giant checks to the champions and the screen flashed the third place, second place, and winner's names. Five figures. Six figures. That cardboard was going to bounce.

A heartbeat shy of the spotlights, Gregg

stopped, realizing she was behind him.

"Have you found it?" She saw more than heard the words. The money. He wanted to know if she'd traced it.

She shook her head. No.

He cursed, barely a movement of lips, and shifted bloodshot eyes toward the sea of champions, all of them toweled off and bandaged, some limping but without braces or wraps. They flaunted their injuries, held them as proudly as the fake checks in their hands. Their eyes glistened in the spotlights, anticipating the announcement they expected to follow the money. The ultimate prize.

What would Gregg have wanted from Logan in this moment? A wife who would support him. Silently, Nora moved to his side. Their hands brushed and turned toward each other at the same time, clasping in the darkness at the edge of the light, a world apart from the spectacle onstage. His palm was moist. Sweat beaded on his forehead. The emcee looked up at the screens and C.J.'s amplified voice filled the stadium.

Twenty years ago, there was a fighter who won every title, defeated every challenger. She redefined her sport for a generation of athletes to follow.

A montage of clips showed Logan in the ring, pummeling opponents, sending them to the mat like jump-cut dominoes. Next to her, Gregg wasn't watching the screen. He still scanned the champions, looking through the faces for one he couldn't seem to find. C.J. muttered in his other ear while her prerecorded, magnified voice carried through the driving music of the montage.

The world wanted her strength. They craved her vision. And so Strike was born.

Flash to a ribbon cutting, Logan and Gregg side by side yet somehow Logan was the only one in focus. Then fighters lined up in a room full of body bags, the Minneapolis club, the first place Nora had ever seen Logan in the flesh. Roundhouses, bags flying, Logan's head thrown back, white teeth against her dark mouth, silent laughter in close-up.

It was oddly exhilarating to watch Logan's image fill this entire stadium, and be the only one who knew why she was gone. The grip on Nora's hand tightened. She looked at Gregg's profile, the desperation suffocating his features as he shook his head at whatever C.J. was suggesting. She'd done that, too.

She's trained tens of thousands of fighters, and challenged millions across the world to step into the ring.

"Logan is missing." He still faced forward, but Nora knew he was talking to her now and his grip became almost viselike. "The police think I did something to her. They found her car."

"Have they searched the park?" It was out before she knew she'd said it aloud.

"Yes, but it's too dark now to —" He broke off.

Like every legend, she created a legacy greater than herself, to inspire and fuel generations to come.

Staring blindly ahead, Nora retracted her hand. She stepped back, and bumped into someone behind her. Apologizing, she sidestepped them and refused to make eye contact with Gregg, who was reaching out to stop her. He was blocked, though, by C.J. pulling on his arm, trying to get him to move to the podium where the emcee waved them over. Nora's heart pounded, her breath sped up. Then Logan's voice boomed into the stadium, and the roar from every section and every aisle made Nora's hair stand on end.

"Strike doesn't live inside a building or a package. It can't die in the street or a locker room." Gregg froze, and Nora startled at the choice of words. Even C.J. seemed momentarily surprised. "It will live beyond me. It will live beyond you. We may die here today, but the fight inside of us lives on. It lives in every child learning to defend themselves, every woman knocking some shitcan on his ass, every time someone discovers the fire in their fists."

We may die here today. Nora's own fists curled as she turned, ran down the stage stairs, and disappeared into the crowd.

"Strike will endure."

As the film ended a chant rose from the seats, insistent and guttural. It drowned out the emcee. Nora made it to the edge of the floor just as she heard C.J.'s voice speaking over the crowd. She was too busy working her way through the press of suddenly still bodies and half-lowered phones to follow everything being said until she realized the chant had washed out of the stadium like a tide and two words distinguished themselves from the rest.

Nora Trier.

She looked up and saw her own face on the jumbotron. They were hunting for her.

GREGG

During the promo film, C.J. kept muttering the advantages and disadvantages of picking each champion through a brilliant lock-jawed smile. The words rolled like scattered coins in all directions. Hopeful. Symbolic. Raw. Young. I didn't try to chase them down, or assign any of them to the fleet of fighters standing on the opposite side of the stage, worthless checks in hand. Merritt was bleeding in a goddamn ambulance and none of the people left standing could fill the magnitude of Logan's void. None of them shone bright enough to blind this whipped-up, fight-fueled crowd. Every choice was the wrong choice.

My vision was blurring, my head pounding. The only thing anchoring me at that moment was Nora's hand, the firm pressure of hope or at least sanity. I heard myself telling her about the police, pathetic, like a child asking his mother to make it better, but I'd hardly gotten two sentences out before I heard her sharp inhale.

"Have they searched the park?"

Then her hand was gone. She backed into the crowd, eyes wide and instantly averted, a woman who knew she'd said something wrong. The body language was unmistakable. How the hell did Nora know about the park?

I tried to follow her. I needed to hold her in place until my head could process what her body was communicating, but C.J. pulled me in the opposite direction and Nora slipped away. When Logan's voice surrounded us, the crowd screamed. She talked about dying in a locker room and blood-splatter flashed through my head, but it wasn't Logan's blood. Logan was in a park in Eagan where — I finally made the connection — Nora lived. She'd told me the other day when we walked across the Stone Arch Bridge. *I'm married to a cook. I'm a mother. We live in Eagan.*

I caught a glimpse of Nora's hair as she ducked around a group of people and descended the stairs from the stage. My hand was still warm from her grip.

"Tell them Logan's missing."

"What?" C.J. hissed through a seething caricature of a smile. "Are you fucking kidding me? The internet will explode. Some of these people traveled thousands of —"

"We can't pick a new face for Strike until we find out what happened to Logan."

"What . . . happened . . . ?"

As she struggled to make sense of what I was saying, I took her phone out and pulled up Nora's picture from the partner page of Parrish Forensics. "This is a person of interest. Put it on every screen. Now."

C.J. gaped at the phone and swiveled to look behind us. "She was just here. Where did she go? Gregg, what happened to Logan?"

The film ended and as the emcee took the microphone, a low chant started and spread in every direction. *Logan.* It gained volume and rhythm until I couldn't even hear the emcee, who stood inches away from me. *Logan, Logan.*

I shouted directly into C.J.'s ear. "We want an army out there looking for her. Tell them to search parks and suburbs, to turn over every rock, but most importantly, we need to find Nora Trier. Understand?"

"Gregg —"

But I'd already left the stage, walking purposefully down the stairs. I couldn't see Nora, but it didn't matter. I didn't need to run. She might think she was invisible, that a quiet, dark-suited accountant could do something horrifying and slip away unnoticed, but she couldn't hide from fifty thousand of us. I strode in the direction she'd gone, pushing through the groups swarming the aisles, feeling calmer than I had in months.

I know you don't understand. At least at first you don't, but give yourself a minute and forget about me. Who the hell am I anyway? Just another suit, another strange creature speaking a strange language. I want you to consider your life for a moment and the things or people who mean the most to you. You can see them, hovering around you, everything bright and good. Everything you would fight for. Maybe you feel yourself drawn more strongly toward one of them. A grandson. A lover you met in an airport, perhaps. Maybe even a company you dreamed and hustled to life. It's okay. You don't have to explain yourself to me. There's no logic to what we love, to the things that pull at our deepest core. You would die for all of these things, of course, but say you were standing in a flour mill and there was an explosion, an instant rending of death from life. Your fast muscle twitch would take over and throw your incinerating body over that one person, that dearest, most precious thing. It's worth a hundred of you, and the thought finds you in the shadows of every day, both sustaining and destroying you. And it will all be worth it, every sacrifice, every piece of you scorched away, as long as you can see them succeed. You will give everything, and you'll do it with the fire of that explosion in your gut, telling you that you're running out of time, that your chances to feed this great and beautiful thing are numbered, and you don't know how many moments are left for it to be yours.

Strike was that thing for me. My true love. My only child. Two minutes ago I didn't know how many moments I had left with Strike. But now, without even realizing it, Nora had helped me save the one thing that mattered most.

I'd known Nora Trier was special without understanding exactly why. I'd been drawn to her again and again, fumbling with my adolescent gestures, my idiotic advances, but now I saw the truth and it was so much more than I could have hoped for or imagined. She hadn't found the money; she'd found the match to light Logan Russo on fire.

C.J.'s announcement stopped the crowd in midchant.

"Logan is missing."

I passed the concessions, where everyone had fallen silent and vendors froze midtransaction with credit cards dangling forgotten in the air. C.J. outlined the situation quickly, with absolute gravity and poise, and then posted Nora's picture on every TV and jumbotron in the arena, setting the entire stadium into unrest. *Logan. Missing. Person of interest.* Everyone on the concourse began coming back to life, but with purpose now. They started to talk and text, heads craning in every direction.

The rumble grew louder, the kindling catching fire, carrying heat past my body and far into the night. Minneapolis would feel it. The country would feel it. If Logan was dead, Strike would burn in the hearts of the world forever.

When the second-floor exit came into view, I saw a familiar form moving past the security guards. Jesus, she'd gotten through. Was I the only person on the planet who could see this woman? By the time I reached the exit she was halfway down the skyway, rushing toward downtown, and when she saw me behind her, she broke into a sprint.

But she couldn't outrun the explosion.

NORA

She flew through the skyway, throwing her entire body against closed doors and sprinting through open ones fast enough to feel wind against her face. She passed a skeletal looking janitor and two beggars, neither of them Rose, her homeless romantic who'd cackled when she walked through these bridges with Gregg Abbott a week ago. Rose had wanted Nora to take her heart out of her briefcase. If only the older woman could see her now. She lost a shoe at one point and kicked the other one away as she raced over the top of 2nd Avenue, leaving them strewn like breadcrumbs.

It wasn't how she'd planned to conduct the interview, but she didn't have time to deal with the police and an entire city of rabid fans. She needed him alone. She needed him to think he'd won.

Stopping to get her breath at one point, in the middle of a bridge, Nora pressed a hand to her chest and squeezed the Strike badge against her racing heart. She looked through the windows, over the dark street, and saw — in the skyway one block down — Gregg Abbott staring back across the night. He smiled, and she felt something crawl inside her. She started running again and he moved in the same direction. Come and get me.

Passing the turn to the Parrish offices, the route she and Corbett had walked a thousand times, she raced over another street and into the building that housed Strike. Panting now, she used the guest badge that Gregg's assistant had promised would allow access at any hour. The pad buzzed and lit green, but the clearance made her pause. She looked from the security light to the plastic card inside the lanyard; it felt like a piece of vital knowledge hovered just beyond her reach. She could almost taste it. Checking the corridor as she stepped inside, expecting Gregg to burst around the corner at any moment, she closed the door firmly and slipped into the gym.

Safety lights were on in one corner, casting a hollow white glow across the room. The gym was still set up for the VIP party, with two narrow columns of body bags down the sides of the room and the red carpet stretching from the door to the shadowy ring. She heard a noise and automatically glanced toward the floor-to-ceiling windows, but they'd been shuttered, closing out the city beyond.

She crossed to the women's locker room and paused before turning to the men's side instead. Feeling along the wall in total blackness, she found a switch and flipped it, which turned on the pendant lights above the sinks. The showers were dark and empty, their frosted doors closed. The hair on the back of Nora's neck stood up as she moved to the granite bench that ran the length of the room. She hadn't been here since Logan had brought her in to fix her makeup, but she'd been distracted then. She hadn't been able to think clearly, not with Logan clouding the scene, her grief close enough to inhale.

The crime scene photos had been shot from multiple angles — above, on either side, and underneath the bench itself, the camera probably millimeters from the blood congealing underneath the body. The gun was lying next to him, his phone nearby, and his wallet with the Nassau account number tucked in his pocket. But something had been missing. How had no one seen it?

A click sounded in the near distance, making her jump. It could have been the A/C system, or the plumbing, or a door. Nora swiveled to the doorway that connected the gym to the headquarters side of the Strike space, the passageway through which Logan had led her to Aaden's untouched cubicle. The police report indicated that, on the night of his death, no one else had badged in besides Aaden Warsame.

She felt the adrenaline surge before she'd even finished the thought. Racing across the room, she used her own badge to push through into the administrative offices. Dark. Empty. She turned lights on as she ran through the lounge and into the area of cubicles reserved for trainers, the ones she'd instructed her staff not to spend much time in because they didn't fit the fraud profile. The key to the puzzle had been right in front of her, and it had been an actual key. She'd looked right at it.

It took seconds to reach Aaden's workstation, but when she got there, she stopped short. The paperwork littering his desk from earlier in the week had all been cleaned up. The magazines, the weights — disappeared. And the badge, the badge that had been hanging over his dark and dusty computer monitor, was gone. She stepped forward and saw the faintest outline of a rectangle in the dust on the screen. Inadmissible. Proof of nothing. But she'd seen it. It had been here, in the tomb of Aaden's office. She pulled open drawers, checked folders, and felt along the bottom of every compartment. All she found was a box cutter, which she gripped with enough force to wring out a security badge if there had been one hiding inside. Exhaling in frustration, she pocketed the tool and turned around.

Gregg Abbott stood directly behind her, smiling. Nora screamed.

He held up a hand and took a step back, but not far enough to allow her to exit.

"I didn't mean to frighten you, Nora."

"Evidence to the contrary." Fight or flight. While both impulses surged strong, she forced herself to breathe calmly. She smoothed a hand down her lapel, subconsciously moving into fighter's stance. The emergency exit at the end of the corridor was thirty paces away, twenty if she sprinted, but she'd wanted this interview. It could be her last.

"You shouldn't have left the stadium like that. It makes it look like you don't want to cooperate."

"Who cleaned up Aaden's cube? I thought Logan didn't want it touched."

He leaned against the edge of the doorway,

394

like a coworker who'd stopped to chat. "Unless there's a reason you don't want to talk to the police."

"Did Sara do it? Did you tell her to?"

"What did you do to her, Nora? It's okay. I'll understand. No one could understand better than me." His voice was casual, interested. They could be gossiping over smoothies.

Nora shifted. If she wanted to talk about Aaden, she'd have to begin with Logan. "She surprised me in the woods. I didn't go there expecting to confront her."

Gregg nodded, leaning in a fraction, and Nora's entire body tensed. "You didn't plan it."

"No."

"Sometimes these things just happen. All you can do is pivot, and find a way to keep moving forward. For the business."

"You think I killed Logan."

"I have no idea what to think anymore. I'll be honest, Nora, I always had trouble reading you. The consummate professional. You weren't the type I usually had to deal with when it came to Logan's fans, but I guess Celebrity Worship Syndrome can happen to the best of us."

"I didn't worship Logan."

"You felt disconnected. You felt unseen,

invisible. When Logan came into your life, you saw all the things you longed to be. Being near her made you feel alive." His eyes were shining in a way that made Nora want to reach out and shudder at the same time. They pleaded, and they bulged.

Nora backed up as far as possible, until her legs hit the desk. "Which one of us are you talking about right now?"

"What did you do to her in those woods?"

Nora didn't reply.

"Just give me a hint. Is she above ground or below?"

She swallowed. "I'll tell you if you answer a question of mine."

He relaxed again, smiling, which she took for agreement.

"One thing that bothered me was how blatant the scheme was. Twenty million in six months? Someone was going to notice. Even a shitty accountant like Darryl would have caught on sooner or later. The whole thing seemed . . . novice."

"Logan didn't get any degrees in finance. And neither did Aaden."

"Then there's the phrase, 'Please note,' as in 'Please note the new instructions for all future payments and refunds to be processed to Strike Inc.' " She moved her hands as naturally as possible to brace against the edge of the desk. "That phrase appears three hundred and eighty-four times in your correspondence over the last two years. It appears zero times in Logan's profile and only once in Aaden Warsame's. Do you want to guess which email?"

"Please note, Nora, that means nothing." His voice was even but his jaw tightened and he pushed away from the edge of the cubicle.

"It was too obvious. You didn't need an elite forensic accounting firm to find this money. You could've found it yourself, if you hadn't been the one who stole it in the first place."

He took a step closer. "You said it, Nora: it's not what you know. It's what you can prove."

"It was a good plan. Everything in Logan's name: the email, the accounts, an easy trail of evidence pointing to your wife as an embezzler. Accessing her email would've been second nature; you've been handling her business for decades. You could've forced her out of the company and re-invented your empire with a multibillion-dollar deal waiting in the wings. But you didn't count on Logan finding a copy of the email. You didn't know that until we went to her old apartment and saw one of the deposit slips had been balled in the trash."

"I haven't heard a question yet."

"The one thing I still don't know — the one thing Logan didn't even know — was whether Aaden was an accomplice or another one of your victims. She tried to investigate the money in his account and got nowhere. There was no evidence either way, but tonight . . ." Nora looked at the outline of dust on the computer monitor.

"On the night of his death, Aaden badged into the gym, alone, but if he was really alone they would have found his security badge on him, wouldn't they? He couldn't have draped it over his computer and walked back into the gym. The door locks from both sides." She leaned in, face-to-face with him. "Why didn't you leave it with his body?"

Gregg mirrored her, leaning in until they were only an inch apart. "What did you do with Logan, alone in the woods?"

Nora swallowed. "I wanted her to know what it felt like to be invisible. I wanted her to disappear."

Gregg nodded, a small smile on his mouth, and infinite compassion brimming in his eyes. Then he lunged at her.

Nora hitched back on the desk and kicked, a front kick that caught him directly in the groin. He grunted and doubled over and she shoved him back, forgetting all her punches, all the training. All she could think about was getting as far away as possible, but before she'd taken two steps he dove into her, sending them both flying into the desk and crashing onto the floor. A stabbing pain shot through her arm and she cried out, rolling to her other side. When she looked back, Gregg was already swinging. Keep your guard up, she could hear the echo of Logan's voice, but she couldn't lift the broken limb in time.

A cold, heavy object smashed into her face, crunching bone, ripping skin. She fell, and the back of her head hit something else. On the other end of a long, dark tunnel, she heard Gregg's voice, murmuring.

"I'm sorry to tell you, Nora, but they don't ever disappear. Frame them, kill them, it doesn't matter. Somehow they keep coming back."

GREGG

I knocked on the door that led from the Strike offices into the men's locker room of the gym. It took several minutes, but eventually the security pad bleeped and the door swung open, the light behind Aaden throwing him into shadow. We stood for a moment, neither of us moving. The entire building was silent, as if watching, waiting. In the end I was the first one to speak.

"What am I doing here?"

It was the middle of the night on one of those early March evenings when winter in Minnesota is endless, the cold intolerable not for its temperature but its sheer duration. Even Madison, where I'd been today, felt somehow closer to spring.

"Walk in slowly," he said.

I hadn't recognized the number when he called earlier tonight. I'd just checked in to a hotel in Rochester, my impulse lately when traveling by car, to stay on the road as long as possible, away from the penthouse where I was clearly no longer necessary or welcome. Aaden hadn't wasted any time in pleasantries. He demanded to meet in person — tonight — or else he'd go straight to Logan. About what, I asked. Come to the club, he'd said, as though graciously inviting me to visit his summer house. I told him I was an hour away and he hung up, apparently believing the matter settled. I'd spent the drive in alternating states of anger and unease, and when I arrived downtown I took a back, staff-only stairwell that led to Strike headquarters, a route entirely devoid of cameras, and used a spare key a janitor had given me once to access our floor. Not knowing what I was walking into, I treaded as lightly as possible.

"Look, I'm happy to be here for my trainers and staff, any time of the day or night. But I can't help you if you don't tell me what this is about. Are you in some kind of trouble?"

He backed up as I propped the door open and walked into the room, both of us taking infinite care to retain our distance from the other.

I checked the corners of the space, the bathrooms and showers, to see if we were alone. When I turned back around an object was flying at my face. Jerking, I caught it and found myself holding his company badge.

"I quit."

Careful not to take my eyes off him again, I slid the ID into my jacket pocket. "Resignation letters are usually delivered to your immediate supervisor or HR. During business hours."

"I'm not going to be a part of this." He pulled out his phone and hit a few buttons, then showed me a screen too far away to read.

"Sorry, my eyes aren't what they used to be."

"Deposits in my bank account. Nineteen thousand dollars! You're setting me up."

I wasn't the one trying to insert myself into his company. I wasn't taking over his mother's grocery store and sleeping with her on the side.

"I have no idea what you're talking about, Aaden." I shifted an inch toward the door, still open behind me, but before I could move further he pulled out a gun. An actual gun. The entire room refocused, everything else fell into meaningless background, and I didn't hear what he was saying until he motioned with the weapon, assured me it was loaded, and repeated that he would kill me if I tried to leave.

The only other time in my life I'd been near a gun was when Logan wanted to go to a shooting range for her birthday. Those were the early days, when we were still fighting for brand recognition, getting rejected for loans, and I spent every waking moment either arguing with Logan, having sex with Logan — sometimes both, simultaneously — or pushing protein bars on athletes like a drug dealer offering free samples. She sprung the idea when we were on the road somewhere, passing a billboard advertising a shooting range, and we spent an afternoon firing holes in paper people, black silhouettes with targets drawn on their chests. I went for the body. Logan aimed exclusively for the head.

Logan didn't do cake or candles and most years she ignored her birthday completely. ("What, your only accomplishment is that you didn't die?") When she did mark them, as with the shooting range, it tended to be with some sort of challenge. She ran a marathon for her thirtieth and took a polar plunge into Lake Minnetonka a decade later. In the back of my head, as her fiftieth birthday approached, I'd been expecting another Herculean idea. Chin-ups from the wing of an airplane. The Iditarod, maybe. You never knew with Logan and you couldn't compare yourself to her like she was a normal human.

I celebrate my birthday the same way every year, with a scotch and a quiet end seat at the bar while listening to jazz at the Dakota. Never a headliner night. Just a few guys making music on an unassuming Tuesday. I have one drink, jot two or three cocktail napkins' worth of ideas — some personal, some Strike — then I head home, toss the napkins into the fireplace, and start another year. Some of the managers would call it a rebirth ritual, which is why I don't tell anyone about it.

Logan's occasional celebrations, on the other hand, have become marketing gold. We started a Strike marathon team the year she ran, right as the company itself was being born. Her dive into the lake, where they'd chipped a hole through the foot-thick ice, got over ten million views on YouTube and raised thousands of dollars for athletic programs at local schools. I didn't know what she'd planned for fifty, but I'd thought I was prepared for anything and I hoped, whatever it was, we could find a tie-in to Strike Down.

Then, during an early tournament planning session, she announced she was going to spend her semicentennial on the beach.

"I want to get away. Fifty fucking years and I've never cheated winter by taking a vacation. It's time."

Agreement and chatter flooded the room, with more than one question directed at me. "So, where are you going?"

As if we'd discussed it beforehand, like a married couple or even business partners. I didn't know if I was invited, or whether Logan was planning to take Aaden instead. She smiled at me across the table, though, and leaned back in her chair like she was practicing her beach lounge.

"We were thinking The Bahamas."

I booked it, of course, and made all the arrangements. A private, ocean-front villa. Our own butler. Twenty-four-hour room service with high-protein meals, no refined carbs. An endless stretch of white sand and bubbling surf. And Logan didn't have the first clue what to do with herself. It was almost worth the insane cost, just to watch her try to relax and do nothing. While I read competitor data and skimmed construction site proposals, she tossed and turned on a beach lounger, picked at plates of fruit, tried to read a novel, and got up every few minutes to stretch and plod restlessly around the sand. She swam until she tired herself out — in the ocean, not our private pool because that would have been too easy — with the butler anxiously hovering and watching the black dot of her head recede further and further into the waves.

It was a three-bedroom villa, and we didn't go through the pretense of discussing sleeping arrangements. We each took our own rooms and staggered our daily jogs on the beach. We ate together, but when the butler set up a candlelit table on the beach, Logan laughed and made him bring the whole thing back up to the terrace.

By the second day she was already admitting defeat.

"It's too warm here. My brain is melting."

I went through my emails and pulled up a link for a conference call. "This was your idea."

"I thought it would be different. How do people enjoy this shit?" She glanced at my phone and took a sip from one of the ever-present drinks.

"Did you want to talk about structural deficiencies with the Philadelphia club construction manager?"

Another drink, this one longer.

I dialed in early and put the hold music

on speaker, then shuffled a few papers and watched the butler stack towels through the patio door.

"You could drive into town. There's a lot to see and do in Nassau, and it's just over the bridge."

"I don't sightsee."

"You could open an account."

She looked over, the first time she'd looked me full in the face for the entire trip.

"The Bahamas are a banking center. Millions of businesses use accounts here to protect their assets. It would be good for us if we didn't have all our eggs in one basket. Safer."

She got up and went swimming again, striding into the surf like she expected the ocean itself to back down from her.

I left the topic alone, going through the daily reports, running the business that one of us had to run, until two days later she took the keys to our rental and demanded a copy of the articles of incorporation. I emailed it to her with an inquiring look, but all she said was, "I'll be back later. Tell them not to salt the fish so much tonight. I feel like I'm digesting the fucking sea."

And that was all it took. Four days in a paradise luxurious enough to bore the crap out of her and we had an offshore account in Strike's name, bearing Logan's signature.

Aaden instructed me to move slowly toward the sinks. I did, although my first instinct was to run. I'd never had a gun drawn on me before, never felt the jerk of bowel-liquefying fear in my intestines. Clenching my ass, every ounce of manhood on the line, I lifted my hands — still clad in driving gloves — and walked as normally as I could in the direction he indicated.

Overpowering him wasn't going to be an option. I could run ten miles and bench press two hundred pounds, but I was a fifty-year-old man whose knees popped every time I stood up from a chair. He was a twenty-four-year-old who'd been training nonstop for a decade, a machine with reflexes, reach, and speed I could never match. Any overt move would be a fatal mistake.

"February twenty-eighth. Cash deposit. Cedar-Riverside branch. $9,500."

He scrolled down the screen one-handed, the other still training the gun at my chest, and read the virtually identical details from a second deposit before looking up at me, waiting.

"If you need some kind of counseling,

financial or otherwise, I can get you in touch with several people." Keeping my hands up, I edged further over to one of the granite counters and leaned against a sink. The mirror behind me would show him his reflection. It would remind him he wasn't a killer.

"My father died when we were living in Nairobi, already refugees, already unwanted. I have no memory of him." He lowered his phone and considered me, as if evaluating whether I had taken that from him, too. I swallowed, maintaining eye contact, wishing to God I'd ignored privacy concerns and had security cameras installed in the locker rooms.

"My mother knew we needed to leave Kenya. She gave everything we had to a man who promised to secure visas for us, so we could join some of our relatives in Minnesota. She never saw him again.

"I didn't know. I was a young boy. Years later, after we finally made it here and she started her business, she told me about this man. She talked of how pleasing he was, how he sympathized with her situation and had answers, all the news and reassurances she had been seeking. He knew her concerns before she had even voiced them, and outlined in great detail the journey and the *martisoor,* the hospitality, that awaited us here."

Aaden seemed to be looking straight through me now, at a point far beyond the Strike locker room, and I didn't know if the gun was pointed at me or a grifter in Kenya.

"She told me one detail about him in particular, something I've always remembered. I don't know what he looked like, his height or hair or whether he was fat or thin. She didn't mention any of that, but she told me about his eyes, how they never wavered. He was never distracted by the traffic outside or the noise or smells of the building where we were forced to live. His attention was always fixed on her, his prey."

He blinked and seemed to come back to himself. He glanced in the mirror and just as quickly away, shaking his head.

"I was intimidated by this space when I began training here. Not the gym. The fight lives in my blood and I've always known home there." A smile crossed his face. "Logan says I was born in a ring.

"But this room . . ." His gaze raked the granite and tile, momentarily distracted. "All this luxury, a space fit for kings, but not for me, right? You didn't build this for a poor Somali immigrant."

Somewhere in the bowels of the building

a boiler fired up and heat hummed through the vents.

"I saw you for the first time in here, in that exact spot by the sinks. You were talking to some members, and all I could hear was my mother's story. You were so charming, so focused on each person you spoke to it seemed you had no peripheral vision. Only the ahead existed for you. Only what came next.

"And I wondered, as I stood in the corner and watched you, what you would be taking from them. I've wondered it ever since."

His finger flicked, unlocking the safety on the gun.

I didn't look for the Nassau account immediately when we got home. It wasn't part of some evil master plot, but then Logan announced Strike Down, dropping the bomb that she was putting a new face on the company, and my inbox literally exploded. The servers crashed. Our website went down. Every manager at headquarters pulled a seventy-hour week trying to sort out the backlash and frenzy. Everyone except Logan. She holed up with her golden boy, the kid who claimed he was entering the tournament along with thousands of other fighters banging on our doors with dollar signs and dreams of glory shining in their eyes. Logan didn't lift a finger to help any of the other entrants. She refused to do any of the promotional work we'd discussed, instead devoting every free hour to Aaden Warsame.

No, it wasn't an evil master plot. It was a note scribbled on a cocktail napkin in an Atlanta hotel bar and burned in the fireplace. A plan born from the conviction, long festering, that Logan was not only holding the company back but actively sabotaging what I'd dedicated my life to build. She was right when she made the tournament announcement on the blog; Strike wasn't her. Not anymore. And not ever again.

Her tablet wasn't difficult to access. A few nights of guessing passwords, never so many that the computer would lock out, got me to "avocado" rather quickly. It pays to know your wife. From there I found the emails from FirstCaribbean International Bank, logged into the account with the saved passwords on her device, and copied all the information I needed.

I researched the financial side of things on a library computer in the wilds of St. Paul and found the best way, the simplest way, to cut them both out together. An embezzlement. A glaring, obvious one. It couldn't be

412

too complex, or no one would believe an aging kickboxer and her young, inexperienced lover capable of pulling it off. But Logan signed the Magers Construction contract with me, her initials alongside mine on every page, including the one outlining the unusual deposit requirement for each site. She hadn't read a single word of that clause or any other, but the paper trail said differently. In court, she would have had full knowledge of the lump sums paid in advance to Magers Construction and just waiting to be reimbursed.

What would you do? If your wife paraded her twenty-four-year-old lover around the company you'd conceived and hustled and saved and spun from every fiber of your being, and then she publicly announced to anyone with half a brain that she was planning to hand it over to him, to *him,* what would you do? Would you stand quietly in the corner of your own goddamn boardroom and let it happen? Feel your worth in every form drip uselessly from your spinal column? Deflating you. Making you less, and more importantly, making your company less. Would you let her take your vision and give it to some inarticulate child to unravel at his fucking leisure? No. No, you wouldn't.

413

I bought a phone, a burner, and set up the online transfer account with Logan's information. I instructed Sara to hang around Aaden at headquarters, feeding him cup after cup of steaming black coffee until she found out his password. (It was "strike1." Seriously. Not even an odd capital letter. And millennials are supposed to be taking over the virtual world?) I sent the email to Magers Construction from his email account and his computer terminal, in case anyone ever checked the IP address, while the entire office was being treated to a catered lunch. Fielding the confirmation request from Logan's inbox was as easy as logging into her tablet, replying, and going through the same purge. It was the following days that were hardest. Waiting. Not doing anything. I logged into Logan's tablet whenever I had the opportunity, to ensure no further replies came through from Magers Construction. After a full week had passed, I broke down and called their payables department, right at lunchtime, and posed as a clerk to confirm the refunds. While the woman chewed and the keyboard clacked in the background, she looked up the account and confirmed yes — there were three large refunds in queue for approval and did I need to speak to her supervisor? I said no, thanked her for her time, and continued to wait.

Then the money started to flow.

The deposits accumulated, invisible, while I waited for Darryl to eventually notice what was going on. To be honest, I thought even he would have caught on quicker. This wasn't a few dollars here and there from a petty cash box. These were massive quantities of capital. I drove up all other spending, flooring the gas as we sped toward the brick wall. Strike Down got the best venue and vendors, prime advertising through premium channels. We poured money into vStrike, hiring cutting-edge virtual reality programmers. Everyone got bonuses. And I waited, counting down the days to the inevitable explosion, when Darryl or someone — anyone — else in the company, figured out what was going on.

I just never expected it to be Aaden Warsame.

"Aaden, I want you to put down the gun."

He continued as though I hadn't spoken. "You have so much already. Strike. Logan."

"I can't talk to you when you're pointing a gun at me." The unlatching of the safety had made only a whisper of noise, but it was echoing like an actual gunshot in my head. Sweat broke out under my arms.

"What did you want from me?" he asked. "What could you have wanted so much that you had to give me nineteen thousand dollars to get it?"

"Just set it down. Please, let's sit down and talk." I gestured to the benches and to my infinite surprise he shrugged, walked over, and sat.

I stood frozen at the sink until he laid the gun down on the bench and raised an eyebrow at me, a dare. Blisteringly aware I was walking into a trap but with no other alternatives, I moved across the room and sat next to him, well within his reach. The gun lay between us, its barrel facing the lockers.

"The last deposit was two days ago." His voice was low, measured. "My friend and I had met at a coffee shop across the street from my bank. He was studying business. I was studying fighters. And he said, look, white people even go to the bank different. I looked out the window and do you know who I saw?"

He turned fully toward me, rising up as high as his spine would stretch.

"I saw you, Gregg Abbott, telling an Uber driver to double park. I was so surprised to see you in my neighborhood. In any neighborhood. I've never seen you outside this building. It seemed wrong that you could exist anywhere but here. I didn't say anything to my friend. I didn't want to lose face and admit I knew you.

"Then I logged into my account and found this money. Your secretary, Sara — who doesn't bring me coffee anymore — she said you were out of town when this happened."

"The Madison club. Final inspection." And a confirmation with the project manager that $900K of the retainer was coming back.

"Yet I saw you in Minneapolis with my own eyes."

I exhaled, one long final breath. "Can I show you something? In my wallet?"

Aaden's eyes narrowed a fraction, but his confidence overrode any internal warnings. He knew we were unevenly matched. He nodded.

Taking care to move as slowly as I had across the room, I unzipped my coat to pull the wallet out of my vest pocket and handed him a slip of paper. He stared at it, frowning, then shook his head.

"A bank account?"

"A hidden account. A tax shelter. Logan wasn't entirely onboard with the idea. She

417

insisted you should have some of the money. That was her condition for agreeing to it. She . . ." I swallowed and zipped my coat back up as high as it would go. "She cares more about you than she does any of this. Or me. You don't need me to tell you that. You've got eyes."

I pinched the bridge of my nose and squeezed my own eyes shut. "It's somewhat gray — legally speaking — which is why we have to be careful. No paper trail. No traceable transfers. I thought Logan told you all this already."

"No." He sounded unsure for the first time since he'd opened the door to the locker room. Like a kid. I heard the scrape of paper as he folded it. "I'm keeping this until I've talked to Logan."

"Fine, but only Logan. And, for God's sake, put it away. Don't leave it lying around. Keep it somewhere secure."

I heard the rustle, felt the shift of his weight on the bench, and didn't hesitate. I grabbed the gun, put it to his temple, and fired. The kickback was nothing, so much less than the rifles we used at the shooting range for Logan's birthday, but I let it fall out of my glove anyway and clatter to the floor.

Gurgling noises, as if underwater, or

maybe I could only feel the vibration of them in the white space after the blast. I stared at the tile, my mind still playing out the other scenario, the one where the gun wasn't loaded and he punched me across the room. Shock. Anger. I would stagger back to my feet, telling him I knew it all along, that there was no way a good kid like him, an elite kickboxer, would have relied on any weapon other than his own body. Then I'd throw the gun across the room in disgust, calling his bluff I might have had to haggle with him to keep him from going straight to the cops. Make him think he was blackmailing me, which would only look better in the end, but risky. Too dangerous to have him out there with a story, a counter-narrative to the one I'd spent so much time and effort crafting.

This was better. Once my hearing returned and the other scenario faded into an unnecessary future, I surveyed the scene. The blood and skull and brain matter had all splattered in the opposite direction, a good deal of it hitting the lockers and dripping down to the floor around his body. There were only a few drops near me or on my arm, but — since Aaden had been reaching to stop me — there were a few on his right arm, too. Good. His phone had fallen out of his jacket pocket, face up and providentially still unlocked. Sometimes things just fell into place, like meeting Nora in Atlanta. It was almost enough to make me think there could actually be some benevolent deity in the sky, lining up the shots. But that would have diminished my role in what happened. Luck isn't divine intervention. Luck is preparation meeting opportunity.

With one gloved finger, I scrolled to his log and deleted the record of his call to me. He hadn't texted anyone since 7:00 p.m., and there were no messages in the last two days about his bank account, Strike, or me. I emptied his trash then locked the phone. Checking my shoes for dirt, blood, or anything that would leave a mark, I backed out of the locker room and closed the door.

Let me be crystal clear. I never wanted anyone to die. I'm not a monster. Aaden Warsame had his entire life ahead of him. He had talent and opportunities, regardless of Logan's attention. The members liked his classes and even I could admit he was a natural mentor for the Strike Next kids, especially the ignorant boys who thought they couldn't look up to anyone without a penis. Aaden transitioned them into the fold, and when he watched the female trainers with the concentration and respect they deserved, the boys followed his example, letting the misogyny drain silently out of their fists.

He could have had a good life, the life his mother had dreamed for him when they fled Somalia. Instead he chose his father's path. And like his father, he died because of it.

I didn't bring the gun into that room and I didn't go there intending to kill anyone. Any semi-coherent lawyer could argue I was the real victim, and I acted in self-defense.

Here's how the entire plan should have worked, if everyone had simply complied with the outline I'd written on the cocktail napkin.

Phase 1. Spend an aggressive amount of capital on key expansions to the company: a) doubling our clubs, b) branching into virtual entertainment with differentiating technology, c) taking the brand to the next level with a world-class event.

Key Note: no element in Phase 1 can produce income immediately. They must each require significant upfront investment, which will drain the company's resources and force the theft to light.

Phase 2. Cash flow problems lead to discovery of fraud. Privately hire accounting firm to investigate and conclude that Logan and her lover embezzled millions. Commence civil lawsuit and force Logan out of company. Discreetly circulate internet rumors about Logan's character and state of mind, framed with easily confirmed facts about previous physical altercations to give appearance of legitimacy.

Phase 3. Supplant new charismatic female face on company. Externally: rebrand with international appeal, focusing on kickboxing strongholds (Japan. Brazil. Germany.). Internally: tighten all financial and administrative controls. Implement stock ownership plan for all employees. Begin collecting revenue from Phase 1 investments.

Phase 4. Take on the world.

I wouldn't have left Logan destitute. We had a prenup, so she would have walked away with all her endorsement money. She and Aaden could have bought an island and turned it into their own Enter the Dragon–style paradise somewhere in the South Pacific. It would have been an opportunity to reinvent herself, a chance to start over, get back to her fighting roots with her boy lover at her side. A happy ending for everyone. Don't tell me I'm not thoughtful. I saw a path forward for all of us and none of those paths led to a pool of blood and brain tissue on the Strike men's locker room tile. I'm not a killer. But I'm not a coward, either. I will do whatever needs to be done for the company. For Strike.

That, my friends, is living your brand.

Nora

The darkness lifted and Nora became aware of pain. Pain first, the kind that came in waves with the promise of an ocean behind it. Then odor — sweat, copper, and the bite of rubbing alcohol. Something wet and sticky underneath her and an uncontrolled hitch in her chest. She concentrated on steadying her breathing, until the need to know more intruded, as always, and she had to open her eyes.

Mats came into focus, and then the ropes enclosing it. She was in a ring, the Strike ring, with a single spotlight shining a circle of light and leaving the rest of the gym in shadow, or at least that's how it seemed. Objects wavered in and out of her vision, the mats blurred, and she blinked furiously, trying to orient herself.

She lay in a fetal position, and when she moved, her top arm screamed. She'd never broken a bone in her life — no sledding accidents or falls on the ice as a kid — but she had no doubt her forearm was fractured. The desk. Her arm had hit Aaden's desk when Gregg tackled her.

"How are you feeling?"

His voice came from behind her and she struggled to push herself up to sitting. Gregg leaned on a stool in the corner, texting. He didn't look up. She blinked at the phone and then saw a gun resting in his lap.

"I apologize. The #WheresLogan hashtag is exploding. A hundred thousand retweets of the tournament's call for help, and it only posted an hour ago. I have to participate, obviously, even though I've got the one person who knows where she is right here." He paused, scrolled. "Nora Trier isn't trending. Yet."

One of her eyes didn't want to open. Nora reached up with her good hand and felt the area gingerly. It was swollen, and her nose was stabbing little shocks across her face. The skin itself felt alien, entirely unlike her own flesh. When she drew her hand back, her fingers had blood on them.

Gregg looked up and concern laced his eyebrows together. "I'm sorry about that, too. The only comfort I had, with the Aaden episode, was that it was instantaneous. He couldn't have felt anything. I have to tell myself that every night, like a bedtime prayer before I can sleep. Sometimes it still doesn't work."

He was admitting it. She blinked, and tried not to react to the news that she was alone in a dark room with a murderer. The exit signs glowed from what looked like a mile away.

"He let you into the locker room with him that night. You killed him."

"It wasn't part of the plan, believe me."

"What was the plan?" She turned her head and even that small motion made her nauseous. If she could make it out of the ring, she might find cover behind the columns of body bags flanking the red carpet, but she wasn't going to outrun a bullet. As she stared into the dark rows of bags, they seemed to be moving of their own accord. She closed her eyes.

"Are you still investigating, Nora?"

"Managing my expectations."

He laughed once, a warm, genuine sound that made her go cold. "God, I love so much about you." She heard him stand up and move closer. "The gym was the only option now that the situation has . . . evolved. I need to know everything, and that requires time and privacy. This is the ideal place, actually. Draw the blackout shades, disengage the security cameras, turn off the badge sensors on the doors, and we have a perfect interview room. It's soundproofed, because Strike gyms are never a nuisance to our neighbors, and the ring is disinfected daily. Cleaner than a hospital." He breathed out a satisfied sigh. "Ask and Strike will provide."

Nora rocked herself to all fours, letting her head hang heavy and biting down on the urge to whimper.

"Take it easy. There's an ice pack next to you."

She opened her eyes again and saw it, sweating in the spotlight. Applying it to her arm, she braced herself and rose to one knee. The room spun. She moved the ice pack to her head.

Gregg watched her with tender detachment, like one would a wounded sparrow floundering on the ground. He held the gun in one hand, pointed at the floor. He wasn't going to use it, though, not yet. He said he needed to know everything, and that meant she had leverage. She still had time.

"He confronted you about the money?"

Gregg didn't answer.

"Was he blackmailing you for more than you'd agreed, or did you frame him, too?

427

Was he an innocent party in all this?"

"Innocent is a strong word for most people."

The cold focused her, steadied her, but she closed her eyes again and sat back on her haunches, pressing the ice pack harder, wishing she could bury it inside her head. "Logan confronted me, too."

She heard him move and when he spoke again, his voice sounded closer to the ground, on her level. "What happened, Nora? You can tell me."

Slowly, she did. She told him about Logan finding the email and recruiting Corbett, the chain of transfers across the Caribbean, and how Corbett had — in a fit of conscience — moved the money beyond even Logan's reach. And then, how Logan had responded to his ultimatum by cracking his skull against an alley wall.

"She surprised me in the middle of the woods near my house. She'd come there two nights in a row, waiting, wanting me to recover the money for her." Nora lowered the ice pack and stared straight into Gregg's eyes. "I didn't plan to hurt her."

He moved closer, an arm's length away, still holding the gun at his side. "Don't think it'll upset me if she's dead. If you killed her. I'd be the last person to blame you." He crept nearer, a bald appeal stretching across his face. "Can't you see how alike we are, Nora? You would protect your company, too, if you had a partner who was trying to throw Parrish away. You know you would."

She forced herself to inch forward, mirroring him. "What happened with Aaden?"

The story came haltingly at first, short statements she had to coax out of him, but once he got going the details began pouring out: his simple cocktail napkin plan, Logan's birthday trip and the Nassau account, Magers Construction, deposits Aaden wasn't supposed to be able to trace, everything that led up to a gunshot in a locker room. Ten minutes passed, then fifteen. The ice pack turned warm in Nora's hand.

When he finally finished, he looked exhausted.

"I drove back to the Rochester hotel. I got rid of the clothes I'd been wearing and that's when I realized Aaden's badge was still in my pocket. It should have been in the locker room with him. I didn't know if the police would notice it was missing, but by the time I got the call and drove back they'd secured the area. I draped it over his computer while everyone else was in the gym.

"When I fall asleep, though, I still have it." He swallowed, squeezing the handle of the gun until the tips of his fingers were white and bloodless. "I can never get rid of it in my dreams."

Nora set the ice pack aside, trying not to shake. She'd gotten exactly what she wanted — the truth, at last — but the more he'd told her, the more certain she'd become of one thing: Gregg Abbott wouldn't have confessed to anything, the fraud or the murder, if he'd planned to let her leave this place alive. She couldn't outrun him, and no one had come to help.

"What are you going to do with me?" She still used her interviewer voice, the low, dispassionate tones that made discussing her own death sound like a restaurant decision. "Two bodies at Strike in the same year? I doubt Detective Li will sign off on a second suicide so quickly."

He pushed all the air out of his lungs, as though the oxygen itself was hurting him. "This isn't what I wanted, Nora. If you'd just followed the evidence and found the refunds, it would have been fine. How much easier did I have to make it? Logan even confessed to hiding the money, for Christ's sake. None of this had to happen."

She didn't know what it was, his tone or

the insidious shift of blame, but all at once everything stopped. The tremors. The fear. Her attempt to draw out the interview until she could somehow find a way out of this room. There was no way out. One way or the other, this ended here.

Finding her balance, Nora rose. She forced her broken arm to lift and shifted until her whole body aligned into a fighter's stance.

"No."

"Nora, don't make me use this." He stood, too, and the gun twitched in his hand, but he didn't raise it. He was sweat-slicked, sick, and maybe even a little afraid. Good. She licked blood off her lip and flexed her good arm.

"I'm not making you do anything." The words ground out from the depth of her gut. "I've never cheated. I've never stolen. I never put a gun to anyone's head and pulled the trigger."

She jabbed with her good arm, landing the blow in his shoulder and backing him up a step.

"None of this" — she shot a fist at his chest, and then another to his gut — "is my fault."

It never was, not Sam White, not her parents; she'd never done anything to deserve any of it. The adrenaline coursed through her, burning with the need to fight, to stand up for once, even if it was the last time she did.

He's going to kill me anyway, she thought, hearing Henry's voice from the day she'd watched him play his video game. His opponent had been unbeatable, yet he'd attacked anyway. He'd charged ahead, fearless. Hot tears stung the cut on Nora's face. She hadn't written him any letters. She hadn't told him how proud she was. She'd failed him a thousand ways, but if she was going to die, at least she'd die big. Just like Henry had taught her.

"You can't win this, Nora."

"It doesn't matter." She sent a hook to his head, putting more power behind it, but he blocked it this time. "Hit me, shoot me, I don't care. I'm going out big."

Without warning, she lunged for the gun. The room tilted as they struggled, both pulling at the weapon until he grabbed her broken arm and she screamed.

Shoving her back, he pointed it at her heart. His hand shook. "Where's Logan?"

"She's right here."

The voice came from outside the ring. Nora spun around and the room itself seemed to revolve. Cool and collected, the body bags flanking her like a guard of honor, Logan walked out of the shadows and onto the red carpet.

"You need to go."

The last rays of sun filtered through the trees into the hidden meadow. Frogs and cicadas had begun to sing, the only sounds now that Henry had run home. What would Nora have given, a week ago, to share a moment like this with Logan Russo? But last week her shoulders wouldn't have tensed like they were doing now, her feet wouldn't have shifted to seek the high ground. Last week she would have shied away, embarrassed by the storm of emotion she felt whenever she was in the same room as Logan. Today every muscle in her body vibrated with tension, begging to take down the woman standing in front of her.

"Excuse me?"

Logan had just finished telling her the entire story — stumbling upon an email with her signature that she'd never seen before, investigating the money the police had found in Aaden's account, and bribing Corbett to help her move the stolen millions at the exact moment Gregg would need them the most. Aaden was dead, Gregg was framing her, and she was going to make him pay. Nora listened without comment, weighing the testimony against the evidence she'd already compiled, and came to one conclusion.

"If you're telling the truth —"

"I am," Logan bristled.

"There's only one way to find out." Nora shifted. "All the evidence points to you right now. You're a giant target, but if we take the target away, we discover what lives behind it."

Logan moved in a wide circle, skirting the edges of the trail around Nora, who pivoted, keeping Logan in her sights at all times.

"I don't run away from my problems."

"I don't run away from mine, either, even when they've nearly killed my best friend."

"He ran into that car himself. When I was going through his wallet looking for the twenty million dollars he fucking hijacked, he freaked out and ran."

"You're claiming you didn't hit him."

Logan rolled her eyes. "I pushed him, once."

"Like this?" Nora stepped in and shoved her by the shoulders, simultaneously surprised that she'd done it and that Logan had let her.

"No, it was more like this." Logan's arm came out of nowhere, a single palm strike to Nora's chest. She didn't have time to block it, but she hooked a foot behind Logan's leg as she fell and in the next moment both of them were sprawled in the dirt.

"Oh god." Nora pressed a hand to her chest, feeling her heart convulse.

"Are you okay?"

Logan propped herself up, looking down into Nora's face with a mixture of concern and suppressed amusement, and Nora punched her.

Logan's head flew back, but she caught Nora's wrist before she could land another shot. "Fuck. Nice. That was a good one."

A drop of blood fell from Logan's nose onto Nora's shirt, drawing both of their gazes before they looked back at each other and the fight, in that heartbeat, was over.

"I was jealous," Nora admitted, realizing how true it was. How irreversible everything became when she said it out loud. She'd been drawn to Logan since the moment she'd first seen her, compelled closer and closer without letting herself understand why. She rubbed her free hand over her chest as the pain faded. "I wanted you to notice me. To choose me."

"Obviously I fucking should have. Brains, balls, and a right cross to write home about.

435

Tell me, Nora Trier," Logan loosened her grip on Nora's wrist and brushed a leaf out of her hair, "since I'm putting myself in your hands, what would you have me do next?"

Somewhere in the distance a firework went off. Nora startled and glanced up the trail, afraid for a split second that Henry had returned with more fireworks, but the meadow was empty. When she looked back, Logan was staring at her mouth. She leaned down, hovering for an endless moment, giving Nora time to decide.

The kiss was a revelation. Nora opened to it, her body humming at each point of contact with Logan's, and every vibration was tuned to the same word. *Yes.* Nora reached up and wound her arms around Logan, pulling her closer, taking more.

Later, as the sun disappeared behind the trees and the mosquitos began to attack, Nora pulled Logan to her feet and ran a hand down her arm, linking their bruised and dirty knuckles.

"Are you ready for the spotlight, Nora?"

She left the meadow side by side with the fighter she'd loved for so long, the fighter who might be playing her, who could have made all this up just to punish her husband. And Nora smiled, knowing the truth hovered so close, that — whatever it was — she would be the one to find it.

"Are you ready to disappear?"

Logan stalked the length of the red carpet toward the ring where Gregg and Nora both stood frozen. Gregg still pointed the gun at her, but she didn't care. Logan had come for her. After she'd slipped through security at the stadium, Logan had blown up her phone with texts.

They live streamed it.

Get out of there.

Now.

Where are you?

Nora told her to calm down and wait, but she hadn't. Thank God she hadn't.

When she reached the end of the red carpet, Logan stopped. Gregg's attention was fixed on his wife. He didn't notice Nora slide her good hand into her pocket.

"I thought you coerced Aaden into helping you, that you tricked him or threatened him. I thought he killed himself over the guilt." Logan's entire body shook with fury. "He was just a kid, and you murdered him."

Gregg's mouth curled into a sneer. "I've got ironclad evidence of your embezzlement, of laundering money around the world, and you have nothing on me, Logan. Nothing. Strike is mine."

In reply, Logan lifted a hand into the air, revealing her phone and the app that was still recording, that must have been recording Gregg and Nora this entire time.

Gregg swung around, pointing the gun from Nora to Logan.

Nora didn't think. She didn't hesitate. She pulled the box cutter out of her pocket and plunged the blade into the side of his neck. The gun went off, deafening her, and one of the body bags behind Logan shuddered with the impact of the bullet. Gregg stumbled and grabbed his throat. Dark columns of blood seeped from between his fingers, but she didn't see him fall. She'd already turned to Logan; Logan, who had refused to leave town; Logan, who'd found her in time to save her life; Logan, who slowly lowered the phone and stared back at Nora as her husband choked and writhed.

ALIVE

July 12, 2019

This is Logan and yes, spoiler alert, I'm alive. For all the fans who didn't believe the police announcement, or the Associated Press story confirming my safety, or the pictures Strike posted to show everyone I'm actually fine, I get it. It's been a little crazy lately. So keep your guard up and follow me over to this live feed.

The embedded link goes live, showing Logan sitting in a low chair with one knee up and an arm cocked on top of it. The plaster wall behind her is white and alive with the skittering shadows of sunlight filtered through waving trees. Logan wears a tank top and shorts, and her skin shows no marks or wounds. Her hair is slicked back, her face makeup-less as she looks unblinking into the camera.

"It's me. I'm safe. Thank you.

"Thank you to the literally hundreds of thousands of you who responded to the appeal at Strike Down and were looking for me last week, and that includes the good people at the Minneapolis PD.

"Let me set the record straight. I wasn't kidnapped. I wasn't murdered. I didn't go early onset dementia and wander off into a lake, not yet anyway."

Logan pauses and narrows her eyes at the camera.

"Someone I once trusted with everything was trying to take me down. That person failed. That person is gone, and I have one message for all of you watching today.

"Fight. Everyone. Who. Holds. You. Down."

Logan glances off camera, her expression softening, before she turns her attention back to the feed.

"I've learned a lot in the past few weeks, some of it wrenching, some of it beautiful. I've learned there isn't one kind of strong. Strong is a refugee making a home for her family on the other side of the planet. Strong is putting your entire career on the line for someone you believe in. Sometimes strong is even letting someone else fight for you, trusting them with your life."

Tears run down Logan's face. She doesn't wipe them away.

"No matter what strong means to you, find it. Find your strength and if someone tries to take it away from you, hunt them down. Make them fight. Be the one left standing.
"And never, ever apologize for winning."

Logan leans in and smothers the camera with her hand. The feed ends.

NORA

The beach was too white. It blinded, even from the shade of a wind-battered palapa, and made it almost impossible to see her laptop screen. Nora's eyes watered as she looked away, into fronds as wide as her arm-span where tiny green lizards darted around with the speed and precision of humming-birds. Beyond the palms the green stretched back and up, rising into a volcanic peak. In all the years she'd tracked money to Nevis, this tiny speck of island that cast shadows large enough to obscure billions, she never imagined it would be lovely.

Hurricane season had just begun, the innkeeper told them at check-in, but over-head the sky glowed a faultless blue. The beach was deserted except for two figures boogie boarding in the surf. She listened to them play while she typed, until a noise behind her made her turn and that simple movement drew perspiration down her

442

body, sticking the paper-thin sundress to her skin.

Logan walked out of the stucco building's shaded terrace. She dangled a tablet from her fingers, like a frisbee she was getting ready to launch over the waves, and jogged the few steps down to the chairs Nora had set up under the palapa. Dropping the tablet on a vacant chair, she leaned over and closed Nora's laptop with a decisive click. The whine of the computer's fan shuddered off.

"I was working."

"We're taking a break." Logan flashed a grin and pulled two beers out of a cooler. She cracked one and took a long pull before considering Nora, who sat bolt upright at the end of her lounge chair, drumming the fingers of her good hand on the top of the computer. Setting her beer down, Logan stepped closer and tipped her chin up with a finger. She rested the other, unopened can against the side of Nora's nose. When Nora had checked it in the bathroom mirror this morning, the gash had been crusted black. Healing.

"The swelling's already gone," Nora objected, even as her eyes drifted closed.

"The cold still helps. It's too fucking hot here."

The trip had been Logan's idea. She didn't trust intermediaries, she said, so that morning she and Nora had walked into the Nevis bank, proven Logan's identity to access nineteen million dollars, and sent wire transfers to every winner of Strike Down. Then they closed the account, ending the chase and concluding Nora's investigation, before walking back to the hotel together.

"It's eighty degrees and sunny with a light breeze. Most people would say that's perfect."

"I'll take a blizzard any day. You know you're alive when your face is freezing off."

"Speaking of," Nora murmured, and Logan moved the can gently from one side of her nose to the other, aligning aluminum to bone.

"It's going to be a little crooked from now on."

"The nose or my business?"

Logan snorted. Eyes still shut, Nora covered Logan's hand with her own and held it for a moment, absorbing cold and heat together, before moving the can away.

"I don't know what I'm going to do now. My career has been built on independence, on neutrality."

"But you're a partner." Logan picked up her open beer and took another drink.

"What are they going to do, frame you for embezzlement?"

Nora smiled. "Nothing so creative. Accountants prefer meetings, and voting, to force out the people who risk the company's reputation."

She'd stopped by the hospital before leaving town. Corbett's condition had stabilized enough for him to be moved out of the ICU, and the doctors were optimistic. Physically, he might recover. Professionally, they were both finished. Neither Jim nor Rajesh had contacted her since she'd briefed them on the full details of the case, holding nothing back, and she knew they must be reeling. One of their partners had organized an illegal and unethical laundering of funds. The other partner had convinced a client to fake her own disappearance, and murdered another client by stabbing him in the jugular. The only real question was how long the paperwork would take to revoke her CPA.

"Some risks are worth it." Logan's smile melted from her mouth into her eyes, which seemed to glow as she studied Nora. She offered her beer and Nora drank.

A laugh from the beach drew both of their attention.

Mike had wiped out and was flopping

theatrically at the water's edge as Henry gleefully paddled over to him on his boogie board. It wasn't immediately obvious, at first glance, who was the adult and who was the child. When Henry reached his father, he dove on top of him and the two began wrestling in the waves. Henry eventually won, pinning Mike and sitting up, shouting, his rail-thin arms thrown wide in victory.

"Detective Li called." Logan picked up her beer again, watching the man and child splash back into the water.

Detective Li had been the first officer on scene after Gregg's death. He'd taken one look at the body and the two women sitting next to each other at the edge of the ring, Logan stone-faced and Nora holding a fresh ice pack to her arm with blood trailing from her temple, nose, and mouth, and asked what the hell had happened. Nora gave the same account she would provide to the partners the following day, with all the composure of an expert witness — how Gregg had framed Logan and Aaden for embezzlement, killed Aaden when he discovered it, and tried to kill Logan for the same reason. For his company.

"So you killed him first." Detective Li glanced at the blood splatter in the ring and then back to Nora, clearly skeptical. She wondered if she should cry, or exhibit more emotion in order to convince him, but all she felt was a searing numbness. In the end, they didn't need oral testimony. After getting Nora's text, Logan had left Bilan's place in Little Mogadishu and arrived at Strike halfway through Gregg's confession. Reactivating the security sensors, she'd crept into the gym and started recording. It was low-quality, barely audible, but the words were distinguishable enough to be damning. Logan had texted Detective Li as soon as she'd realized Gregg had a gun.

"I told you to stand back and wait for us to arrive on scene."

"He was pointing the gun at Nora," Logan said as they listened to the end of the recording. The series of garbled noises seemed meaningless, but Nora could see his eyes bulging, hear the body falling. She thought of how Aaden's badge had haunted Gregg, and wondered if this would be her picture, if his dying face would be the one she carried into her dreams every night, but then Logan's hand found hers.

"I'm taking this woman to a fucking hospital. You can find us there later, or talk to my lawyers."

Nora's nose and arm were fractured. She had eight stitches in her temple where

Gregg knocked her out with the butt of the gun. Her right incisor was missing and she was treated for a mild concussion. The forensic team found no hair or skin under her fingernails, but the knuckles on her good hand were bruised. For a Strike fighter, those were defensive wounds.

Aaden's case had been reopened and the police were going through the evidence in light of the recording and Nora and Logan's statements. Detective Li had called with an update.

"Gregg's prints were found on the bank information in Aaden's wallet. And the closed-circuit downtown cameras spotted him walking toward the building about a half hour prior to the estimated time of death."

"Is it enough?"

"It'll never be enough." Logan's jaw, in sharp profile against the white sand, tightened. "If Gregg could die a hundred deaths, it still wouldn't be enough. I'll see him in every bag I hit for the rest of my life."

Nora drew a breath. "I meant, is it enough evidence?"

One short nod. "They're ruling it a homicide."

They fell silent, passing the beer back and forth. Logan's streaked face caught the reflected light of the sun off the water. Echoes within echoes. Waves from waves. Henry and Mike continued to surf, oblivious to the women under the palapa, one sitting straight-backed at the foot of the chair, the other standing with legs braced wide.

Logan drained the can and set it aside. She turned and Nora sensed her eyes running over the sickly green skin above her cheeks, the stitches and crusted, soon-to-be scars. She'd never been beautiful, but she hadn't been prepared for the looks on the plane and from the islanders, some side-eyed, others openly staring. Her face had been a magnet in the bank this morning, drawing stark and uncomfortable attention.

"Come on." Logan tugged her elbow.

Nora smoothed her good hand over the laptop. "I have a lot of work to do before they fire me. I need to hand off clients and finish the Strike report. Your management team deserves a full presentation of what happened, along with recommendations for implementing adequate controls."

"I'll need some recommendations on whose asses to can, too."

Nora smiled. "Noted. But after that, I've got to get my résumé in order. Figure out what I'm going to do once I'm not an accountant anymore."

"You don't have to worry about that." Logan tossed the laptop aside and pulled Nora to her feet, leading her over the sand and toward her family playing in the sea. They looked so happy to see her coming.

"Why not?"

Logan squeezed her hand and looked at Nora as no one in her life had done, as though she was cut from something precious and rare. Despite the bruises, despite the broken bones, cuts, and fractures, she felt suddenly and achingly whole.

Beaming, Logan brushed a strand of Nora's hair aside. "Because you're the next face of Strike."

ACKNOWLEDGMENTS

So many people helped bring this story to life. Some knew it. Others didn't. I won't bore anyone with the details of my stalking, just know at some point in your life, the odds are good that a writer will be watching you. Thank you to Stephanie Cabot, my sounding board and coach, who provided an unfailingly honest and generous first read of this story. You make all the books possible. I owe thanks to several other tremendous readers — Ellen Coughtrey, Jane Wood, and Therese Keating — who each helped shape and refine the narrative until it actually became the thing I'd imagined. This book wouldn't exist without the support of my amazing editor, Emily Bestler. I'm so grateful to have another book published by Emily Bestler Books. Thank you, Emily, Lara, David, and the whole team at Atria for all your hard work and enthusiasm. You make my dream job even more dreamy.

451

Thank you to the accountants I've learned from and had the privilege of working with over the years: Sarah Fjelstul, Paula Pogreba, John Brejcha, Rhonda Lee, Grant Tullo, Megan Kalina, Kelly Groon, Beverly Kile, Sharon Amundson, and Dick Root. They are the funniest, smartest, most caring people, and I doubt most of them would murder anyone. Thank you to Alex Moreno for chatting about insurance with me, and to the Association of Certified Fraud Examiners for their invaluable courses and publications. Thank you to Sarah from ilovekick boxing.com for reading an interview in which I mentioned I needed to research kickboxing, and offering her gym as the ultimate learning experience. I'm indebted to the awesome trainers at that gym, Rae, Wendi, Noelle, and LaDonna, who taught me how to throw down. Thank you to the people and places of Minneapolis, from the Mill City Museum to U.S. Bank Stadium. I'm so grateful for the amazing women crime writers I've met along the way, whose work constantly inspires me, and for all the readers who've thrilled to these journeys through the heartland. Let's see where we go next.

ABOUT THE AUTHOR

Mindy Mejia is a CPA and a graduate of the Hamline University MFA program. Her debut novel, *The Dragon Keeper,* was published by Ashland Creek Press in 2012. She lives in the Twin Cities with her family, and is the author of *Strike Me Down, Everything You Want Me to Be,* and *Leave No Trace.*

EE